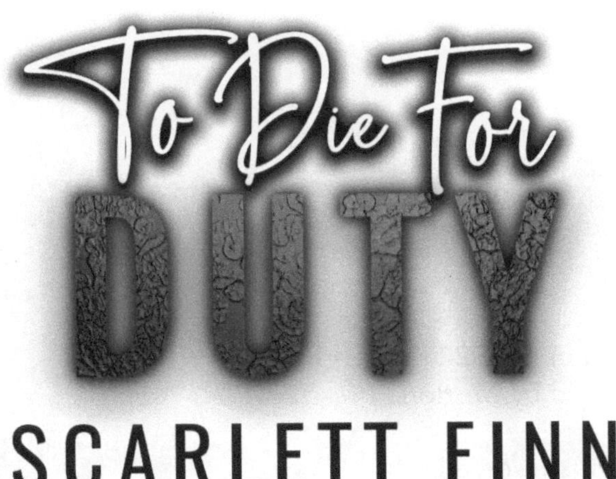

SCARLETT FINN

Also by Scarlett Finn

TO DIE FOR...
TO DIE FOR TRUTH
TO DIE FOR HONOR
TO DIE FOR VIRTUE
TO DIE FOR DUTY
TO DIE FOR LOVE

GO NOVELS
GO WITH IT
GO IT ALONE
GO ALL OUT
GO ALL IN
GO FULL CIRCLE

KINDRED SERIES
RAVEN
SWALLOW
CUCKOO
SWIFT
FALCON
FINCH

LOVE AGAINST THE ODDS STANDALONE COLLECTION
SWEET SEAS
HEIR'S AFFAIR
RESCUED
MAESTRO'S MUSE
GETTING TRICKY
THIRTEEN
REMEMBER WHEN...
RELUCTANT SUSPICION
XY FACTOR

EXILE
HIDE & SEEK
KISS CHASE

THE EXPLICIT SERIES
EXPLICIT INSTRUCTION
EXPLICIT DETAIL
EXPLICIT MEMORY

WRECK & RUIN
RUIN ME
RUIN HIM

MISTAKE DUET
MISTAKE ME NOT
SLEIGHT MISTAKE

NOTHING TO...
NOTHING TO HIDE
NOTHING TO LOSE
NOTHING TO DECLARE
NOTHING TO US
NOTHING TO SAY
NOTHING TO GAIN
NOTHING TO YOU
NOTHING TO THIS
NOTHING TO DO

THE BRANDED SERIES
BRANDED
SCARRED
MARKED

RISQUÉ & HARROW INTERTWINED
TAKE A RISK
FIGHTING FATE
RISK IT ALL
FIGHTING BACK
GAME OF RISK

FORBIDDEN PREQUEL DUET
ALL. ONLY.
ONLY YOURS

THE FORBIDDEN NOVELS
FORBIDDEN DESIRE
FORBIDDEN WANT
FORBIDDEN WISH
FORBIDDEN NEED
FORBIDDEN BOND

LOST & FOUND
LOST
FOUND

ONE

"YOU'VE GOTTA MOVE FASTER, LADY."

Styx tugged on her arm, forcing her to keep going. Try as she might to keep up, their fitness levels were just too disparate. It didn't matter that she ran every day and tried to build up her strength with whatever random items were lying around camp. She was not Olympus strong.

Her bare feet slowed them down, which was probably the only reason he'd let her stop to change in a hidden corner not far from camp. All the while she'd been aware of him hissing at her to hurry up.

"We have been moving for an hour," she said, out of breath.

That was a guesstimate. Given it felt like a week to her tired legs and scraped up feet, an hour seemed a reasonable suggestion.

"It hasn't been that long," he said, still dragging her in his wake.

With each forceful, prompting tug, he came closer to jerking her shoulder right out of its socket.

"We haven't heard shooting or fighting," she said. "It could've been Garrick and the other guys."

It suddenly occurred to her that every step they took

away from camp would have to be taken in reverse when her guide decided it was safe to return. Not only that, if they did hear shooting, she'd want to be close, in case Daire needed her.

"Stop!" she hollered, yanking her hand free of his.

Styx whirled around to grab for her again, but she leaped back, preventing him from getting hold of her. "This isn't a game, Tess. We need to move."

"Why? Where are we going? You and Daire were supposed to go on a hike, not us. Just tell me what the hell is going on."

His scowl betrayed his impatience, but he added a disgusted exhale just for good measure. "We don't know who was en-route to camp. If it was Garrick and he wants to take down Zeus then we might have an ally. It could just as easily have been Zeus come to obliterate us."

"Shouldn't you be down there with them?" she asked, thrusting an arm behind her, pointing at their path. "You need to help them."

"Hades has to be there to deal with whichever principal showed up. If it was Zeus, there's a chance he can keep him talking. Then Ares might be able to sneak up, do what he can."

Some sick part of her was excited about the potential outcome that could erase their worries so soon.

Except it wouldn't be that simple. "There were vehicles, more than one," she said. "I don't know how many, but that means more than one guy."

"Yeah," Styx said, pushing his shoulders back.

His resentment about her slowing him down began to make sense. To him, she was dead weight. It was only then, illuminated in the shards of moonlight breaking through the trees, that she realized their pace wasn't the only thing angering him.

"You're mad at me."

"Yeah. You need to build up your stamina, start endurance training."

If her father hadn't been so adamant about not training her every time she'd asked, maybe keeping up wouldn't be so difficult.

"Make the case to Harry when we get back," she said, peering into him. "But that's not it. You're mad because you want to be there. You want to be back at camp."

"With my unit? Yes," he said. "I do."

Her presence meant his assignment was babysitting instead of murder.

"Then go," she said, leaping out of the way, stopping just short of grabbing him to push him back down the incline. "Get your butt back there."

"You need to be protected."

She opened her arms. "No one's going to get me out here," she said, figuring if she was lost, there was little chance of anyone else finding her. "I'll stay right here. I won't move."

It wasn't wrath or upset that surged through her. Hope bloomed over every other emotion. She wanted Styx with Daire. Wanted the brothers to have someone watching their backs. If that meant she had to spend a night in the woods on her own, so be it.

"My orders—"

"I don't give a damn about your orders," she said, swallowing the lump forming in her throat. "Think about it. I want you down there and you want to be down there. No one expects you to be in the shadows. If they're in trouble, they need you sneaking up on them. Don't you think they'll forgive you for disobeying orders if you save their lives?"

"No," he said, his expression relaxing some. "Hades would never forgive anyone for disobeying orders for any reason."

"Daire will forgive you."

He licked his lips before smiling. "For leaving you in the middle of nowhere on your own? Have you met him? What's the thing he says about eyes on?"

Anything that reminded her of their relationship gave her a thrill. "His eyeline. It's easier for him to keep me safe if I'm in his eyeline."

Actually, it was her who'd put it that way first. In all the time Styx had been racing ahead, dragging her along, she hadn't been in his eyeline. She might have told him that, except he was only just beginning to chill. Probably best not to be antagonistic.

"Right. And he can't do that right now 'cause he's busy watching Hades's ass and making sure you're not pursued."

Some of that anger was creeping back in.

"Do you think I like being the weakest member of the herd? Slowing you all down?" she asked. "I don't want you here. I want you with Daire. I always want you with Daire because I know you watch each other's asses. Harry refuses to train me to protect myself in any way. I know how to handle a weapon, but he won't even give me one of those."

"You'll have to learn," he said, the hood over his eyes descending further when they flicked to her abdomen. "If you have something other than your own life to protect."

Turning around, she started to go back the way they'd come. "I am not talking about that with you."

"You're going the wrong way," Styx called after her. "We're not going back there."

"You can go wherever you want," she said, knowing she'd be of little combat help if anything was going down. "I am going back."

"Stop," Styx said, grabbing her shoulder to whirl her around. "You are so goddamn stubborn."

"I will do whatever it takes to protect the man I love," she said, vehement in her certainty. "Whatever it takes. If that means putting myself in the path of a bullet, it's what I'll do."

Maybe all she'd be able to do. If she went down as a human shield, it would be her choice. Harry would only have himself to blame for not giving her a fighting chance when he refused to share the tools to do anything else.

"And if you're carrying his child?"

Talking about a potential pregnancy was one thing, factoring it into decision making when it might not even exist was a step too far.

"Then Harry will be pleased he doesn't have to worry about it," she said because her father was damn sure she should never carry Daire's kid.

Standing in the darkness, braced to hear any hint of a

ruckus near the distant camp, the situation became so real that a new kind of gravity weighed on her.

"Daire won't let—"

"You have to look after him," she said, feeling the true burden of what it was to be loved by a man who felt responsible for everything. "If something happens to me, you have to promise, you can't let him self-destruct."

"Maybe you should've thought of that before."

Styx had been the one to accept them without hesitation. Harry didn't like her and Daire being together for a bunch of reasons. Most of which she understood. What she didn't understand was why Styx had chosen that moment to judge something that he'd never had an issue with before. Usually, he was their supporter. He put himself in the position of mediator, using careful comments to talk down Harry or Daire when they were building themselves toward a confrontation.

Breathing out, she sagged. Her whole body revolted against the idea of getting embroiled in another argument. "Please," she said on a sigh. "He's your brother and he loves me. He didn't choose to and I didn't force myself to love him… We know that it's crazy. We know it breaks rules and is a ridiculous position to be in when the weakness could get us killed. Please… don't make him fight you too. He's already fighting on so many fronts."

"I'm standing here with you. Not him."

"And if I had the energy to argue with you, I would. But your brother led me one way, screwed me senseless and then dragged me back. You've had me racing up this damn mountain like there's gold at the summit. I just don't have it in me to justify myself to another judgmental ass… What can I say that will make this better? Nothing. I can apologize for loving him or for *making* him love me." Which wasn't something she'd done on purpose. "But will it change anything? I'll still love him. He'll still love me and we'll still be racing away from any chance of being there for him."

Styx came closer, relaxing his grip on her shoulder. "I'm sorry. You're right, I know, I… He says you focus him. Me bringing you up here was as much his idea as Hades and it's not just about your protection. If Ares could fight and watch you at the same time, he'd probably tie himself to you." As he smiled, so did she because Tess couldn't deny that was probably true. "If he knows you're up here, safe with me, then he can focus. You don't want him searching camp for you after every punch, trying to keep you in his eyeline while assholes are sneaking up on him."

"No one can sneak up on Daire," she said, thinking of all the times he'd heard potential danger long before she'd detected a whisper. "He's always alert."

"Until you're in the mix," he said. "Maybe when you're alone he can do it, but remember what happened when I made that crack about joining you in the shower in the Miami apartment? I did that on purpose, to show how he can be distracted by you. And that was just a comment. Imagine what would happen if he saw someone hurting you, detaining you."

He'd go nuclear. "God, this is a mess," she said, backing up to sit on a fallen log. She needed the rest and time to think. "How can we do this? I mean, how can I ask him to stay focused and still be around to distract him…?" Running a hand up over her hair, she pushed it from her forehead to look up at him. "Do you think I should leave?"

He frowned. "Leave?"

"If I lose myself, if no one can find me—"

"Ares will find you," Styx said, coming over to join her on the log. "He found you before, remember? That was before he was crazy in love with you. I bet he knows you better now, so it would be easier to hunt you down. If you split… Shit, Lady, if you split, I don't even know what he'd do. No, that's a lie, I know what he'll do. He'll drop absolutely everything to track you. He won't care who's pursuing him or what's being missed while he's doing it either."

"He hates it when things are missed."

"Yeah, he does." Styx put an arm around her. "You think leaving will make any of this easier on either of you? Here, with the unit, you have allies who can protect you. Until we have Zeus or he's dead, you can't be anywhere except with us… You just have to trust that when we say run or hide, that we're doing it because it's best for you. We give you those orders or drag you away because it's what's best for the whole. We've considered all the outcomes and scenarios, and everyone is where they're best placed to do the most good for the unit. If you're given an order, you have to carry it out. We have to trust that you'll carry it out."

"Or…?" she said, peeking around at him.

"If one soldier doesn't carry out their orders, they're not trusted by the others. That makes them a liability. In your case, I'd bet Hades would be just as willing to tie you up and stuff you in a closet, if it meant your protection." Tess didn't doubt her father was capable of that. "In the case of a ground assault, the orders were to put you in the truck and drive… Imagine how far from camp we'd be then."

Too far for her to avoid a meltdown. Leaving Daire behind like that would probably end her. "Least my feet wouldn't be all cut up," she said, figuring he knew just how loathed she'd be to drive away from her love.

Styx shirked the pack from his back. "Are they bad?" he asked, sliding off the log to crouch in front of her and unlace her boots. "You picked good footwear."

"I'm not an idiot," she said, watching him pull off the boot and then peel away her sock. "I knew what Harry meant. Most of the damage was done before… when Daire was bringing me back."

"'Cause you lost your shoes out there?" he asked, smirking as he examined the sole of her foot. He propped her heel on his thigh and reached over to retrieve some kind of ointment from his pack. "And your panties?"

She gasped. "You were spying on me getting dressed?"

He laughed. "They were hanging out of your sweater pocket when we stopped."

Please God let that be the truth. "You're brother's a real gentleman."

"My brother will have his ass handed to him when Harry finds out you were getting busy in the woods," Styx said, rubbing the ointment into her foot.

The massage felt good. Even the sting of the

medicine didn't diminish it. She tried to remember the last time she'd had any kind of massage… and came up short.

"Us going out there gave him valuable intel… sooner than he'd have got it if we just stayed at camp."

He took some bandage from the pack and began to wrap her foot. "And the sex?"

"That was… me," she admitted. "Damn it's always me tempting him over that line. He's right about me. I am a temptress."

"Doesn't seem to bother him." He finished with one foot, putting her sock and boot back on before moving to the other. "You know Hades didn't have a chance to say, but…"

"Say what?"

"Even if it is Garrick down there with Olympus guys, Hades doesn't think it's a good idea to be open about your relationship. Not until we know more. Until we're sure they're on our side."

Because if they weren't, then learning Daire had a weakness they could exploit, one they wanted to exploit to get JARR anyway, would be a coup.

"I can do that," she said, noting his surprise in the way his focus jerked up from his task. She laughed. "What? You think I've never hidden my love for him? Maybe it's not easy and maybe I don't always like doing it, but if it's best for him…"

Most days, she thought Daire would be better off having never met her. She never believed the opposite. But hiding their feelings, as best they could, should at least offer a glimmer of protection to him. Otherwise, she may as well just hand herself to her enemy and tell them to threaten her to win Daire's allegiance.

He went back to treating her foot. "Okay, but I'm just saying, you weren't great at it in London."

"I didn't know I had to be great at it," she said. "I didn't know you were looking for signs. Besides, I've learned a lot since then. I can fake it."

Styx snickered. "Wait 'til I tell Ares that."

She socked his shoulder. "Don't challenge him to prove otherwise. You just told me to keep us a secret. Might be difficult if you're brother's not on board. I'm not great at saying no to him."

More than once she'd tried. Since their early days together when he was Danny, if he wanted her, he got her. She didn't even have to be thinking straight to be seduced. Her mind could be anywhere. Her stress level high and still her Heart would wheedle his way in.

"I know a good spot not far from here where we can set up camp."

"Camp?" she asked, concerned and relieved. "You're not going back to help them?"

"Whoever is down there," Styx said. "Hades needs time to assess the situation. If it's safe, when it's safe, they'll let us know."

"There hasn't been any fighting."

"You keep saying that, but it doesn't prove anything. If they've been taken—"

"Taken?" she repeated, slammed by horror. "Oh my God."

Who would have the ability to steal trained professionals like her love and Harry? Maybe it wasn't that simple. Drugs could be in the mix and they had no idea how many men had descended on their allies. Anything was a possibility.

"If they've been taken," Styx said, deliberate in his intention to finish the sentence he'd started. "They'll need us to go get them."

"That was Harry's order? If they were taken, we should go get them?"

"No," Styx said. Putting her foot on the ground, he stood up, brushing his hands together. "His order was to run and hide you."

He offered her a hand, which she took to let him pull her onto her feet. "You literally just said no one should ever disobey a direct order."

A wild and mischievous smile took his lips as he leaned in closer. "Yeah, but I'm a rebel, haven't you heard?"

Disruptive was the word Daire had used to describe his brother. As much as she wished Styx would use that angle of his personality to return them to camp then and there, she had to trust he knew what he was doing. It wasn't easy. Sometimes she wanted to go against Daire just to be there with him. But she didn't doubt he was smart and careful. She needed to have faith in him and his abilities.

Camping for one night wouldn't be the end of the world. She just couldn't make any promises about how much she'd sleep knowing that she'd left her love behind.

TWO

THE TEMPERATURE PLUMMETED at night. Maybe it was her mood or just that she'd taken the Beast and real blankets for granted. She did sleep. At some point, the anxiety overtook her and she passed out. Waking up cuddled next to Styx was a shock, but not one that bothered her after she shoved away from him only to realize how cold it was without his body heat.

They hadn't lit a fire or eaten anything either before setting up the tent or after waking. On the ground, huddled in Daire's sweater, she watched Styx pack everything into his big Bergen backpack.

"Can we go back now?" she asked.

It had been the first question on her mind the moment after she opened her eyes, but she'd held off from asking it. Unless he answered in the affirmative, her mood wouldn't lift.

"Let's find out," he said, fastening the backpack and slinging it onto his back. "Come on."

He started to stride away, so she scrambled to her aching feet to rush after him. "How will we find out?" she asked, noting that they weren't going up or down.

From what she could tell, they were heading toward

the water, though the rise they'd ascended would leave them somewhere on the ridge. That was just fine. The thought of an early morning swim in potentially frigid, near freezing water didn't appeal in the slightest.

"I have a scope."

"What does that mean?"

It might be a relief he wasn't yanking and tugging at her like the previous night. Except for the fact she had little choice but to follow him. Yesterday, she'd been ready to rush back into camp to do whatever she could for Daire and Harry. In the cool light of a dewy morning, she understood how dangerous that could be. Presenting herself, their weakness, could do more harm than good.

"It means we have to look for a sign," Styx said, pausing where the trees ended, though there was another ten feet to the edge of the ridge.

He hunkered down and took something from the thigh pocket of his pants. A little telescope. Crouching with him, she looked out over the ridge. The water and their height separated them from the camp, but it was visible in the distance. The Airstream wasn't difficult to see, especially when it caught a glint of the sun rays still scattering themselves wide, maybe only an hour or two after first appearing.

"What's the sign?" she asked, eager to know what they were looking for. Though without the scope, all she could really see were shapes and colors. "Can you see other vehicles?"

"Two," he said, "which isn't bad. Means no more than ten."

Those didn't sound like the best odds. "Ten against two?"

He glanced away from the scope to look at her. "I'll remember to tell Ares you doubted him."

"I don't doubt him," she said, standing up when he did. "I just prefer it when there isn't the chance he had to face off against ten automatic weapons."

Styx tucked the scope away in his thigh pocket again. "We didn't hear gunfire, remember? And that those vehicles are still there suggests they weren't taken."

"Doesn't mean they're not being tortured though, does it?" she asked. "They could be tied up over there, beaten, anything." When he started to move again, she followed. "That's it? Don't I get to see?"

"No," Styx said. "I saw what I needed to."

"What did you see?" she asked, wishing his pace was more urgent. Last night he couldn't move fast enough, that morning he was much more leisurely. "Are we going back?"

"What do you think?"

Glancing around, she took note that they were descending rather than the opposite. "We are going back. How do you know it's safe?"

"Last night you were all for rushing down there. Now you're scared?"

"I'm not scared," she sneered. "I do want to go back. I just want to know how you—"

"The tailgate was down."

She thought about that for a second. "The tailgate was down?" she asked. "On the truck?" He nodded. "And that's the sign? How do you know they're not just unloading something?"

"Because it was down when I checked earlier too. Everything's in the same position."

"Wait, how did you…? When did you check earlier?" As far as she knew, they'd been together every second since leaving camp. "You left me alone in the tent?"

His smirk didn't amuse her. "I was careful, Lady. No point waking you… I went back and forth between the tent and the viewpoint a few times."

So sleep must have found her sooner than she thought. Either that or he'd slipped her something. "If you knew it was safe last night, why didn't we just go back?"

"Orders were to keep you away all night. We need a cover story and us out on a trek worked."

"So we were out on a trek," she said. "An overnight trek? Together? Alone?"

Telling the new arrivals they'd split because they feared the newcomers' intentions wouldn't be the best way to start a new alliance.

"Yeah, what's wrong with that?"

"If I was going on an overnight trek with anyone, alone, it wouldn't be you."

"Yeah, it would," Styx said, still smiling. "'Cause Hades would never let you and Ares go off together, chances are, you wouldn't come back."

True story. Not for a while anyway. Tess was good at tempting her lover into bed, and at tempting her Heart to go against his better judgement… which maybe wasn't something to boast about. More than once he'd reminded her that all she had to do was ask and he'd take her anywhere she wanted to go, even if that was a million miles from the security of their unit.

Their unit. That seemed like a joke. Even if those who were at the camp were loyal to Harry and Daire, she wouldn't know them. Wouldn't know it. The only thing that she could trust was Daire's word. If he told her to trust the people there, she would. Not that she'd be comfortable with them. Chances were those people would have to go into battle with her Heart. They could be responsible for him keeping or losing his life.

She couldn't be argumentative. She had to be the perfect, amiable hostess. Those men, whoever they were, either wanted to end her love or protect him. Even though she couldn't admit to anyone that Daire was actually hers, she wouldn't give anyone any excuse to be combative. Unit cohesion was the most important thing. She could smile and laugh and be a silent companion to the group. Yeah, it might not be her natural state, but she'd do it for Daire. For his life.

Retrieving one of the power bars from her pocket, she opened it up to start eating. Styx glanced at her, then the bar. "You want one?" she asked, plucking out another to offer it to him.

He took it to begin eating. "Where did you get those?"

"The Beast," she said.

"Panties and power bars, maybe you're not an idiot after all."

She just sneered at his snicker. "I'm surprised you don't have food in that big pack of yours."

"I do," he said, chomping on the bar she'd provided.

"Then why are you eating mine," she said, lunging across him. "Gimme that back."

He just held his hand out of her reach. "You offered."

"Why didn't you offer me yours?"

"I don't know how long we'll be out here," he said. "I wasn't just gonna start handing things out before I knew whether we were going to camp or hike to town."

The prospect of hiking to town was so daunting that she didn't even dare ask how long it would take or the distance from here to there.

"Daire always feeds me."

Another scoff of a laugh escaped him. "Yeah, but I think he'd object to me feeding you the same thing the same way."

She frowned. "What are you—" Realizing what he meant, she threw the back of her hand against his arm in a gentle slap. "Yeah, that's disgusting. I would object too… So would you when I bit down hard."

They kept on going. Both finished their food and Styx took the wrappers to stuff them in his pocket.

"Did you and Ares talk out there or was there only one thing on your mind?" he asked and glanced her way. When she wasn't quick to reply, he kept going. "I know you think it's none of my business, but the truth is, if you're carrying an Olympus kid—"

"Elysium."

"What?"

"That's what we decided to call it," she said, retrieving her water bottle.

"You want to call your kid Elysium?"

"No!" she said, lowering the bottle from her lips. "Olympus is dead. It won't come back in its previous form. So we decided to call the new organization something else. Elysium is what we came up with."

"You had time out to talk and you brainstormed company names?" he asked. "You guys have some weird idea of dirty talk."

"We were done with sex by then."

Truly they never were and she didn't think they ever could be. Just thinking about him got her ready for another roll in the forest and he was nowhere in sight. Still, thinking about how she felt out there compared to how she'd felt the previous day when they were both in camp, there was more zing in her step. Whatever happened, she felt ready, invigorated, prepared to take on the world. The biggest difference between that moment and yesterday's was the duration between intimate bouts.

That seemed a pretty good measure to her of just how important sex was in their relationship. She'd done her duty by refilling his stores not long before they were descended upon. Except with Styx's message from Harry that they should keep their relationship under wraps, they may not have a chance to refill those stores again any time soon.

"You're really not gonna tell me?" Styx asked after they'd gone another few yards.

"Tell you what?" she asked. "What is it you want to know?"

If anyone should be giving him information about their relationship, it should be Daire. Still, she wanted to at least know what the guy was so curious about.

"Are you pregnant?"

"I don't know," she said because it was a straightforward answer. "How would I know that? I've been stuck out here for eleven days now. Harry and me were with Asclepius before that, traveling from Miami, which we left just a few hours after you and Daire. When would I have had the time to do a pregnancy test or see a doctor?"

"But it's possible?"

"Anything is possible," she said. "You must've heard us having sex. Telling you we were together wasn't a prank. We really are together."

"And you're not careful? Hades seemed to think you used rubbers."

"This is exactly the conversation I didn't want to have," she said, catching a loose leaf from a low branch as they passed. "Daire said it, our methods of birth control are our own. Besides, nothing is a hundred percent."

"When was your last period?"

"Not your business," she said in a sort of sing-song voice, figuring Daire would prefer to control the flow of information to his own family.

"Okay, but say you are, what would be the plan? Would you keep it or... not?"

Again, still not his business, yet she understood everyone's need to plan ahead. "It doesn't feel good to be evasive," she said. "But I don't have answers. I can't promise anything until I know something."

Anticipating her honest reaction in a hypothetical was impossible. Maybe she would be so fiercely protective that she'd run and hide even from Daire. Maybe she'd be flat out terrified of what might happen to her and her child. Maybe she would consider aborting if the reality of carrying Daire's baby overwhelmed her. She couldn't really see it going that way, but no one knew anything for sure until they were in a given situation.

THREE

IT TOOK MORE THAN twice as long to get back to camp as it had to flee the previous night. She wouldn't have minded the same pace both ways. They didn't go straight back to camp either. Although she noticed they were taking an indirect route, she didn't say anything. He'd have his reasons. Though he'd said the signal it was safe to return was on show, he may assume the situation could've changed since they last checked.

As they came around a tall bundle of boulders, they almost walked straight into someone. A guy… Broad, built solid, definitely Olympus. The rifle in his hands was already pointed their way, but Styx raised his hands then lunged forward to grab the barrel to throw it aside.

Thinking there was going to be a fight, she almost leaped back behind the boulders. Before she did, the men started laughing and slapping their palms together.

"I should've taken that shot," the guy said.

"You hesitated," Styx said. "Hades will love that." He stepped aside to grab her shoulder and haul her forward. "Pandora, Coltrane. Coltrane, Pandora."

"Harry told me you were out here," Coltrane said, scanning her figure, not in a sexual way, it seemed he was curious. "And that we had a passenger."

"She's a little more than that."

Styx kept hold of her when he and Coltrane fell into step walking in the direction of camp.

"Yeah. She's our ticket back. Sure can't live like we have for the last year," Coltrane said. "We shouldn't be spread all over."

"Guess we know where you fall on the debate about the future," Styx said. "Garrick with you?"

"Yeah."

"Who else?"

"Boze, Lowe, Zip, Milo." Those were the guys who'd been in Vegas. Minus Albany. "Rice, Kingsley."

Styx stopped to look at his colleague, letting her go as he did. "Kingsley is at camp?"

"Yep," Coltrane said, smirking. "You are in for a rough ride, buddy."

The normally relaxed Styx tensed, she didn't see it in his form as much as the almost sulking scowl that took over his features. "Whatever."

The guys started to walk again, so she hurried along with them. Quickly adding everyone up, they had nine soldiers and two principals. Not bad odds… though she couldn't be sure of that until they knew who Zeus had working for him.

"What is Garrick's plan?" she asked, figuring that if they were going to walk the rest of the way together, she could at least try to figure this Coltrane guy out.

He glanced at her, but only for a second. "I heard you weren't shy."

Damnit. During their walk, hadn't she told herself to be a happy, friendly, easy person to get along with? That didn't really gel with an interrogation. Already it seemed that she was making enemies. The whole damn situation was frustrating. If she couldn't get answers from others and she wasn't allowed to talk to Daire, how was she supposed to be kept in the loop? Her father sure wouldn't be having any heart to hearts with her. Garrick was his equal and both of them were superior to the soldiers. They'd take the reins and everyone would follow orders.

Everyone else anyway. She might not want to rock

the boat while they were in training camp. But it was her blood they'd need for JARR. She wasn't going to just trot along and offer it unless she knew it wasn't going to be used for anything nefarious.

"Would be interested to know how he got you and Rice on board," Styx said. "Don't think you took him at face value."

"Boze got us on board. Him and Lowe. 'Cause if P had rocked up on his own…"

"Yeah, that's what we figured."

"Felt good to see Ares again, I gotta tell you. Wouldn't say it to his face but…"

Styx and Coltrane shared a snicker. "Yeah, guy already thinks enough of himself."

It was difficult not to get in on the teasing when they were talking about her love. She figured she'd let the boys be boys and refrain from letting them know that Daire had the goods to back up his confidence and then some.

"So what's the plan?" Coltrane asked Styx.

That was annoying. So it was presumptuous for her to ask about Garrick's strategy, but just fine for Coltrane to quiz Styx on theirs?

"I leave that to the higher ups," Styx said. "I go where they point. Kill who they point at."

"Yeah," Coltrane said. "We've got guys still out there… We'll need to bring them in. You got numbers?"

"No," Styx said on a shrug, planting a hand on her back to push her forward a few steps, so she didn't lag behind. "No way to know."

"Can't say I'm sorry we were on Zone when this happened. Wish the damn thing was better though… We've lost guys, right?"

"You can bet on it," Styx answered. "You hear about Albany?"

"Yeah. Should never have happened. What the hell are we doing killing our own? What was he trying to do? Was it a warning?"

In her opinion, Zeus obliterated the Vegas house in the midst of a temper tantrum. There was no denying he'd been pissed, at her specifically. That meant she had to accept some level of responsibility for Albany losing his life.

"Who knows what's going on in his crazy head," Styx said.

"Someone needs to figure it out," Coltrane said, coming to a stop. "This is as far as I go."

"Stand alert," Styx said, smacking Coltrane's upper arm in what was probably supposed to be a friendly gesture.

Coltrane turned to go back the way they'd come. She was still watching him when Styx took her arm to guide her back onto the route to camp.

"Why isn't he coming back to camp?" she asked.

"Because he's on perimeter duty," Styx said. "It's his duty to keep everyone inside safe."

From that side anyway. The only way anyone would know where they were, or be able to sneak up on them, was if there was a mole in camp. Given they'd just taken on a bunch of new members, that was a possibility. Just because Styx shook the guy's hand didn't mean she trusted him.

"I don't know how you do this," she murmured. "The paranoia is driving me insane."

"What do you have to be paranoid about?" Styx asked. "You think your guy's gonna let anything happen to you? What do you think he would do to the rest of us if we let it happen?"

"Who is Kingsley?" she asked, recalling his reaction to learning that guy was with them. "What does he have against you?"

"Nothing," Styx said. "Quit asking questions."

"You know, I'm really going to try to get along with everyone. But if I think you guys are cutting me out or on the wrong path—"

"What?" Styx asked, stopping to whip her around toward him. "You wanna be careful before you threaten anyone around here."

She swallowed, not because she was afraid, but because she didn't want to get emotional and start an argument. It would be dangerous to be distracted by an argument any time, but so close to camp, when they hadn't declared themselves, that would just be stupid.

"It's not a threat," she said though could forgive him for thinking that. "I know you have a lot to consider. But, at the end of the day, it's my blood that's needed to free JARR." He frowned. "Regardless of what happens to me after, that in itself is a big responsibility and it's on my shoulders, no one else's."

"You're going to be protected. Ares wouldn't—"

"We have no way to know how this will play out," she said. "And I'm still not convinced that I can trust what either side will do with the information stored in JARR. It's temptation. Even with the best intentions, there will be..." The hue of his frown became something else; his attention began to drift. "What?"

"JARR," he murmured. A second later, he closed his eyes and hissed out a breath. "Goddamnit." Grabbing her wrist, Styx tugged her along, much as he had the previous night. "Come on."

Their pace was as punishing as it had been on their departure. Whatever had occurred to him, it had changed the urgency of their journey.

"What?" she asked, jogging to keep up. "What did you figure out? What are you—"

"We've gotta get back. We need to talk to Ares."

They did? Tess didn't know why, but if they were heading for her Heart, she didn't have any worries about whatever would happen when they got there.

Camp wasn't much further away. Within ten minutes, they broke from the thin line of trees that tapered from the end of the woods behind the Beast. Styx didn't slow down. There were people dotted around. One by the water. Another at the tree line. Someone else wandered in the distance, near the path into camp.

When they were noticed, the various people paused to look their way. They probably wondered who'd gotten through the defenses. At least they would until they recognized Styx. Once they did, they went back to their patrols.

By then, she had noticed who was standing next to

the Beast. Her Heart. Standing alert, just as he had the first night she'd met Harry. Styx didn't have to drag her half as hard when she had Daire in her sights. He didn't flinch. It was incredible how he could be so aware and yet completely ignore them at the same time.

They were no threat; he knew that even better than those patrolling elsewhere. As they came closer, Styx swung her around to put her body in front of his. As a shield, there wouldn't be a better one against Daire, if it wasn't for the fact that she was a head shorter than Styx. Kind of left an important part exposed.

Putting Daire at the entrance to the Beast was smart if Harry and Garrick were in there, which it seemed safe to assume. It was their roving headquarters. Ironic that Daire was the one who'd acquired the thing, yet he was the one most often kept from the inside.

Harry wouldn't mind if his most valued lieutenant overheard whatever conversation was going on inside. Well, he'd mind least if Daire heard anything. And the guy on the door was the last line of defense. If any enemy got through their patrols, they'd have to face Daire before getting to the valuable principals. Daire wouldn't let that happen. It was as simple as that.

Styx's pace didn't let up until they got right up to Daire who didn't move away from the door. His momentum was such that he actually propelled her right up against Daire. Her Heart still didn't flinch and Styx didn't pull her away, so there she was, stuck in a sandwich between the brothers.

"You're not getting in," Daire said.

He seemed to be looking straight ahead and definitely wasn't looking at her. But his brother was blocking her Heart's view if his intention was to keep an eye on things.

"We missed something," Styx murmured, laying his hands on her upper arms.

The comment caused Daire's blind focus to shift to his brother. "Missed what?"

"JARR," Styx said. "We missed something."

From the twitch in his brow, she could tell her Heart didn't understand. His brother didn't seem to be in any hurry to fill him in. Although she didn't know what Styx had deduced, she did know what had sparked his comprehension.

"I said it was a big responsibility on my shoulders," she said, ignoring how Styx's grip strengthened. "That I wasn't sure I could trust either side with it. Even with the best of intentions, it's temptation and it's on me if it gets out there."

Styx's hands slid a little higher. The brothers remained fixated on each other. "It's on her... if temptation—"

"Shit," Daire exhaled.

Trying her best from her restricted position to get some hint of what was going on from either of them, all she saw was Styx slow nod. "What?" she asked, frustrated. "What is going on?"

"We have to keep this close," Daire murmured so quietly that she almost didn't hear him.

"My Heart."

On a blink, his attention dropped to her. "Styx told you? We keep this under wraps."

"I don't know what either of you are talking about," she said. "Safe to say I can't tell anyone something I don't know."

"I mean this," he said, a tinge of longing polluting his otherwise severe gaze.

"You wanted the guys to know."

"Things have changed," Daire said, setting a glare on his brother. "You've gotta keep her in your—"

"In my eyeline, I know," Styx said.

The conversation was so quiet, so discreet, it was obvious they didn't want any hint anyone could listen in, even those in the trailer.

"Kingsley gonna be a problem?" Daire asked.

That name again.

A tremor of tension vibrated through Styx. "No. No problem."

"Pandora comes before everything else," Daire said, demonstrating exactly how to threaten someone.

"I get all of the aggravation and none of the sex."

Her Heart wasn't amused by his brother, she inhaled

through her nose. "No one's getting any of that any time soon," she murmured.

If they were a secret, they couldn't take the risk of anyone catching them in an intimate position. They didn't have only Styx and Harry to concern themselves with anymore. There were others. Highly trained others. Who may or may not be loyal to them.

"Take her to town with you," Daire said. "Do not let her out of your sight."

"Why are we suddenly so worried about me?" she asked. "I know we've been worried about me for a while, but you should share whatever you've just figured out… Share it with me. You're the only two I trust here anyway."

"Keep it that way," Daire said.

Behind him, the door made a sound, so Daire stepped aside to let it open. Her father stood on the threshold.

"You're back," he said to her.

She opened her arms. "Apparently I am."

He nodded to the side. "Inside." It was automatic to look at Daire for permission. "Tess."

Her father obviously wasn't impressed with her reaction. Inching forward, she didn't let her father's glare intimidate her. It actually helped her out. While he was glaring, trying to berate her without words, her hand moved closer to Daire's. Her pinkie brushed his, which was quick to respond, stroking hers in return before they curled together.

She needed his love. Needed his strength. It didn't matter if they could acknowledge each other. As long as she knew he was there. Close. With her in their love, she would battle whatever tried to tear them down.

The stairs weren't out. She guessed that was why her father offered her a hand. "You're needed inside. Come on."

Her relationship with Daire wouldn't stay secret for long if she refused her father's request. Her Heart must have had the same thought because his finger drifted away. So she slapped her hand onto Harry's, letting him pull her up into the trailer.

Garrick was seated at the dinette. Already she hated it. The more Olympus contaminated her safe space, the harder it became to leash her emotions. In any other circumstance, she'd tell the intruders to get the hell out of her home. With their veil of compliance still shrouding each of them, all she could do was smile.

She glided across the space toward him, "Mr. Garrick," she said, saccharine sweet, offering him a hand. "Always a pleasure."

The Beast's door slammed shut as he joined his hand with hers. That was her chance. Maybe she didn't want these men in her home. Maybe she did need a shower and a change of clothes. But everything else would wait while she took the opportunity in front of her. Information. Intel. It was the key to survival.

FOUR

"SEEMS LIKE A LIFETIME since we last saw each other," Garrick said, releasing her hand to gesture at the dinette seat opposite his. "Would you like to sit down?"

His smile became more of a grimace as she clenched her jaw. The Beast was her realm. Her home. No one invited her to do what she wanted there. She had entitlement there. Daire had entitlement. That was it. No one else.

Still, pleasant, amiable, that was the plan. She slid into the seat as her father came over to prop himself against the counter next to them. Folding his capable arms, he took his time assessing them. Under the scrutiny of both men, she wasn't sure she liked it.

She was an easy scapegoat. If anyone wanted to accuse her of something, she didn't have much ability to defend herself. There were eleven Olympus agents in her midst. One of whom she was sleeping with. Another was her lover's brother. They were about the only two she could rely on. On the morning's descent, she'd told herself not to measure odds when she didn't know them for sure. Now she did: three versus nine. Considering that she was one of the three, they weren't that favorable.

"Do we have a plan?" she asked, rather than wait for

them to accuse her of something. "More training?"

"Your father believes it's necessary," Garrick said, linking his fingers on the table. "I think we need to keep moving."

Given that they'd been there for ten days, Tess wouldn't be averse to going elsewhere. Except her opinion didn't really matter on the training score. Her father was the one who knew his men. Anything that better prepared Daire for what would come, she was in favor of.

"Moving where?" she asked. "Do you have a destination in mind?"

"Now that we have numbers," Garrick said. "We can approach what needs to be done with the proper consideration."

That he was so forthcoming was appreciated, though it did raise her suspicions. "I didn't expect you to be honest."

"What do I gain from lying to you?" Garrick asked. "Your father tells me you know about JARR. About the blood."

Glancing Harry's way, she wondered why he'd revealed anything when he was so sure it was necessary to be discreet in other areas.

"My blood," she said. "That you need my blood to access JARR. Yes, I know."

Garrick drew in a breath. "That's probably for the best. Your compliance will make this much easier."

"Just because I know doesn't mean I will comply."

The man opposite her frowned. "You expect us to leave JARR where it is? Beta is not secure."

"Neither is Gamma," she said. "Any Olympus site could be compromised... Unless you expect to continue your work under Zeus's command."

"You don't?"

"I've never been Olympus," she said, sliding her hands along the width of the table to grip the end with one. "I don't intend to work under anyone's command."

"You want your freedom," Garrick said. "I'm sure that could be arranged. If you comply—"

"Is that what you want? To order some of your men

to take me to Beta? To retrieve JARR?"

"We might be able to secure you at Beta," Harry said. "If we get into the system—"

"Access and function are limited with Minotaur offline."

"So we get Minotaur online," she said, knowing that whether she went by choice or through coercion, her future journey would feature the Beta site at some point. "If it helps our cause, helps us maintain control of the site, we should do it."

The descent of her father's brow suggested he hadn't expected her to be so open or willing.

"It's not as easy as that," Garrick said. "Someone has to be there, inside. That involves a series of deliberate moves, not something a layperson would be capable of... Most Olympus agents wouldn't be able to get into Beta while it's on lockdown."

"Ares could," she said. Although the code name was rancid on her tongue, she was proud of herself for remembering to put distance between her and Daire. "He could do it."

"Yes," Garrick said. "He could... if we had the necessary keys. Harry tells me the Scepter is not in his possession. As far as we know, Zeus still has the other two."

Not true, but she made a deliberate choice not to look at her father. Her poker face wasn't that great.

"He'll retrieve them," she said. "Task Ares with getting Minotaur online and he'll do whatever is needed to achieve his objective."

"He always does," Harry said. "But he has his own agenda."

"The Titan chip will be crucial for the Gamma site," Garrick said, surprising her with his knowledge. "I heard it was taken."

Such a prominent piece of tech being taken was the kind of thing Garrick would know. He probably had an alert set up to inform him if any secure site was compromised.

"And you think that was us? Maybe Zeus has it."

Garrick wasn't so quick to share his thoughts

anymore. "The objective is to retrieve JARR and Minotaur from the beta site. We have to be conscious that Zeus will want both. We also have no idea where the loyalties of the Six lie."

"Liberating JARR and Minotaur while Zeus is on the warpath is dangerous. We have to deal with him and, like Harry said, find out the position of the Six."

"Do you know where they are?" she asked.

Styx had known where they were. Though that information wasn't necessarily the most up to date.

"Yes," Garrick said. "Most of them. They're lying low. Holed up in a remote lodge in New England."

"Why?" she asked. "Doesn't that make them vulnerable?"

"Two and Five are new to the organization," Garrick said. "They'd be too easy to eliminate and they have to feel protected. It's on the others to prove how they value their newest members."

"If they don't, we risk Two and Five backing out. Losing their money wouldn't be great, but—"

"The possibility of them exposing Olympus is the real worry," she said. "It could cause all kinds of trouble. We don't want that."

"No, we don't."

She focused on Garrick. "You said 'most of them.' Who don't we know about?"

"Four," Garrick said, glancing at her father.

"Slipped the net?" Harry asked to which Garrick nodded. "Those we do have locations on, they have to be our first stop."

"Agreed," Garrick said. "I think we should get on the road as soon as possible."

"We need a plan," Harry said. "We can head that way, but I'm not sending anyone in until we've run drills and assessed unit cohesion."

"We lost a man. They're hungry."

"We lost more than one," her father said. "And I understand their need for vengeance. But we should never take emotions into the field. We also have to give them the chance to go to Zeus's side, if that's what they want… We could encounter him at anytime, anywhere. They have to understand who we're fighting here. Anyone switching sides mid-battle could fuck with the rest of the team."

"Our people are loyal to you," Garrick said. "Nothing I've seen since we found them has suggested otherwise."

Which would be exactly what a double agent would want them to think. Whether they'd come up with a plan with Zeus or just went to his side when the opportunity arose, they'd have to be careful of who they trusted.

"They'll be loyal," Harry said. "Until they're scared… We don't know how this will play out or who Byron will have protecting them." A former president would have plenty of military and intelligence connections. "Things could turn fast. If we're not on top, if we're facing execution—"

"I understand what you're saying," Garrick said. "But I stand by my original assessment. The only person who will be given the chance to turn is Ares. Zeus won't care about anyone else."

"There's no underestimating how important experienced agents are," Harry said. "Z's never been against taking prisoners."

As she knew from her stay in London. "Can't we discuss this stuff while we're traveling?" she said. "We need to start making progress."

"We can't deliver Pandora to Zeus," Harry said to Garrick. "There is a chance he's with the Six. If he's there, courting their loyalty, taking Pandora to him will be doing his work for him."

"I will not be tucked away and hidden."

"You may have to be," her father said. "We have the numbers to protect you somewhere safe now."

Shock and anger snapped her attention around to him. "I'm strongest with the unit. Most protected here."

With Daire. That she didn't share aloud. There was no need, her father heard the truth of what she was saying, that was obvious in his expression.

"If we have to launch a full assault on the lodge where they're holed up, it will be all hands on deck. We can't have a base. Can't have a vulnerability."

"So you agree with the plan to send me to beta?"

"Launching a full assault at the lodge would be a dangerous plan," Garrick said. "We have to divide and conquer. Split them up… tempt them into the open."

"Sending me to beta would tempt Zeus out," she said. "Like Harry said, it would be doing his work for him."

"Especially if he has the keys, yes," Garrick said. "I think the best way to assess where Zeus is and who is loyal to him would be to send you to Las Vegas."

That startled both her and her father. "To the gamma site?" Harry asked. "Tess has never been there. It's not operational."

"No," Garrick said. "Her boutique is still in her name… Her suite still hers."

"How?" she asked.

Almost two months had passed since Three, also known as Hugo, gave her access to a boutique and suite in his exclusive hotel.

"He hasn't been back to Vegas since the explosion. If Zeus did that intending to tempt him out, he failed. There was good reason for that," Garrick said, leaving a few beats just to raise their suspense. "Fundamentally, Hugo Balfour is a coward… Facing Zeus himself? He doesn't have the nerve for that."

"But you think if he hears Pandora is in Vegas…" Harry muttered.

"He'd be more likely to approach her, especially knowing how valuable she is to Zeus… to all of the principals," Garrick said. "He could act as ambassador."

"And get us into the lodge," Harry said, both intrigued and invigorated. "We could waltz on right past security without ever firing a shot."

"We don't know if Zeus is with the Six," she said. "Even if he is, he wouldn't be so stupid as to send Hugo into a trap."

"He wouldn't walk into a trap himself. Three is more expendable," Garrick said. "Zeus is curious, just like the rest of us. Even if he suspects it's a setup, he will want to know our plan. And don't forget that he does still need you."

For the blood and because she'd made a fool of him. Well, technically, that was Daire because he'd been the one to take Zeus's guy down. Still, she doubted that Zeus would make that distinction.

"It's a balance," Harry said. "The reward has to be greater than the risk."

Both principals present seemed to be of the same mind. "Where you're concerned, Pandora, the reward is high. You are the key to JARR, which he needs more than anything else."

"Whether Zeus is at the lodge or not, Three will look to One, to Byron, for direction…" Harry said, thinking aloud. "We shouldn't bet that he'll investigate alone either. Byron could send some of his people to protect Three. That would reduce the number of security guys at the lodge… We should send some agents up there to do recon, just in case."

She frowned. "So I go to Vegas and wait for Three and a bunch of mercenaries to come for me, while you and the rest of Olympus descend on this lodge to take down the Six?"

"We can't hurt the Six," Garrick said. "Harry's right. We should send a detail up there, just to watch and learn what they can. Meanwhile, we send you to Vegas with your own security detail… And we wait for Three to come to you. When we have access to him, we'll discuss the situation, ask him to take us to the rest of the Six or talk to them on our behalf. The ultimate objective is to secure their loyalty. If we have control of the Six, Zeus will be weak. He won't be able to hold out forever."

That plan assumed Zeus wasn't already puppet-master of the Six. "He might be at the lodge with them," she said. "He could already have their support. What do we do then?"

Harry crossed one ankle over the other, apparently as interested in the answer as her.

"We know that Zeus can't return to command," Garrick said. "For one thing, none of our lives would be safe."

"If you don't want him in command, you have to kill

him," Harry said.

"We could take him prisoner. There are facilities at the gamma site capable of holding him."

"Hold him for what?" Harry asked. "It's not like he could ever be released… Why would we keep him alive? He doesn't have anything we need."

If Zeus was with the Six in New England, the plan to transport him from one corner of the country to the other would present him with opportunities to manipulate his way out of their control or escape. She didn't like to think any of the Olympus agents would be so careless, but anything was possible. Zeus shouldn't be underestimated.

"You want time to train and the rest of us need progress," Garrick said. "There is room to compromise here… If we take Pandora to Vegas, try to tempt Three out, that could afford Ares the opportunity to go to beta… to restart Minotaur… if we had a key."

The depth of those last few words was concerning. It almost seemed like… either he knew, or suspected, that Harry wasn't giving him the full story. That might be worrying except she couldn't fault Garrick for being suspicious. He was right. They weren't giving him the whole story.

Harry shook his head. "No, we can't spread ourselves that thin. We only have nine agents."

"They can be deployed in teams of three," Garrick said.

Her father didn't seem to be convinced. "When is the time to train?"

"You don't have to be present for training. Ares and Styx can act in your stead. Give them temporary command of each detachment."

That meant splitting the brothers up. With Harry at the head of one group, Daire at another, and Styx directing the last. She was torn. As much as it would be useful to have someone she trusted monitoring each of their splinter groups, she didn't like the idea that none of the three would have someone watching their backs.

And who would she want with her? Anyone who knew the truth would assume Daire would be her first choice.

But that might not be the smartest thing for him or for her. She'd distract him and without Harry around to make sure Daire stayed focused, they could end up in trouble.

Her father had proved he would kill for her. Styx seemed happy to kill whenever the opportunity arose. But Garrick wasn't likely to want to go anywhere other than Vegas and did she need both principals? Probably not.

"I want forty-eight hours with them," her father said. "Then we move out."

"Agreed," Garrick said, standing up to shake Harry's hand.

The men were happy, she wished she could be as optimistic.

FIVE

THE PRINCIPALS WENT OUT to do whatever they did with their people, which gave Tess the chance to shower.

On opening the door to reach for the towel she'd left on the end of the bed, she heard a male cough and then a familiar voice.

"Eyes front, asshole."

Recognizing that voice in an instant, she was quick to wrap her towel around her body and jump out of the stall.

Yes. Just as she'd thought. Daire. Her man was there, propped against the counter where Harry had been earlier. Unfortunately, he wasn't alone. Styx was sitting at the edge of the dinette, his feet in the aisle.

Both men were looking her way when she tossed her wet hair from her face. She was aware of that, but only focused on the one she walked toward.

Her smile was instinct. "You're not supposed to be in here," she said, noting from the corner of her eye that the day shades were all pulled down. "If you wanted to break the rules…" Sliding her arms around his torso, she held herself against him. "You shouldn't have brought your brother."

Styx laughed behind her. "'Cause when the trailer starts a' rockin'…." he said. "How long do you think it would take for the unit to figure you guys out then?"

The reminder they were again a secret put a damper on her mood.

Daire caught her chin and tipped it up to kiss her. "It's temporary," he said, running his thumb across her lower lip. "Just until we figure out who we can trust."

"Maybe Hades changed his mind," Styx said, though she was more interested in admiring her love than listening. "He told us to come in and wait, he must have a reason."

"Aggravating me," she said, skimming her fingertips up Daire's chest and over his shoulders. "We could pull the screen in the bedroom."

"Listening to the two of you having sex through a door is bad enough, that flimsy piece of fabric won't do jack… And Harry will be back any minute."

Giving up on the hope that she might get to lie down with her Heart for a while, Tess spun around to sink back against Daire, using him as her own leaning post.

"They want to split the unit into three. One group go to the lodge in New England where five of the Six are holed up. The next goes to the beta site to reactivate Minotaur and the third goes to Vegas."

"Why Vegas?" Styx asked.

When Daire's hands met her hips, there was such obvious hesitation in them that she grabbed both to force his arms around her. They were alone, except for Styx. Her Heart was aware of his orders and those meant he wasn't to acknowledge her. Tess had to remind him that the rules weren't his gospel anymore. They had to take the chances to be familiar whenever they had them.

"Because former president Byron could have the whole Secret Service protecting them where they are. The idea behind going to Vegas is divide and conquer. Hugo will come after us to find out what's going on and we can convince him to act as ambassador and recruit the Six to our side."

"Zeus has Byron," Styx said. "Somehow he got him and I don't see that changing… Not unless we find out what he's got on him. And Byron is the key to the Six." He frowned. "How does he think us going to Vegas will get Three there? The guy's house is a crater."

"It's you," Daire said, his chest rumbling against her back. "Little Red?"

Oh, he was talking to her. Tess tipped her head back so far it bumped him.

"Yes. Apparently, Hugo never got around to telling his people I wasn't coming back."

Which made sense. The guy was in London with her until he wasn't and not long after that, his house blew up. Hugo Balfour had other things on his mind; all of them more important than her frivolous boutique.

"They want you to go there and start over," Daire said, the depth of his voice suggesting he wasn't sold on the plan. "You're the lure."

"Could work," Styx said. "Lady never screwed him, he's got unfinished business."

Anticipating her Heart's objection, she tightened her grip on his hands. "Hugo won't be screwing anything. I'll have Olympus people watching my tail."

"Us Olympus people?" Styx asked.

She shook her head. "The plan is for Harry to command one of the detachments. You two get the other two."

"We play rock, paper, scissors for who we get under us?"

A gruff, almost smug cough/laugh came from the guy holding her. "I won't fight you for Kingsley."

All expression left Styx's face. "You can take her."

That sent a jolt of shock through her. "Her?" Dropping Daire's hands, she stepped away from his embrace to turn and face him. "There's a *her* in your ranks?"

His serious look became something lighter as amusement danced behind his gaze. Rather than say anything, he dipped down, full of confidence and kissed her.

From a gentle caress, his need grew to an urgency in time with him driving his fingers into her wet hair and cradling her head to pull her tighter to him.

As her arms coiled around his neck, her towel loosened. She should care that Styx was there to watch, but her whole world existed in that kiss.

It didn't matter anyway. Her own senses didn't have to be at their peak to protect her modesty. Without breaking the kiss, the moment her towel began to slip, Daire's free hand jumped up to catch it at her cleavage. Always aware, her Heart just kept on thrilling her.

Breaking their passion, Daire paused to steal another soft kiss. "You gonna use that tone with me 'bout other women again?"

Still a little dazed, she just shook her head while her tongue darted out to capture every last remnant of their kiss.

Her father came stomping inside and stopped just beside her as the door slammed shut again.

"What's going on?" Harry asked, looking her up and down. "Where are your clothes?"

"I don't know," she said, addressing her father as Daire tucked her towel in tight. "They just melt away when my lover is near me."

Her father glared. "I sent his brother in with him to make sure you didn't get up to any of that bullshit."

"Didn't work," Styx muttered.

Harry groaned out his anger. "You two have to cool off. I told you that—"

"Don't yell at him," she said, putting herself in front of Daire. "Why do you always blame him for everything?"

"I have high expectations."

Of Daire, not of her, she got that message loud and clear.

"So do I," Daire said. "You want me to lead a detachment to the beta site and send my primary to Vegas...? My potentially pregnant primary to Vegas?"

Alarm gripped her father. "Do not talk about that here," he hissed.

They couldn't afford to have the same fight over again. Anyone outside could overhear.

"Styx goes to Vegas," Daire said. "He goes with them."

"Because you don't trust me to look after my own daughter?" Harry asked. His glare snapped onto her. "You shouldn't be sharing privileged information."

Her mouth opened in shock. "I don't! I would never share anything privileged."

"Then how did these guys find out about the plan?"

She inhaled but stopped when Daire laid his hands on her shoulders. "What you and Tess consider privileged is different," he said. "Anything she knows, she'll share with me."

When Harry's eyes met hers, she immediately looked away. Too many things were going on. She needed a night alone in private with her guy to get everything out.

A whole night alone with him. Imagining it put her in a daze. Had she ever spent a night with him? Oh, it was surreal to think that he'd ever been wholly hers. They'd taken those nights together for granted.

"That's love, Harry," Daire growled behind her, signaling she'd missed something while daydreaming. "It's trust. There's nothing I wouldn't tell her either."

"It's naïve."

"Can we fight about relationship rights and wrongs later?" Tess asked. "We may not have much time alone…" She glanced around. "Why are the shades down?"

"Because we need privacy," Harry said, striding past her to swing into the dinette. "You need to get dressed."

His abruptness came off too much like a disapproving father. Still, it was her instinct to look at Daire for direction.

"Yes," Daire said, bowing to kiss her bare shoulder. "Go put your clothes on."

"You have to stop doing that too," Harry said as she went past to head into the bedroom. "You look to him for guidance."

She didn't need anyone to tell her that.

"And I look to her," Daire said. "We're partners, Harry. In everything."

Partners? She smiled as she retrieved underwear and clothes. He was right. They were. They'd endured a lot. As she turned intending to close the screen, a thought struck her.

They'd survived.

Everything.

Their relationship had survived everything the universe had thrown at them. The lies. The misdirection. The danger. Despite people coming for them or ripping them apart. Despite her father's disapproval and missions and murders, they were still together. Still in love.

If they'd got through all of that, they could get through anything. They'd held together. Made it.

Marriage. Pregnancies. Plans or not. Whatever came next, whatever Zeus did, whether they kept their lives or not, it didn't matter. Their love was a forever love that didn't care about beating hearts or oxygen. Whether they ended up in Tartarus or the Elysian Fields, their love would endure.

Harry was going over everything they'd discussed with Garrick, she listened in from behind the closed screen while getting dressed. Her hair was still damp when she opened it again, but she didn't want to muffle their conversation with her blow dryer.

"Reach any conclusions?" she asked, hopping up to sit on the counter next to where Daire was propped.

In her eavesdropping, she'd heard most of what they'd said but thought it would be polite to afford them the opportunity to loop her in.

"Yeah, that you're sticking with Styx," Daire said. "And Harry is going to fourteen."

Again with the numbers, Tess guessed they related to states or specific locations. "How long?"

They'd survived without each other before. If she had to choose between having a timescale or not, Tess would definitely go with the former. It wasn't just for her piece of mind either. If Daire told her how long they would be apart, she'd have a timescale for raising the alarm. Harry might not listen to her, but if Daire said four days and she hadn't heard from him by day five or six, she'd drop everything to get to him.

"I don't know, baby," Daire said, laying his arm across her lap while still looking at the dinette. "Which key you want me to use?"

"I don't know if I like this idea of revealing that we have the keys," Tess said. "This whole thing could be a big fake out."

"You think Garrick's playing us?" Styx asked.

"Harry said there's no way to know how people will act when they're scared. Even if Garrick thinks he's on our side now, who knows what he'll be when Zeus shows up."

"We won't tell him we have the keys," Daire said.

"Then you'll have to let your team think you're going somewhere to retrieve it."

"To retrieve the Scepter," Styx said. "'Cause everyone except Zeus still assumes he has the other two."

Everyone may or may not include the Six. They didn't often get involved in the inner machinations of the organization. When they did, it tended to end in disaster.

"We should tell him the truth," she said, speculating on what it would mean to allow whoever was with Daire to believe he was going after Zeus to retrieve a key.

It would mean tracking and eyeballing him. Too dangerous. Tess didn't want to take the risk Daire and Zeus would face each other while her Heart had such little backup.

"Lady, I don't think—"

"If we need Minotaur up and running, then we need a key," she said. "Garrick is not stupid; the Scepter has to be somewhere. The alternative is sending Daire after Zeus. Both of them know he doesn't have a key, so what would be the point?"

"I'll kill him," Daire said.

Tess grabbed for his shoulder. "No. You can't confront him, not while it's just you and two others. You need the unit together before you face him."

They'd just been talking about how Zeus could be protected by Byron's people or how he could be at the lodge in a stronghold with the others.

"She's right," Styx said. "If Daire has to track down Zeus and chase him all over, there better be a purpose beyond misdirection. All he'd be doing is lying to our guys the whole time. You're already so sure they won't trust him when they find out about him and Pandora. We can't pile more reasons on."

"Okay," Harry said, accepting their reasoning with

surprising haste.

Either the guy was in an especially accepting mood, or he'd already come to that conclusion and just wanted them to believe it was their idea.

"He doesn't have to know anyone lied," she said. Anyone except her. "Just tell him I hid it… That I was scared to tell you guys."

"Why would you have confessed the truth now?" Styx asked.

"Because we have to make progress. I already told him that… I was just keeping the information to myself until it was needed… which is now. Plus…" Sliding her arms around Daire's neck, she rested her chin on his shoulder. "If you don't have to chase phantom Zeus around in an epic fake out, you'll get back to me quicker."

To chase Zeus, Daire would first have to find out where he was. Checking out the options, doing whatever they did, it took time. Tess didn't want him out there, away from her, for longer than he had to be.

Inhaling, Harry drew his eyes away from the couple. Clearly them showing any kind of familiarity pissed him off, even though they were alone.

"You have to go into town," Harry commanded Styx. "We'll be training for the next couple of days, then hitting the road. Won't be any time after today."

"Sure," Styx said, probably unperturbed because it had been his role to do supply runs while they'd been there anyway.

"Take Kingsley."

That sent a blink of surprise across his face. Harry didn't see it, he was looking at Daire again, but Styx's reaction intrigued her.

"We've got our work cut out," Harry said to the man in her arms. "We need to get everyone in shape, cohesive—"

"In two days?" Daire asked. "Good luck."

"When we split, it will be up to both of you to keep training going… We need our people to have confidence in our leadership. We're going into battle."

"We'll put together a program," Daire said, giving her

leg a squeeze in a prelude to moving away.

She knew it, so tightened her hold, pulling him back to her hard.

"He has work to do," Harry said, standing up.

"Yeah," she said, nuzzling the back corner of his neck closest to her. "And there's a good chance we won't be alone again before he has to leave me."

Twisting around, Daire found his way between her thighs and took her face in both hands. "We can still walk away."

Every time he got the chance, he reminded her that she was his guide. Just as he was hers. Tension rippled around the confined space. Of course it did, Harry and Styx relied on Daire; he was part of their unit and vital to its success. She noticed it, but if Daire did too, he showed no outward sign.

"I want you to have support," she said, stroking his body, hip to waist. "I just need your promise that you'll come back to me. It's supposed to be you go, I go."

He pressed his lips to hers in a gentle kiss before crouching lower to align their eyes. "Once Minotaur is back online, things will start to happen fast. It doesn't only help us, it helps Zeus too. All of us will be more vulnerable. Whoever I have to kill to get to you, I won't blink. You should know that by now."

"I do."

"If you're vulnerable, I need to be there."

"We'll have to get the timing right," Harry said in the background. "We can't equip him while my unit is still traveling to the lodge. How far away is the Scepter?"

Her eyes were already on Daire's and they didn't flinch. "Not far."

"Tess—"

"I'll tell Daire. No one else."

Her Heart smiled. "You want an excuse to be alone with me again."

That wasn't the only reason, but he was right. Garrick could know that she'd been keeping the Scepter's location a secret. They needed to reveal that semi-truth for the mission and to show Garrick some form of trust. But Tess was no fool. Telling Daire meant giving the information to someone she trusted rather than someone she didn't… doing it alone… that was just a bonus.

"We don't have time for games."

"Yeah, who has my list?" Styx grumbled. "I should get going."

Tess snatched a quick kiss from Daire and then eased him aside to jump down from the counter. "I'm coming too."

"You're not going anywhere," Harry said.

She glared at him. "Standing around here watching you and Daire put your men through their paces… or making a plan to put them through their paces, isn't exactly riveting. I have laundry to do and—"

"You can do that in Vegas," Styx said. "It's a quick in, out. There's no way I'm hanging around longer than I have to."

It wasn't like him to be in such a bad mood, but she couldn't focus on that. "Okay, fine," she said. "But I'm still coming." She spun around to Daire. "Do you have the truck keys? I need money. Oh, and you'll need to make sure all the Beast tanks are filled and emptied."

"Always do," he said. "And there's money in the nightstand."

"Okay," she said, her lips curling higher.

It was nuts that she just couldn't take her eyes off him.

Her Heart wasn't oblivious and he stared back until amusement warmed his expression. "What?"

"Nothing," she said, snagging his pinkie with hers. "I love you."

"I love you too," he said, narrowing one eye. "Doesn't usually make you stare."

Shrugging, she scooped a hand under his to raise it up so she could kiss his knuckles. "These hands are going to save our lives."

"Probably more than once," he said, curving his hand around her cheek. "Sure you're okay?"

Exhaling all her tension, Tess forced herself to move away from him to go up the trailer. "So long as you come back to me, I'll always be just fine," she called over her shoulder.

There was money in his side of the nightstand, tucked in a clip in the back corner. Not a whole bunch of money, but enough that if they were to be robbed, the perpetrator would be satisfied they'd found a stash. Smart. Her Heart was so goddamn smart.

By the time Tess returned to the living area, the door was open and Styx was the only one there waiting for her.

"You ready?" he asked, still wearing a grump. "We've gotta get moving."

He went outside without waiting for a response and Tess was left wondering. His mood had soured after Harry told him to take the Kingsley woman. Styx really hated the female Olympus agent and Tess was intrigued to know why… Almost as intrigued as she was about the woman herself.

Going into town with Styx meant she'd be safe. Going with Kingsley gave Tess the opportunity to do her own kind of recon on the enigmatic woman.

SIX

RIDING IN A TRUCK that wasn't Daire's felt odd. But not as odd as the air crackling around inside the cabin. They'd been driving for a while. Styx and Kingsley up front with Tess seated in the back. So far, no one had said a word. The two agents hadn't even looked at each other.

It was nice to have a mystery that didn't involve death… Well, as far as she knew it didn't involve death. There was something going on between the agents. From what she'd heard, Tess assumed it was animosity. Now, actually being close to them, she suspected something else.

Renee Kingsley was a beautiful woman. With dark red hair and a figure all women would envy, the female Olympus agent was ready for action. She exuded a badass vibe. Somehow it managed to scream "don't mess with me" without making her completely unapproachable.

"So…" Tess said, seated in the middle of the back, she looked from one profile to another. "Have you been with Olympus long, Renee?"

"Kingsley," Styx said. "Don't use her first name."

It was only then she realized Renee was the only agent whose first name she knew. Except Daire, but he was as unique to her as he was to everyone in the organization.

"Is it a distance thing? How come they don't have code names?"

"In the field we do," Renee said. "But they're the same depending on our role. Infiltration, recon, over watch, backup, ordnance."

"Oh, I get it, so rather than name the person, you name the role," Tess said, thinking that she liked this Kingsley already. The smile stayed on her face until she realized why that made sense. "Because you've lost so many agents…"

Maybe they started by giving all agents code names. Daire's mom had one, she remembered that. But if every time an agent was lost their code name was retired, eventually they would run out of options, or the names would get too weird— there were some complicated names in Greek mythology.

"It's more efficient," Kingsley said, telling Tess she was right without actually saying the words. "How did Ares track you down?"

Her brows rose. "I don't know. I never asked him."

If Kingsley was going to ask questions, Tess would answer them. So long as the agent answered questions in return.

"Did you know about Zulu? Before the Exodus?"

"No," Kingsley said, her head turning a fraction toward Styx who was fixated on the road ahead.

Watching them fascinated her. Styx was never uptight, not like he was in that minute. The only time Daire gripped the wheel that tight was when he was mad at her and trying not to throttle her… or in the early days when there was something more carnal going on in his mind that he was trying to resist.

"Must have been a while since you two saw each other then, huh?" Tess asked, catching glimpses back and forth, trying to decipher any hints of confirmation. "Were you at the beta site when Harry sent the alert? Styx was in the field."

"What's with the history lesson?" Styx snapped. "Just cool your heels."

Her smile came as she sank back in her seat. No way. Styx was definitely hot for Kingsley. Without a doubt.

His mood was telling. Given all he'd done for her, Tess should probably stop prodding at him, but she might not get them alone ever again.

"Kingsley is the first woman I've had to talk to since my mom died," Tess said. "I want to be friends."

"Kingsley doesn't have friends. She's an Olympus operative," Styx said. "We're not friends. None of us are friends."

Dropping her brow in a mock scowl, Tess grabbed for the shoulders of the front seats to pull herself between them. "No, we're just ice-cold killers," she growled, teasing him. When his knuckles flexed on the wheel, she laughed. "Relax. I don't plan to start braiding her hair and painting her nails. It's just nice to be around someone who isn't testosterone high all the time."

"Pan—"

"You're the one who needs to relax," Kingsley said before Styx could get to chastising their passenger. "It's smart for her to know the people around her. One day soon we'll probably be expected to protect her life. She has to know if we have the balls for it."

"Or the loyalty," Tess said. "All of you have been scattered since the Exodus."

"And anyone could've gotten to us in that time," Kingsley said with a nod. "I understand. Like I said: smart… There's also the chance we're just so flat pissed at Harry that we'd do anything to punish him."

Not an unfamiliar tale.

"The time away made you soft," Styx snarled at Kingsley. "Since when were you a sharer?"

"Maybe that's just what I want you to think. Maybe I'm lulling you into a false sense of security."

Pissed, eager for revenge, but playing it cool and friendly, ready to strike at the moment for optimum carnage? It was possible.

"Harry is her father," Styx stated, still with that edge of anger quaking his words. "One word from her and you're outta here."

Tess caught Styx glaring at her in the rearview. He

wasn't talking about Harry. He was talking about Daire. He couldn't say it because they'd all agreed the relationship should be a secret, but that was the message he was trying to convey to her, not to Kingsley.

Yeah, he was telling Kingsley to watch her ass because Tess wasn't as benign as she seemed. But he was also telling her that he was aware of her power. It was a power that she hadn't considered. Daire asked all the time if she wanted to leave, reminding her that his loyalty was to her before everything else. But what would happen if she told her Heart that someone shouldn't be trusted or someone should be hurt or cast out?

Styx wanted Kingsley protected. Tess just wondered how far he'd go to ensure that.

"You're assuming I'll let either of you get back to camp alive," Kingsley said, her shoulders moving in what Tess guessed was a smug show. "Or that I trust either of you."

That was a good point and one she hadn't considered. Kingsley had been in the cold since the Exodus. While they were taking the time out to assess if she was still trustworthy, it made sense that she was doing the same.

Being an agent, Kingsley wouldn't know about the blood. She might not even know about JARR's existence. If she was out of the loop, she'd be more suspicious and with good reason. When Tess didn't know what was going on, she felt less secure, more unsafe. Despite Kingsley's obvious capability, the woman was still human and vulnerable to attack. She should be suspicious and expect Harry and the others to prove themselves dependable.

If Styx was attracted to her, maybe that was mutual. It didn't mean that Kingsley should trust him by default. There were times Tess's faith in Daire wasn't absolute and they'd been with each other, supporting each other, for months.

"Let's just get this done," Styx said, speeding up. "The sooner we get there, the sooner we get back."

And out of the confined space of the truck. Those minutes she'd had alone with Daire were all the more frustrating knowing that they might not come again. If there was something between the couple in the front, Tess bet Daire knew about it. Brother would confide in brother; they'd told Styx about their relationship before anyone else. Her Heart hadn't been against his brother knowing either.

Was it just an attraction, maybe a flirtation? Was it one-sided or mutual? Had they consummated their attraction? Were there feelings involved? All of her questions kept piling up. Their relationship was their business and Tess wouldn't win any points by blurting out her suspicions, not while Kingsley was around. Tess didn't know the woman well enough to tease her yet. Styx she would tease, just as soon as she got him alone.

***

GETTING HIM ALONE didn't take long. They parked the truck when they got into town and Tess was left inside while the two agents conversed at the hood. She guessed they were trading tasks, making plans; it was fascinating to watch.

The obvious distance they kept between them wasn't conducive to a clandestine conversation. It put a smile on her face. Were they so paranoid about being near to each other? She wondered what they feared: that they'd be found out or that they wouldn't be able to restrain themselves? Both she understood and had experienced in her own relationship. Usually around the time she and Daire became a secret, for whatever reason, Tess would suddenly want to touch him more than ever. Maybe it wasn't that she wanted it more, she just became more aware of it when he was off limits.

Kingsley was the first to walk off, so she guessed Styx would be sticking with her. Daire probably threatened him against letting her out of his eyeline. That and Styx wouldn't want Tess peppering Kingsley with questions… which she probably would.

His reasons didn't matter so much. It worked out for her either way. Styx would be easier to get rid of, easier to distract. Her suspicions about the couple were the perfect fodder.

So in almost the same second Tess hopped out of the truck, she began to ask questions.

"Talk about amateur," she said, twisting toward him as they walked down the street, away from the truck. "How the hell could you let yourself get involved with a colleague?"

That was damn close to what he'd said to Daire on confirming their relationship.

"Stop talking shit," he grumbled.

"Oh, come on," she said, grabbing his arm to give him a shake. "Doesn't all of this tell you that if you have feelings for her, you should tell her?"

"Not everyone is loved up and stupid, Lady. We've got a list of things to do today; I don't need you stirring up trouble. Your dreamboat isn't here to have your back, don't forget you're on your own."

Smiling, she looped her arm through his. "You know it's impossible for you to threaten me, right? I mean, I guess you can threaten me, but it's impossible for you to actually scare me."

"How's that? Because my brother would kick my ass if I hurt you?" He glanced down at her. "You should know that I've taken a bunch of beatings in my life. Ares and me used to fight all the time. I'll factor that in if I decide to hurt you… it won't stop me doing it."

Maybe that was true. In their line of work, it was sort of a given that there was a chance of getting hurt. A beating from Daire would probably be a walk in the park compared to whatever Styx and the beauty with balls had been through. She hadn't asked questions about what took him from peak fitness and hadn't asked Daire. It didn't feel like her business and there was too much else going on. But she cared about Styx and would like to know. It must have been some kind of hell. Olympus had put him through the wringer, but he still loved it more than the family he'd been born to. That much was obvious in the way he rejected having any other name.

Still, she couldn't afford to let herself feel sympathy for him. Tess's point was to be so annoying, he'd give her some time alone.

"I think she's nice," Tess said.

"You met her an hour ago."

"So? I can size people up fast," she said, noting the

twitch at the corner of his mouth. "We could double date! Does Daire know about—"

"When the hell does Ares ever take you out?" he asked. "You guys ever had a real date, just the two of you?"

"Plenty of times," she said, though they were more of the her and Danny in the Beast variety.

If they ate out, it was either fast or with other people. Having the Beast to support them meant they didn't have to go to external places even when they were on the road. Appearance-wise she'd probably made more effort for Styx when she met him at Fox Den than she ever had for Daire.

"Yeah, right," Styx mumbled.

"He's a great cook. When this is all over, I say we get together, just the four of us. Daire will cook, we'll have a bottle of wine… or three. Get to know each other, you know? We're family after all."

"He hasn't married you yet."

Not discouraged, she grinned up at him. "He will. You know it."

"He probably will. How long 'til you think he regrets it?"

"Is that what you're worried about? Regretting making a move? Believe me, buddy, you'll regret not making one way more than you will giving it a shot. There are no promises. I can't tell you that it will work out for sure. No one can. But even if Daire and me were over tomorrow, I wouldn't take back what we had… He's my epic love story. My soulmate. My one and only."

"Okay," he said, pushing her arms away from his to put some space between them. "If you break into song, I'll knock you out."

"If you're scared you'll screw it up, talk to Daire. He knows exactly how to seduce a woman, no matter her mood. Sometimes I'm happy and he teases me, other times I'm so mad I can't look at him… but he still finds a way into my panties."

"I don't need tips."

"Aww, it's okay," she said, trying to take his hand. "I'm not judging you. Everyone needs some help sometime…

I'd bet Renee likes a guy to be more forceful, not like scary forceful just… confident."

"You met her an hour ago," he said again.

She shrugged. "I know, I just think—"

"Are you going to be like this all morning?"

"Probably," she said, stopping to point across the street. "Oh, drugstore." She succeeded in taking his hand when she tried again. "We need to—"

"No drugstore on my list."

"There is on mine," she said. "I'm almost out of shampoo and Daire needs razors… Oh! You should get condoms. Lots of them, 'cause those suckers run out fast."

He blinked down at her, his expression blank. "For real?" Tess just smiled. "Okay, fine. Go to the drugstore, you've got twenty minutes and I'll be back this way to get you. Just wait outside. Don't go anywhere else. You see anything that freaks you out, just hang by the counter, near the staff and be ready to scream. Don't wait until someone approaches you, that way they get a chance to threaten you, just scream."

She saluted. "Yes, sir."

Styx just glared and shook his head. Teasing him was fun, in its own way. Most of the time that was as far as it went. That day was different. That day she needed to shirk him for a specific reason.

Checking for traffic, she bounced off the sidewalk and hurried across to the drugstore. Twenty minutes should be enough time, but Tess would make the most of every second.

SEVEN

ZIPPING UP AND DOWN the aisles, Tess grabbed everything that she could possibly need. None of it was that important. Daire and Harry were taking their detachments to the middle of nowhere, she was going to Vegas.

They had drugstores in Vegas.

What they didn't have at camp and what she needed: privacy. Rounding the corner, Tess came face to face with the purpose of her visit. Pregnancy tests. Standing there staring at them was conspicuous. If Styx got back early or Kingsley tracked her down, they would catch her in the act.

It was stupid. It felt stupid. So she'd been dragging some days and her stomach rebelled once in a while? That didn't mean she was knocked up. The really annoying thing was her implant. Yes, it was supposed to prevent pregnancy, but the damn thing knocked her cycle out of whack too. She hardly ever got her period. Even when she did, it was light and short. A dream for a woman on the go and one who didn't want her sex life interrupted, but a nightmare for giving her a clear measure of whether or not there was a bun in her oven.

She touched as few of them as possible to find the most sensitive ones that could tell her even if it was early. It had to be early, didn't it? She couldn't have been pregnant in

London… could she? The whole thing was just a head fuck.

Taking the tests, and everything else to the register, was easy. Even asking about restrooms didn't agitate her. Once she was in there, stick in hand, waiting for the result, the panic and fear hit her all at once.

In an ideal world, she'd be taking the test with Daire nearby. But she couldn't risk taking it back to camp. Buying the test while she was alone, shredding the receipt and flushing it, her actions were designed to keep her secret. She'd asserted that she couldn't be pregnant. There was no way.

Repeating those things over and over was supposed to put her mind at ease. If she was a hundred percent sure, then she wouldn't be standing there, leaning against the wall, trying not to look at the stick in her hand. She wouldn't even have a stick in her hand.

She couldn't be pregnant. It would be just like her mom and Harry all over again. They couldn't bring a child into such an uncertain world. Such a dangerous world.

Not pregnant.

Of their own accord, her eyes had drifted down and there it was, in plain English. Not pregnant.

Closing her eyes as her chin dropped to her chest, Tess stopped thinking. Her heart was racing. The adrenaline fueled the anxiety that had accompanied her since peeing on the damn stick. She needed to just breathe for a few seconds.

Was it relief? Disappointment?

Daire. She needed him. Wanted him with her. Close.

Having a child would be insanity.

"Goddamn," she whispered to herself.

Time was running short; she didn't have the luxury of pondering. Wrapping the test in toilet paper, she put it in the sanitary waste and washed her hands. The small mirror above the sink was smudged and scratched, but it showed dampness on her face. At some point, she'd been crying. Before or after the test? She had no idea. It didn't matter.

After washing her face, Tess looked at herself again. It was good. They knew once and for all. Or she did. Daire would be pleased. Everyone would. Why did it feel like she'd let him down? They couldn't have a family. Couldn't have normal. That's what Harry had said. He was right.

Admitting that her father was right wasn't easy. History couldn't repeat itself. Getting rid of Zeus might be at the top of the agenda, but Daire would always have enemies. What did that mean? What came next? Surviving a day at a time.

Someone always wants to hurt you.

Be in control.

Everyone is a threat.

"Mom," she whispered.

If she couldn't have her guy, then she wanted her mom. Scooping her pendant from her cleavage, she clutched it in her fist. She would never be a mother. Never have children. Never carry the child of the man she loved. The only way to ensure the security of their future was to decide kids were not an option. Daire would never abandon her. He'd put her above all else. He wouldn't deny her either. That left it up to her to make the choice. Daire or normality?

It was almost funny. Would be if it wasn't so tragic. What did she know about normal? What had she thought? White picket fences and Sundays in bed with the kids were never in the cards for her.

Maybe it wasn't their non-existent child that she grieved, maybe it was the optimism of any stable future that she mourned.

Big picture questions would have to wait.

Grabbing her bags, she left the restroom with a smile on her face. It was important to exude nothing different in her air. When she'd last seen Styx, she was happy, playful, and optimistic. She couldn't be any different when they met outside. The man was a super-agent, so it wouldn't be easy to hide much from him. Luckily, Kingsley's presence seemed to have distracted him from reading too much into anything.

She stopped to buy some fruit juice before going outside to wait for him. The sweet liquid was another distraction. Something to occupy her mind and her hands in case he was watching from afar. No one could know what she'd just done. That was exactly the point of doing the test in secret. Just the prospect of it maybe being true was dangerous enough when no one could even know of her relationship with Daire.

Styx was almost right in front of her by the time she noticed him. "Done?" he asked and she nodded. His brow lowered. "You okay?"

She spread her smile wider and took his hand. "More than okay," she said. "Let's go meet your beau."

EIGHT

TWO DAYS OF TRAINING for Olympus meant two days of not much for Tess. Cleaning the Beast was the first thing she used to distract herself from the commands and noises of exertion that came from outside. It was easier not to think about what Harry was putting his people through. What he was putting Daire through.

It astounded her. Lying on the bed in the Beast, she stared at the ceiling imagining the times she'd lay there with Daire. Dwelling didn't change anything. Their love was secure. It didn't matter if they were physically occupying the same space or not. Yet, time was running short. Every minute was one closer to him leaving her. Soon she'd be on her way back to Vegas. Given all that had happened there, was it any wonder that prospect filled her with dread?

The door opened further down the trailer. She pushed onto her elbows. Harry strode up the central passageway. The door hadn't closed, which she guessed was an indication he didn't plan to stay.

"You wanted to see me," he barked.

Apparently, it wasn't easy to shirk being Stratego. "I did," she said, shuffling forward to sit on the end of the bed.

About four hours ago, she'd stuck her head out of the

Beast only to find it being guarded by Boze. Tess didn't want to be held prisoner. It was tough not to see it that way when the guy demanded to know what she wanted, saying he'd get it for her.

"What's with the bags?" Harry asked.

Her things were packed and stacked on the couch at the end of the trailer. He didn't look that way, but he proved his own skill by letting her know he'd noticed.

"I've removed absolutely every single scrap of evidence that I ever lived here," she said, standing up. "Removed anything that could even possibly identify anyone, anything sentimental or personal… I even took the music out of the truck."

He frowned. "Okay. You're kicking him to the curb? You tell me before you tell him? What do you want me to do? Exile him? Tell my guys to run him outta here?"

"I bet nothing would make you happier. No, I asked for you because if I thought requesting a private audience with him would work, I'd have done it two days ago." Harry wasn't going to let her be alone with Daire, not unless it was absolutely necessary. "I want Daire to take the Beast on his mission."

Harry narrowed one eye. "Why?"

"Because it will make me feel better. I don't need it, I'll be staying in Hugo's hotel, in that fancy suite. If I thought I could get away with staying here, I would. I'd always rather sleep in the Beast. It's about the only place I feel safe these days."

"But you want Daire to travel with it?"

"Because I need to know that he has a safe place," she said. "This is our home. One of us needs to be looking after it. Like I said, I've taken out every trace of me, or a couple, ever staying here. You can't object if it won't compromise him."

"You know he's got this place rigged to explode," he said. "He could make a crater out of it with the flick of a switch."

Why was that relevant? "So?"

One side of his lips rose in what appeared to be

amusement. "Just funny you say you feel safe here when you're sleeping on C-4 every night."

"What's that got to do with anything?" she asked, her fists rising to her hips. "You said Daire was in charge of it. As long as he holds the switch, I'm safe."

Breathing out, her father folded his arms. "You really love him."

"You say that like it's a surprise."

"I just… I'm not used to anyone handing over so much trust to a stranger."

That put a smile on her face. "We've been together for months. Daire's no stranger."

Though Tess was beginning to feel like a stranger. The things she wasn't telling him weighed heavy on her mind. Losing her pressure valve was taking its toll. If she felt it, Daire must be amped to the max. So much rested on his shoulders, not least of which was the safety of every Olympus ally.

"Detachments are moving out today," Harry said.

"You figured out who's going with who?" He nodded. "Who does Daire get?"

His head tilted. "You care more about that than who will be with you?"

"Styx will be with me. I know I'll have an ally. Who does Daire get?"

"Zip and Milo."

The two youngest and newest recruits from what she could tell. "Will they follow his command?"

"Zip can be frivolous, but he knows when to be professional. Milo worships the ground Daire walks on. They won't disappoint." He came closer to lay a hand on her shoulder. "His life means a lot to me too."

Their moment was interrupted by a knock at the door. The thing was still open, so when Harry stepped aside to turn around, Tess saw their guest too. Only he wasn't a guest.

She smiled. "Did you just knock on your own door?"

Daire didn't respond to her teasing and focused only on Harry. "Time, sir."

"Yeah," Harry said, unhooking his base unit from his

belt to touch something on it. "That cargo goes in the Ranger, it'll be Styx's ride."

With a half-nod, Harry indicated her bags.

Daire came inside, scowling. "Sir?"

"At ease, son," Harry said, hooking his base unit back onto his belt. "Pandora has stowed all her things, you need to get them out of here."

Daire's scowl was fierce and didn't let up even when it switched to her. "Where do you think you're going?"

"Vegas," she said, squeezing past her father to approach Daire. "I want you to take the Beast. Everything that's me or us, I took out of here. There is one thing… you'll probably have to burn."

Continuing to the bags on the couch, she slipped something out of a side pocket. Two somethings. Turning back to the men, she held one towards each of them and they came to take them from her.

"What is this?" Harry asked.

"It's mom's last letter to you." His attention flew up to hers. "She must have left it in your place the same time she got the Scepter."

"I knew she always left something."

He just turned the envelope over and didn't make any move to open it. Daire's was more obvious, it bore an address. Still, she moved closer to him.

"I didn't mean to take it from you, I just wanted to remove the evidence from Three's house. I wrote it in London. Most of it is irrelevant now, and if you want me to take it with me or burn it—"

"I want to read it," he said, but only tucked it into his pocket rather than opening it there. His knuckles grazed her jaw. "You look tired."

"Not so easy to sleep with the drill sergeant putting you through your paces all night… I prefer doing that myself."

"Pandora!"

"What?" she asked her father with an innocent shrug. "We have sex. Great sex."

"You've gotta be careful talking like that right now, LR," Daire said to her almost under his breath.

"Okay," she conceded with a sigh. "Can I at least say I miss you?"

It wasn't fair to put that on him. There was nothing he could do to change the distance between them. Distance was supposed to help her perspective, that was one of her mom's lessons, but Tess's lens was always clearer when Daire was looking through it too.

"You sure you want to do this?"

No. Not really. But she couldn't say that and nodded.

Harry grabbed one of the bags and went to the door to whistle at someone. Enraptured by the man looking into her, she didn't see who Harry threw the bags to one after the other.

When they were gone, her father turned back to them, "I'll give you eight minutes," he grumbled, "then we're on the road."

Her father giving them any time was unexpected, though there was business to take care of too. No doubt that was his motivation.

NINE

HARRY WANTED HER TO CONFESS the location of the Scepter. That was the only reason he was walking out and closing the door behind him.

The mood changed immediately. Her mood. The charge of magnetism that always pulled them together grew hot. That zap of electricity was impossible to ignore. They hadn't been by themselves in too long.

It felt weird. Being with him. In the Beast. Alone. Not so many months ago, after losing her mom, she'd believed herself to be alone. That her family was gone. There she stood, in a place she considered home. With the man she wanted to be her future.

"Little Red—"

"Don't," she said, shaking her head, taking a deliberate step backwards.

"Baby—"

"Do not say goodbye to me, Daire Canon."

As she turned, his single stride ate up the floor, he grabbed her face to haul her back, forcing his mouth over hers despite her objections.

Loving him was impossible. Her pushing and punching at his shoulders soon became clawing and pulling.

He couldn't leave her. He couldn't. Desperate for the kiss to go on forever, she dug her nails in and hopped up when he scooped his hands under her ass to lift her. She needed him. Wanted him. Yearned to go back in time.

As he laid her down in their bed, every one of their unions flickered through her mind's eye. The heat and urgency of their first kiss to the motion of their first joining. Being with Danny, in the dark, learning each other's bodies, their needs, the gentle touching and tickling. The laughter. Her pleasured screams. Fingers fisted in their sheets. Mouths on flesh, chests, thighs, gratifying each other, the thrill of climax, the demand and charge, their weakness.

With the same bed beneath her, she parted her legs to welcome him into her body as she'd done so many times. The slick slide of his cock inside her was the greatest pleasure. As he thrust into her, his gaze found hers. She knew it. What he wanted to say. The way he felt. His heart belonged to her, just as she'd handed hers to him. Their love wasn't in doubt. Just their longevity.

Climax ramped up fast, softening her clarity.

There were people outside the trailer. People trained to listen. Not as well as her man, but she didn't want to let him down.

Closing her eyes, tears tracked down her temples as she inhaled and held the breath. Silence. She had to be quiet. For Daire. His people needed to trust him. Needed to be as sure of his ability as her heart.

That motivation was enough. Tumbling over the precipice of bliss, her satisfaction became euphoria when he propelled himself in hard, clenching his teeth to clamp his jaw shut.

It wasn't right that they had to restrain themselves. But the cause was just.

In their bed. In their home. They hadn't even stripped, just linked their bodies in the love that consumed them both.

With his forearms braced on either side of her head, he descended to kiss her again. Slower, his fingers tangling in her splayed hair.

"Your something," she pleaded in a desperate whisper. "My Heart."

"We'll be together again," he said, his lips still on hers. "I'll come back to you."

She clenched her fists in his tee-shirt. "Promise me."

"Baby—"

"Promise me or I won't let you leave."

In that very space, she'd given him to Olympus. Told him that she wouldn't compromise his integrity. But she was his something. He had to know what that meant. He had a responsibility to more than his unit.

"Tess—"

He stopped and did his ear prick thing for a second before leaping off the bed to fasten his pants.

His focus trained down the trailer, he opened a hand backward toward her. Getting up as quietly as she could, she didn't take his hand. Instead, she took the chain from her neck and opened his palm to put his gift in it. He turned as she closed his fingers around it.

"With Mom," she said, ignoring the familiar grief that sped her heart. "In the base. Her urn is the only thing I left in the truck."

And he'd take care of concealing that for her after he retrieved the key.

His frown loosened. "All this time?"

She stepped closer, allowing herself to become more somber. "Promise me."

"Babe…" the chain strewn around his fingers didn't stop him grabbing the side of her head. The warmth of the bullet heated her skin. "You are my something. I will do everything in my power to get back to you as fast as I can. I trust Styx with my life, but—"

"I'm never safer than when I'm in your eyeline."

"No games," he said, gripping tighter to shake her head. "Stay with him. Trust him. Do you hear me? You trust Styx. Before anyone else, you trust him. If anything happens to you, I'll kill him. Let that be on your conscience if you think about playing—"

"I'll trust your brother so long as I can trust you to

do whatever it takes." Her intensity was nothing to his, but she laid it on him anyway. "I don't care who you have to kill. What you have to do. If it means getting out alive, coming back to me, do it. Hesitation gets you killed." Something he'd said on the day she'd met Daire. "I need you. If anything happens to you, there won't be a me left. Remember that. Remember what I said I feared? If you let anyone hurt or capture you, they'll kill a part of me, all of me." She smiled. His last memory of her didn't have to be all anguish. "No one else can keep me in line…" her smile dropped, "or make me happy."

"You're not happy," he said like it was a shameful personal failure.

Stepping in close, she slid her hands up his body. "Every second I'm with you, happiness is all I know." She dug her nails into the fabric. "Promise me, baby. Please."

Conflict was written all over his face. He didn't like to let anyone down. His instinct would be to promise, but was it asking too much? Maybe. Being without his word would be the same as being without breath. Death may as well take her there and then.

London. Was that his worry? The Washington mission had an objective; they'd known their separation was temporary. This was different. There were objectives, sure, but no guaranteed end point. There were so many variables. So many unknowns.

"I love you."

"No." Shaking her head, she pushed his hand from her hair. "I don't want goodbye. I want your word."

Their gazes were still locked onto each other when the trailer door opened. Daire immediately turned, blocking the hallway, putting himself between her and the intruder.

"Alright, geez, at ease."

Styx.

Emotions were high. It was no surprise Daire was defensive.

"What do you want?" Daire snapped.

"Lady, time to hit the road," Styx called out with a dubious, almost suspicious, air. His next words were quieter.

"You better calm the fuck down, brother. You're about to take command."

Of his detachment. Yes. Command. That meant level-headed. Cool. Composed. In control.

Daire stepped aside, which gave her room to pass. He didn't look at her. No wonder, given his refusal.

"Are we set?" she asked, trying to divert Styx from frowning at his brother.

"All set," Styx said, moving away from the threshold, arm outstretched, indicating she should depart.

She put a hand on the doorframe, ready to leave, when her Heart stopped her.

"Little Red…" Daire said, drawing her focus. In the aisle, by the fridge, his eyes remained down for a few seconds before rising to hers, full of vehement determination. "You have it."

His word? In time with a relieved exhale, she smiled. "Right back attcha."

Which was what they said when they couldn't proclaim their love for all to hear.

He winked. How many times had he done that for her? How did he give her comfort, arouse and satisfy her with such a simple gesture? Danny. No longer a betrayal, he reminded her of the simplicity. That all they needed was each other. Not money. Not things. They didn't need a designated destination let alone a fixed aim. Hope. Maybe there could be a tomorrow someday.

His ease vanished when his concentration locked onto his brother. "You stay."

"Figured you'd want your last minute to be with the girl," Styx said, moseying away from the door. "Gee, I wonder what this will be about."

She let herself look at both men again, lingering on her love for a few extra seconds. Goodbye? It couldn't be goodbye. She had to believe they'd see each other again. The alternative didn't bear thinking about.

TEN

"BAD INTEL," Coltrane said.

"Must be," Boze agreed.

"We've been driving all damn day."

"And she hasn't said a word."

They were talking about her and she didn't even care. Being shoehorned into the middle of the backseat between Coltrane and Boze wasn't the best road trip experience she'd ever had. Her travel companions still scored higher than her father in the amiable index, even with their blatant discussion of her.

"You've gotta do better recon."

"My recon's fine," Styx said, pulling into a parking spot in the underground garage. "You two worry about your duties."

Vegas. Again.

Her two protectors got out, slamming their doors practically in sync. Garrick left the passenger seat a second later. Without even bothering to check where any of them were going, she closed her eyes and fought to suppress a shudder.

Balfour's hotel. She'd have to go upstairs and put on a show. Be impervious. Bright. Confident.

"Did you tell him?"

Opening her eyes, she caught Styx looking at her in the rearview. Not that he was ashamed, he didn't flinch when their gazes met.

"Tell who what?"

"I'm guessing it was positive."

Shit. Damn her useless poker face. Guess trying to convince him nothing was going on in the drugstore hadn't worked.

Two choices. Admit taking the test or plead ignorance. Last thing she wanted to do was walk into a trap. Maybe he suspected, that didn't mean he knew.

"I don't know what you—"

"Yes, you do," he said, drawing his attention away to scan the concrete cavern. "We can play with each other or have each other's backs. Did you tell him?"

"You don't know what you're talking about," she said.

"Guess you didn't. Good. That was smart. He won't be able to do what he's gotta do if he's worrying about your uterus."

"Wow, thanks so much for the support, Styx," she said, taking off her seatbelt.

Sliding across the backseat, she opened the door.

"Don't get out until the guys have—"

She got out and didn't shy from slamming the door. Sure, that would draw attention to her, to them, but fuck it. If someone was poised to take them out, they were already paying attention to the truck.

Striding across the concrete garage, she headed for the elevators.

Styx rushed up at her side, stooping to hiss in her ear, "I'm not your lover."

She shoved him. Not that she had the strength to move him. "Of that I'm very aware."

"He couldn't have been here," Styx said. "You think it's better to be together? It's not. Trust me, I'm not thrilled I pulled this assignment either. You're a real pain in the ass."

And it always fell to him to deal with her because

she'd never yield to her father's command. Under Harry, she'd likely rebel even more.

"You think you care about him more than I do?" she asked, reaching for the elevator call button.

Styx swatted her hand away and pressed the button with a knuckle. "We're not in competition. We stay in our own lanes, we'll be fine."

She turned to face him, folding her arms. "Harry took you in—"

"Hades," he hissed through his teeth. "What the hell is the matter with you? You're smarter than this."

"Maybe I'm sick of being smarter. Maybe I'm sick of whispering and tiptoeing around. Maybe I'm sick of being reminded of the bigger picture over and over."

The doors opened behind her.

"You think that will keep him alive?" Styx asked, pushing her into the elevator.

He moved around behind her and clamped a hand over her mouth, pulling her back against him. Like father, like son; the moment reminded her of meeting Harry. She considered fighting, but what would be the point?

Coltrane hurried over to jump in with them. He pressed for their floor with a knuckle while frowning at them.

"We're having a moment," Styx said. "Sometimes this is the only way to deal with her."

"The woman who didn't say a word the whole drive got chatty?"

"Figures, huh?"

That their secure environment kept her quiet while an unsecured one provoked her words? Yeah, sometimes she was contrary like that. Nothing to do with the fact that she didn't want to perform for an audience. That she didn't know these new people. That Daire would assuage her woes rather than aggravate her... most of the time anyway.

When the elevator doors opened, Coltrane ventured on.

Styx took a couple of steps but stopped them on the threshold. "Don't say a word until we've cleared the room."

Always with the rules and procedures. Loosening his

hand, he paused, probably waiting to see what she'd do. She pushed his arm up out of the way and went after Coltrane, who was already entering her suite. Did they have keys? Guess that didn't matter for Olympus agents.

"A please wouldn't kill you," she said when Styx appeared at her side.

"Yeah, hold your breath waiting for that one."

It was a tease and one she appreciated. Having Styx around wasn't the same as having Daire there. He didn't try to be a substitute. Good. Nothing matched up to Daire. No one. How long would it be until they saw each other again?

***

WHILE STYX AND HIS PEOPLE went through the motions of securing the environment, she took a shower. Her luggage awaited her in the bedroom, which allowed her to change. She'd just put her dress on when Styx entered.

"We're all clear."

Sitting on the end of the bed, she bobbed her head, focused on the carpet. Styx came a step closer then grumbled something and turned around as though to leave.

"Have you talked to him?"

Styx stopped. A breath passed, then he went to close the door before looking at her. "No. And I won't." That's what she figured. Asking was better than living in wonder. "You can't do this to yourself. You need to function without him. And you better pray to God he can function without you. In your condition—"

"I'm not pregnant," she said and drew in a breath. "Yes, I took the test, but it was negative."

"Did you tell him?"

"That I took it? No. I want him to function without me too. I want it more than you. You don't know what it's like to be the weight on his shoulders."

"He works out, he can take it."

The joke only managed to rouse a vague smile to her lips.

"He says I'm his something," she said, tucking her

hands under her thighs. "That I make him stronger."

"Doesn't sound like you believe that," Styx said, strolling closer.

She met his eye. "I want to. I really do."

"He's good at this. It's all he knows how to do. It's been his whole life."

"Running and hiding was my whole life until my mom died. After that, without her, turns out I wasn't so good at it."

He sat at her side. "We get this done and you won't have to do that anymore."

"And then what? We can't be together. Our story won't end with a happily ever after. What is he without this?"

"You're insecure? Shit," he said on a snicker. "Never thought I'd see the day."

She thrust up to her feet. "I am not insecure. I know how he feels. How I feel." Spinning on the spot, she raised her arms from her sides. "I don't know what I am without this either. Taking that test…" She shook her head. "I wanted it to be negative until it was."

"You wanna have a kid with him?"

"What life can we give a child?"

"He'd be an amazing father," Styx said. "He has the capacity for it."

His capacity was limitless.

"He's a perfectionist, he's good at everything." Backing up a few steps, she leaned on the entertainment unit. "I don't think I want a kid. And now definitely wouldn't be the right time. We'd get a great big 'I told you so' from certain quarters."

Harry.

Her crooked brow put a smile on Styx's face. "Yep. Sounds about right."

"I can't think about what's next because I can't focus. He's going into the lion's den."

"No one knows that building better than him. No one. It wasn't just the compound or a place he worked, it was his world, his home. He played in those corridors—"

"Hades let him play?"

"On the QT," he said with a half shrug. "He ran around there, hid, explored, lived and breathed it. I guarantee no one knows it better."

"The building isn't what worries me."

"It's what comes next," he said. "Immediately next." Not the big picture, future type next, but what would happen once Minotaur was back online. "He'll wait for the go. He won't move until that comes."

Harry had to get himself and his men into position. He'd observe until he had a lay of the land. Only at the optimum moment would he give his ward the proverbial nod.

"Do you think Balfour will come here?"

"Yes."

So resolute. Just like Daire. Confident. Strong. Steady.

"Will Hades take action?"

"Maybe. Everyone's in holding until someone makes a play."

"Is there more going on here than I know?"

"There's more going on here than any of us knows. Intel is the key to survival. On the flip side..."

"Withholding it..." she said, "protecting it, reduces your rival's chances."

"Theoretically. He's good at this, Lady. Trust me. If there is one person guaranteed to make their way out of this and end on top? It's him. And if he drags anyone along with him, it'll be you."

"I don't like being in the dark. He's the only person who doesn't keep me there."

"I can't tell you what I don't know. I don't know what comes next. Neither does he."

"So we wait," she said, though it was completely unsatisfying.

"A lot of what we do is waiting. Waiting for something to change."

"Wouldn't want to blow your wad too soon."

"Something else my brother does?"

Her smile warmed. "One thing your brother never does."

"I'll take your word for it," he said, moseying back a

few steps. "We good?"

"We wait," she said on a single nod. "Just sit here and… wait."

This was the exact opposite of her mother's teachings. Rather than run and hide, she was standing in the middle of the target setting off flares. She was there. Waiting… for something to change, apparently.

ELEVEN

"FINISH THIS. JUST GET IT FINISHED… Keep working. Focus on what's right in front of you, Tess." At a corner table in the suite's living room, sitting with her sewing machine, she adjusted her fabric. "One second at a time. Keep breathing."

Styx came out of the bedroom and took his time checking out the space. "Who are you talking to?"

"Me," Tess said, selecting her thread. "Why? Who are you talking to?"

"A crazy person, apparently," he said and glanced around again. "Where's Boze?"

Her concentration was on the task at hand. "Room service came up in the elevator. We got you fish."

"I hate fish."

"And life is so unfair," she said, rethreading the machine. "That's what you get for insulting Prince."

But Styx wasn't listening anymore, he was frowning. "When did he leave?"

"When? What do you—"

"How many minutes?"

Startled by his abrupt anger, she shook her head. "Three, maybe four."

"It doesn't take three minutes to get a tray. Up. Move."

He extended an arm toward her, gesturing as she leaped up, knocking her chair over in the process. But she wasn't quick enough. After two steps, the door opened.

They braced to see who'd walk in.

Boze. Boze. Please be Boze. All the praying in the world wouldn't deliver them their ally. No, her protector wasn't the entrant. Given who walked in, she doubted Boze would ever be going anywhere again.

"Zeus."

The name came from Styx's lips, but she was the one under the principal's focus.

"Let the games begin," the bastard said.

That was one way to put it. Oh, the smug sonofabitch, whatever he had up his sleeve, however he'd swung this…

"What do you want?" she asked.

He'd be there for a reason. The agenda may be hidden, but his satisfaction was not.

"Nothing I can get from you," he said, oozing smugness.

Damn, she wanted to smack him in the face. The goddamn, motherfucking—spurred to action, she started toward him. She hadn't thought through what would come next, so it was probably best that Styx grabbed her back.

"What's the play, Sherwood?" Styx asked.

The depth of his growling tone took her aback. She'd never heard that baser voice. Despite the teasing about his inability to scare her, an actual chill went through her. That focus. The precision. It reminded her of Daire.

"No play," Zeus said. "We need your assistance in a small matter. Something that will only take a few moments, providing you comply."

"Where's my guy?" Styx asked.

He wouldn't comply. The certainty of his stance was so overpowering that she'd guess even if it was in his best interest, he wouldn't comply just for the principle of rebelling.

"Don't worry about him," Zeus said, admiring the

room with a sneering confidence that pushed her closer to the edge.

What was going on? She'd got the best of him not so long ago. Her. A tiny, trifling, insignificant woman. Hadn't he learned his lesson about underestimating her? With the power of Styx at her side and her Heart backing them up from afar, there was no way Zeus could win whatever game he was starting.

"No way you took him down." Styx's lip curled in disgust when he scanned the so called security around Zeus. "These tools are a nuisance, not a threat."

Good point. Boze was good. And, yes, Zeus had numbers, but the ways onto the floor were narrow. Even if Boze had been overwhelmed, he'd still have raised the alarm. Unless… maybe he ate a bullet the moment the doors opened.

She liked Boze. Liked all of them. Somehow this, especially this, felt like it was on her. The decision to come to Vegas hadn't been solely hers. Still, they'd got it wrong. Oh so wrong. Weren't they sure Zeus wouldn't leave the security of wherever he'd been hiding? What had changed?

"I thought the same thing," Zeus said. Those around him didn't flinch. "I got myself an upgrade. Guaranteed to deliver."

"An upgrade?"

She didn't get what that meant either, but it was the edge of suspicion in Styx's voice that set the hairs on her neck on their ends.

"Only one soldier is needed to win this war. You know it. We've all known it since the beginning. Securing the alliance was equal to achieving victory."

Alliance? She didn't get it. Why was Zeus doing that creepy side smile thing? Byron? Yeah, he had him. Everyone knew that. The former President would be responsible for present security and Zeus had just acknowledged they were not a force worthy of intimidating Olympus agents.

"So we should just give up now?" Styx asked, mocking the principal with ease.

Could it be Harry? No, her father couldn't have been playing her all this time. Though if the three Olympus principals were in cahoots, the agents would be compelled to follow. They were Harry's crew. His band of certain allegiances. Every operative, from what she'd seen and heard, still held Harry in high regard… regardless of him abandoning them at the Exodus.

The principals combined with their control of the underlings would reduce her chance of resistance to nil… unless Daire got to her fast.

"I don't want your surrender," Zeus said. "I want what you stole from me."

What Styx stole? Her heart rate rose higher. The keys. How did he know Styx was involved in that at all? Zeus shouldn't even know Styx was in London. His intel had improved since they'd last seen each other.

"You mean what *I* stole," Tess said. "Scared to admit to your men that you were beaten by a woman? An untrained woman?"

Smug herself, she folded her arms. While her confidence rose, Styx moved, just a little. He put his shoulder in front of her. Like he was trying to block her? To protect her? Like he'd promised his brother he would. A week. If she died only a week after leaving the Beast, Daire would not be impressed. The brothers' relationship had been tested in the past, but never by something like that.

"You think a lot of yourself, Miss Walbeck," Zeus said, using her father's last name. "Too much… You overestimate your abilities."

"Do I?" she asked, without backing down. "And you're going to tell me which ability I've overestimated?"

"I don't need to," he said, slipping a hand into his pocket. "Your desperation was my greatest ally. Your need to cling." His smirk became much more amused. "Your need to mean something to someone… to anyone. It blinds you."

Confused, Tess was distracted by Styx moving another few inches, blocking more of her. She could hardly see around him. What was he…? Styx left her mind when she noticed Zeus retrieving something from his pocket. No. That looked like… The Scepter. Was it possible? Copying the keys was impossible… It had to be. If it wasn't, why wouldn't the three principals have done that straight away?

"What is that?" she heard herself ask.

Holding the metal circle at the end, he showed them the object. "You should know what it is. You kept it hidden in your mother's urn for months."

No. Her stomach clenched. The instinctual reaction joined a surge of adrenaline that got her clinging to Styx's arms. He glanced her way, but she could only stare at Zeus.

"Babe?" Styx murmured.

"I only told Daire," she whispered, digging her nails in to gather strength. "What did you do to him?"

Her Heart wasn't supposed to be taken down, not like this, not by Zeus. Daire was the strongest. The best. The fastest. The smartest. Her throat narrowed. She couldn't cry, couldn't give Zeus the satisfaction, but damn it felt like her heart was about to give out. Breathing. In and out... She was shaking, every part of her, he had to see it, the bastard.

Raising his chin, Zeus called out, "Bring her!"

Her? Who was...?

The men blocking the door parted to allow someone inside. Kingsley: hands bound, mouth gagged. The bruises on the disheveled agent sickened her as much as the woman's red, wet eyes, and obvious disarray.

As the dressed-in-black agents pushed and pulled at their prisoner, forcing her toward Zeus, Styx tried to go to her. Rushing around him, Tess pushed on his chest, holding him back. She understood. She did. But rushing over there could be exactly what Zeus wanted.

"No," she whispered, laying a hand on his cheek, trying to get him to look down at her.

He wouldn't, he was fixated across the room at the sickening sight. They had to be smart. She didn't know what the hell that meant or what to do or how to get out of his... Did it matter? If her Heart was hurt, if he was lost, she wouldn't be capable of another step.

Raw shock seized Styx's expression. So... open. So unguarded. So... out of character.

Despite fearing what she might see, she couldn't resist the instinct to turn, to see what hit Styx so hard.

She couldn't…

"Our primary instrument of success," Zeus said, following it with a snicker as he slapped a hand onto the back of the man who'd just stopped at his side. "Wielding the God of War guarantees victory."

The God of War… Ares.

It couldn't be. She was standing there. Looking at him. But…

"Da—"

Styx grabbed her and yanked her back so hard that the word didn't get out of her mouth. With an arm hooked over her shoulder, Styx held her back to his torso. His fingers curled around her chin, not quite on her mouth, reminding her of how quickly he'd be able to shut her up.

It was Daire. Right there, next to Zeus. Proud. Unhurt. The disciplined Ares… She didn't understand.

"You fuck," Styx said, taking over the confrontation. Her approach would've been far more confused. Styx wasn't cutting his brother any breaks. "This has been it the whole fucking time… Because Hades screwed you over? You fucking prick, it's always Olympus for you. Fuck the rest of us, right?"

Her Heart just stood there. Staring straight ahead. She'd seen him soldier before. Seen him switched on, ready to take orders from Harry.

This was different. He was taking orders from Zeus. No. She couldn't… Closing her eyes, she turned her head, convinced this had to be some kind of nightmare. Her love. The man who'd taken the heart she'd offered. Daire. Her Heart. Were they really standing on opposing sides? She couldn't even look.

"You're a man who knows what it is to be captive, Styx," Zeus said. "Because you can be useful, as your brother—"

"He's no brother of mine," Styx spat the words. "He's a fucking coward. A dickless cunt, who can't fight his own damn battles. You gonna let this fuck speak for you?"

"Ares respects the hierarchy," Zeus said. "He won't speak unless I give him permission."

"Yeah," Styx growled. "Like I said, a dickless cunt."

It couldn't be true. When she'd thought he might be dead or hurt… Would that be better than this? Better than witnessing his betrayal… again. This situation wasn't without precedent. Could it be Danny all over again? Was Daire his true identity or was it this cold, blank soldier detached from everything around him, everything except the chain of command?

"Should I take that as your answer on joining us?" Zeus asked. Still holding her, Styx drew back then lurched forward, spitting in Zeus and Daire's direction. "Nice. You always were impossible."

"Then put a bullet in me. Finish it."

"We would. I would," Zeus said. "I'll give Ares that order in a second… after you tell us what you did with the other two."

The keys.

Zeus needed them to move Minotaur… and to extract JARR.

Her hands rose to Styx's forearm. Maybe she was looking for comfort or maybe she wanted him to understand that Zeus planned to take her with them. Styx knew the location of the keys. But her, she wasn't expendable. Not until they had JARR.

"Yeah, right," Styx said on a revolted snicker. "Let me write down the coordinates for you."

Zeus drew in a breath and glanced up at the impassive Daire. "I knew it was too much to hope he'd have them on his person."

"He'll be easier to search when we have the girl," Daire said.

He didn't flinch, his eyes didn't flicker. The girl? Was he talking about her? Asshole! Motherfucking asshole!

Her weight lurched forward, but Styx jerked her back. "Don't rise to it," he said into her hair and surprised her by ducking further to murmur in her ear, "We're in the field until I say otherwise, Lady."

The field. With her love. Against her love. Grief couldn't begin to… Losing her mother had devastated her.

Losing Danny was a kick when she was down. London was an inconvenience compared to… Her love. Her Heart… She couldn't believe it. Couldn't… Damn the tear that slipped from the corner of her eye.

This wasn't the plan.

He'd given his word that he'd come back to her. This wasn't what she'd meant. Wasn't what she wanted.

But that man, the one who'd hesitated to give her his word… He wasn't the man in the room with her.

"If they put up a fight…" Zeus said, "it's likely you'll kill one of them."

"There's only one exit and we have it," Daire said. "He's alone. He can't win a fight… never could against me."

"Let's go now," Styx said, throwing her to the side.

"No!" she called out, clutching his arm. "Don't! They'll kill you!"

Then what the hell would she do?

"Let them kill both of us," Styx yelled toward them. "Kill us both! Watch your beloved Olympus founder! Go! Do it!"

"No!" she called again, clinging to his wrist with both hands, using all of her weight to pull him back. "Please!"

He stilled. "La—"

That was all she heard before the sting of pain hit her arm.

Letting him go, she grabbed for the spot only to find a dart. Just like the one Albany had used. "Styx," she exhaled and fell forward into his arms.

TWELVE

COOL AIR SLITHERED ACROSS HER from… somewhere. Her head hurt. Not in a typical kind of headache way, more like a dull, uncomfortable throb muddied by a fog of confusion. It was familiar. The Whist? A derivative of…

She sat up fast.

Styx.

Daire.

Zeus.

No one was around. She was alone.

A familiar sensation. But this wasn't alone like before. It was alone accompanied by the chilling truth that the man she loved had betrayed her.

Her mother's omissions caused harm, but they weren't malicious. What else could she think about Daire's decision to throw in with Zeus? About him seducing her… convincing her of his love… It was beyond cruel.

Taking her time about replaying the previous few days, her equilibrium began to return. With a calmer eye, she scanned the room. The walls were concrete, painted pale gray.

No windows, only vents. One door. On the opposite wall was an opening, a doorway sans door. The furniture was odd. The twin bed was attached to the wall on a concrete plinth. She didn't get it. The institutional feel of the cold decor was juxtaposed with typical bedroom furniture. A couple of dressers, soft furnishings on a short loveseat flanked by end tables.

What was this place? Where was she?

Okay. So she remembered the Beast. Saying goodbye. Vegas. Zeus. Daire… Ares.

The man in that Vegas hotel room wasn't her Daire. Finally she understood the code names. From her lover, she didn't want to be separated. The stranger standing with Zeus? She was eager to forget him.

How could it be true? It couldn't be.

Drawing up her knees, she supported her elbow on them and pushed her hair back over her head.

Whatever was going on, she had to get out. Herself and Styx… and Daire. What could she do to get out of wherever she was?

Not much.

Because it seemed like the right thing to do, she got up and checked the door. Yeah, it took a second to find her feet, but at least her suspicion was confirmed. It was locked.

Damn.

So she was a prisoner.

What else would Zeus do with her? Really.

They needed her to access JARR. Styx? They needed him to reveal the location of the keys.

Nothing made sense.

Opposing Daire didn't feel right. If he wanted to side with Zeus, why hadn't he taken her with him? The only explanation was that he didn't want her with him.

Resisting the urge to sink down onto the floor, her next port of call was the doorway.

The same concrete walls awaited her, though they were lined with shelves and drawers, like a closet. And not one usually found in such an industrial space. The bathroom beyond didn't have such a homely feel. A manufactured homely feel, none of it was genuine.

The matte concrete vanity and clinical steel towel rail—

Manufactured.

Her thoughts caught up with sense.

Olympus Beta. That's where she was. With the Scepter in their possession, Minotaur would be online again. That paint.

Rushing into the bedroom again, she took it in with fresh eyes. The color on the walls was the same as that in the corridors of the building she'd visited with Danny. She'd gone in with Danny and come out with Daire.

Who would she leave with the next time?

Styx, at least, she hoped.

Where was he? What were they doing to him? Did Harry know their predicament? That Daire had double crossed him… again?

The back of her legs hit the bed. She dropped to sit on it.

Alone.

Again.

Was Daire in the building? Was Styx? What the hell was going on?

***

EVENTUALLY, SHE FELL ASLEEP. There was little else to do. Of course, she dreamed of Daire. Her Daire, not Ares. When she awoke, alone, reality crashed back in. She lay listening to the quiet rush of air coming through the vents. Were those the same vents Daire told her about? The ones that could release poison gas and shut so tight no air could get in?

They could kill her in a snap. Just like that.

JARR was the only reason Zeus had kept her alive. If Styx gave them the location of the keys, he'd be useless. Maybe he was already dead. Just like she would be when JARR was accessed.

No.

Squeezing her eyes closed, she pictured her Heart's face when they last made love. Reminded herself of the taste of his kiss. The certainty in his gaze.

Daire loved her.

So what if he had to be Ares? She'd told him to do whatever it took to get back to her. That's all this was. Right?

The words he'd written in his letters… the truth of his burden in the Beast when she'd given him to Olympus…

What a stupid mistake that turned out to be.

She'd asked him to run away with her. Why hadn't they split right then?

They could be together. Alone. Somewhere hot and exotic. Somewhere far from the danger.

At last she got it. Like completely got it. Her mother had run not only to protect her child but because it was poison. Olympus was poison.

Maybe it had a righteous purpose. Maybe it had started out that way. Whatever it was now, its purpose had been warped to serve individual agendas. Everyone wanted something. Some were just more honest about it than others.

There was only one thing she wanted. One man.

Being in the same building as him without sleeping in his arms was unsettling, especially when his comfort and counsel would make everything better.

It niggled at her.

If this was all part of some elaborate ruse… If her Daire was actually her Daire… why hadn't he told her the plan?

Time to talk had been sparse in their last days together, but they'd had those moments right before parting.

The last thing they'd done before his apparent betrayal was have sex.

Again. More precedent. Danny had sex with her one last time before revealing he wasn't Danny.

Everything was messed up and only one thing could make it right. One man. She just needed a minute with him. Thirty seconds. A flicker of time alone with him.

A noise came from near the door. No, not near, the door itself. She leaped off the bed but had no plan beyond that. Fight? Flight? Freeze?

In the same second the door opened, the lights died. No windows. No illumination. It was disorienting, which had to be exactly the point.

Blinding light from beyond flashed so bright she covered her eyes.

"Some things never change."

Styx!

The lights were back on. The door closed. And her friend was… a mess.

"Oh my God," she said in a rush of breath.

The swelling and bruising of his face left little to the imagination. The gash above his eye trailed blood from his temple all the way to his chin. Other than that, it was difficult to tell where one injury started and another began.

Though he tried to disguise it, she saw him wince on stepping forward. His face wasn't the only part to have received the brutal treatment.

Rushing over, she grabbed his arm to coil it around her neck. "What did they do to you?"

Her outrage had to be obvious, but he snickered and took his arm back. "Nothing I haven't been through before."

"Before?"

Glued to the spot, she watched him continue toward the closet. His gait was slower, sometimes a little shuffling, but he didn't flinch.

Only once he'd disappeared did she jump to it and hurry after him. She found him in the bathroom, shifting the angle of his face like he was admiring the handiwork in the mirror over the vanity. Was he impressed? No. Although he examined the mess he'd been left in, he seemed indifferent to it. Like it was all another day at the office. Sometimes he and Daire were more alike than first glance would suggest.

"When did you go through this before?" she asked, going over to run the cold water, figuring he'd want to clean up.

"A bunch of times."

"In training?"

He pushed her aside with a forearm to take control of the sink. "Them… and others."

"You've been beaten. They hurt you… Who would…? Because you wouldn't tell them where the keys are."

"Yep," he said, turning up the faucet.

"I don't understand," she said, shaking her head, watching him scoop up some water to wash out his mouth. "This can't be what you signed up for. Who are you being loyal to right now?" He spat out blood and water and scooped up some more. Infuriation heated her angry panic. They were captives. At the mercy of Zeus who was clearly insane. "If you tell him—"

"He'll kill me," he said, his attention cutting to hers. "That fucker is with them. That gives me one card to play."

"So play it," she said, going closer. "Join them. Join their cause."

One corner of his lips curled. He grabbed the towel from the rail as his back hit the wall and he slid down to sit on the floor.

"They don't have a cause," he said. "They have a leader. They're two different things. I didn't sign up to suck Sherwood's cock… apparently your ex isn't so squeamish."

Crouching next to him, she wanted to get it. "Zeus is Olympus, right? If this is what he wants, it's your responsibility to follow him."

Nowhere in any of her thoughts, in her wildest imagination, had she considered joining Zeus or asking Styx to join him. Not for a second. Yet… In his current state, it was easy to see that the only chance he had was to prostrate himself. To hand himself over to Zeus's command. To submit. To surrender.

The notion closed her throat. How could she ask Styx to do something she'd never consider? Except, if he didn't, she was talking to a dead man. While fearing for his life, it wasn't easy to maintain certainty.

"He's not Olympus," he said, clenching the towel in his bloodied fist.

"He's your superior," she said, pushing his hair from his temple to check a wound at his hairline. "You do as your superior tells you."

His blink was slow as he met her eye. "Technically, Ares is my superior."

"There you are. Do what he tells you," she said and

softened. "Please… Isn't that the way of Olympus? Doing what you're told by those above you."

Her heart raced. In the melee of dealing with her and Daire's messy emotional entanglement, she'd missed just how valuable the others she'd met on their journey had become.

"The wrong thing for the right reason. That's what being Olympus means."

Why did it sound like he meant that? "Olympus is gone," she said, sinking onto her butt. "It's finished, remember?"

"You know where you are right now?"

"Beta," she said. "I figured that much out."

"Olympus isn't something you give up because things get tough. It's in the fiber of us."

What the hell? "How could you still want to be a part of it? Of this madness? And if you do, why didn't you just tell Zeus where the keys are and join his ranks?" Like Daire had. She wasn't ready to say that out loud yet. "How can you be loyal to Olympus without fidelity to Zeus?"

He wiped the blood from his lip with the back of an index finger. "You don't get it," he said on an exhale, letting his head bump against the wall. "The vow we take. The sacrifice. It isn't in the name of any one man. It's not about following Zeus or Hades or any of them. We vow to die for the whole. To sacrifice ourselves to doing what's right. No matter the cost." Daire might think he was paying that bill, but he wasn't the only one. "If Olympus was about Zeus, I'd tell him what he wanted to know. If it was about Hades, I'd have taken down the jet before it got here."

Jet? They'd been on a jet? How long had she been out? Damn the Whist.

"And this?" she asked, gesturing at his injuries. "This isn't from looking out for your own best interest. What is it for? Why withhold?"

"Sport," he said, but she didn't appreciate the joke. If it was one. "We do this kind of thing as training. I can take a beating. I can give one out too. I've been taken captive before, been a hostage. Sometimes, if there's nothing better to do, it's fun to play it out. Test the limits. It increases endurance, stamina, resolve. Makes you stronger for the next time."

What a way to live life. What a way to exist.

"Sport," she said, believing him while at the same time being incredulous. "This isn't a game."

"Life is a game." His indifferent mood soured. "You know, you fuckers are supposed to be smarter than me. How come I'm the only one who gets it? You have to play to win. You're in it for you. Only you. Your motive has to be clear in your head. Know your objective. Friend of mine... sort of friend, anyway, he narrows it down to one goal. Whatever it takes to achieve that goal, that's what you do. No deviation. Stay on the path. No wavering."

Daire used to say she didn't waver. What was this moment? It wasn't so easy to be sure and determined when they were living through the looking glass.

"When were you last taken captive?" she asked, hoping to learn more about the man before both of them lost their lives.

Any second could be their last.

"In this last year," he said. "After the Exodus."

Her shoulder bumped the wall. "The fuck me figure woman?"

He exhaled a laugh that became a hint of a smile. "Got me out of there."

"You needed Daire and he wasn't there."

Which may have garnered resentment.

"I don't need anyone. I could've got out of there if I wanted to. If I'd had something to fight for, I'd have been out in a snap. But what was the point when I had nothing to be out there for?"

Something. Wasn't she Daire's something? Could it have been a lie all along? She didn't want to believe it. Who would? Yet, if he trusted her, like he'd claimed to trust her... If their love was real... He'd have clued her into this play. He wouldn't have kept the details from her, he'd have shared them. Whatever was going on, all she could rely on were his words to her in the Beast.

But if her love was her love, why was she sitting there worried about Styx's life? About her own. The Daire she knew wouldn't sacrifice his brother. He wouldn't watch his brother die and do nothing. Did that mean her Daire wasn't real?

Maybe he'd told her about JARR as misdirection. She'd have needed to know anyway, right? They needed her blood to access the system. Looping her in wasn't some huge display of trust, it was necessity.

But damnit, she shouldn't be doubting him… How could she not? He was on the other side of her cell. Free while she was captive. If he loved her, why would he be allowing her to go through this?

Frustrated, she wanted to yell at the universe. Being "in the field" she couldn't even discuss her conundrum with Styx. If Daire was truly working for the other side, screw him, she didn't have to keep secrets. But if he wasn't, if this was a ploy, she couldn't risk blowing it for him by yapping about their relationship when anyone could be listening.

"He's gone."

She'd disappeared into a daze and was pulled out by the statement. "He's gone? Who's gone where?"

"You're thinking this is all some big misunderstanding," he said, pushing away from the wall. "It's not."

"I don't think it's a misunderstanding."

Planting a hand on the wall, he rose to his feet and returned to the sink. "Whatever cozy, homey shit you were thinking before this, I'm here to tell you it's bullshit. I told you in London it was part of a larger play, didn't I?"

"All's not lost," she said, fighting to find some hope. "When Hades hears—"

"You saw Kingsley in that hotel suite, right?" he asked. "Who was she detailed to?"

Harry.

"He's in on it?"

Sucking in a fortifying breath, this time he bent over the sink to splash water on his face. "He's in a worse state than me," Styx said. "They had him bound and contained on the jet. I'm betting the only reason he's still alive is to watch you die."

Shit. "But I… how did they—"

"They didn't." He drank some water from his cupped hands before shutting off the faucet. "Who would he trust more than anyone? Who would Kingsley allow to approach her?"

"Daire," she whispered. "Zeus used him to get to them."

"Daire isn't Daire," he said. "Not the guy you thought he was. It was a lie. Every minute you spent with him."

"No, you don't—"

"Harry's the second smartest guy I know," he spat. "How'd he create such a dumb whore?"

The venom hit her for six. "What? How—"

"It was bullshit! All of it! From the beginning!" Sneering, he looked her up and down. "Z's right, you were so fucking desperate—"

"So this is on me?" she argued, leaping to her feet. "Do you think I knew this was his plan? That it was any plan? This isn't close to anything we ever discussed."

"It doesn't matter! It doesn't matter. Goddamn, do I have to spell everything out? He was playing all of us, from the start. The whole point was to sniff out the Scepter and you handed that right over without blinking. This was what they wanted all along. I wouldn't be surprised if H was right."

"Right about what?"

Despite his anger, and while checking out the split in his lip, he answered, "That Z got Ares at the Exodus. Tracking you and your mom sounds exactly like a Z kind of plan. And Ares would be the only one capable."

"No," she said, backing up. "I don't believe it. I won't."

"Geez, does beauty wash out the smarts? What does the guy have to do?" He raised his hand to her face to show her his torn, bloodied fingertips. "Does this look like fun? Like date night? They won't get what they want from me, so it'll only get worse. Maybe you'll be next. Who knows?"

Her stomach lurched. "He would never hurt me."

"Maybe," Styx said with a 'who cares' shrug. "Some might have said that about me... about H."

Stalled, the words didn't seem to... "You said Harry

was in a worse state. What does that mean?"

"What did I tell you about the field?"

"What does it mean?" she asked, rushing closer.

"Those at the top enjoy their work too much. Your great love is good with his fists… better with a blade… he really excels with the needles. And a razorblade? Forget about it."

"What does…?" She sank back a few steps. "You don't mean… he wouldn't."

"Guess you've got to see it to believe it."

"You think he'd hurt Har—Hades? He wouldn't."

Styx snorted. "Who do you think did this?" He opened his arms for a second to present himself. "Now get out of here. I'm taking a shower."

She didn't move. Couldn't get over the idea that… How could the man she loved hurt the brother he loved with such ease? And his mentor, the man he considered his kin…

His words echoed in her memory. *"Horrific violence, baby… Murder… I'm capable of murder… I've committed murder."*

Capable and witnessing its truth were two different things. Queasy, her hand rose to her belly. Her Heart… or was he? Could it have been a lie from the beginning? He'd never asked her for the Scepter, of course not. Just like playing Danny, he positioned himself and waited… for something to change.

Trust.

Would it be her undoing?

THIRTEEN

CERTAINTY WAS A MYTH.

Pacing, Tess did a terrible job of hiding her anxiety. How many hours had passed? How long had they been ensconced in their concrete tomb?

A life on the run might come with a trail of negatives. One positive she hadn't considered? Freedom.

The only tether she'd had was her mother and that wasn't like this. All her life, they'd been in the air. In the world. Out there. Free to roam. Nomad was a label she'd used in her head, but she hadn't appreciated the value of that existence.

"Why?" she whispered. "What the hell…? Out. We need to get out… How?" If Daire was there. If he was with her, he'd have them out already. He'd never be able to watch her drive herself nuts… Would he? "Just keep thinking. Keep moving. Stay alert."

"Quit it," Styx said from the bed. "You're amping me."

After his shower, he'd lain down in the bed. He'd been there since. For hours and hours. Maybe. There was no way to tell time. Another thing that drove her crazy.

Her skin itched right through to her bones. "Sorry I don't find it so easy to shrug off being imprisoned," she said, her fingers moving in another show of nervous energy. "Shit. How long do you think we'll be here?"

"You asked me that already."

Yeah, and she hadn't been satisfied with the "*how long it takes*" answer. How could he be so damn calm?

Her spirit was broken already. Her sanity was slipping. "We need to get out of here."

"Good luck with that," he said on an exhale, linking his hands at the back of his head. "There's no getting out of here, Lady. Not in anything less than a body bag."

She stopped, her jaw relaxing at the same time. "That's your answer? You want me to calm down and that's your answer?"

"I'm a realist. You should get used to it."

She frowned. "I thought you said you could get out of this if you wanted to."

"I said I could've got out of other places," he said. "This is Olympus."

"So? That makes them invincible?"

"What did I tell you about this place and your former squeeze?"

That Ares knew it better than anyone else. Being up against him limited their chance of freedom because he'd played out every eventuality as a kid, probably just for fun. How could someone escape? No one knew the site better than Ares.

Going to the bed, she sat next to Styx, trying her best to contain her apprehension. "What is this room?" His eyes moved to her though the rest of him stayed loose. "I mean, do you know where we are in the building?"

"Yep."

"Okay, good," she said, grabbing his thigh. "Where are we? Tell me."

"You don't want to know," he said, his gaze drifting away.

"I do…" Glancing around, she took in the features of the odd space again. "It doesn't make sense. None of it makes sense… This is Olympus Beta but…" Shaking her head, her confusion only grew. "What's with the pillows and the art?" The framed pictures on the walls weren't exquisite art, they were basic, child-like. "Oh my God, is this his room? His childhood bedroom or something?"

"Warmer."

His lack of communication infuriated her. "Would you just fucking tell me?"

"We're in the field."

Which meant what? "You think they're watching us? Listening to us?"

"I know they are," he said, meeting her eye again. "So you better can it."

The questions or the pacing and muttering? It wasn't so easy for her to switch off.

"I've never been taken prisoner before."

His next blink was slow. "Yes, you have… You just don't remember it."

"I don't remember it," she muttered, scanning the room again. "Oh my God…"

"Yep," Styx said.

They weren't in Daire's childhood bedroom. They were in hers.

Leaping from the bed, she rushed to the dressers to open drawers. Clothes. Children's clothes. Dolls. Paper. Pictures painted by an infant.

Backing away from the horror, her hand rose to cover her mouth. "Oh my God."

"This room was locked up when you left. No one had clearance. 'Cept maybe the principals."

"Why open it now?" she asked, fixated on one of the pictures stuck to the wall above the furniture.

"It's psychological torture, I guess," he said, at ease. "What do you think it's doing to Hades to know you're in here?"

He was right.

They were in the field and shouldn't be talking about it, but she couldn't contain her next question. "You're sure he's still alive?"

"He'll be alive until you're dead. Wouldn't surprise me if Z had Ares do it."

Whirling around, her shock was difficult to hide, not that Styx was looking at her. It couldn't be true. Wouldn't be… Daire. Her Daire? He would never hurt her… Except she'd have been as sure that he'd never stand by while she was shot full of tranquilizers. That he'd never be party to her being locked up against her will. A lot wasn't what she thought it was.

Accepting that Daire wasn't the man she believed him to be would help. The sooner the better. Why couldn't she do it?

"How do I know where one man ends and the next begins?" she asked, approaching the bed again. "I never knew him at all, did I?"

"Don't beat yourself up, I called him my brother for two decades. Anyone deserves the Dumb Fuck Award, it's me."

Which led her thoughts to someone else.

She stopped by the bed. "How do you think H feels?"

Betrayed by the boy he'd raised.

Their eyes met. "He'll be dead soon too. Least we won't have time to wallow in the humiliation."

"That really makes you feel better?"

Instead of responding with words, he breathed out and extended an arm toward her. Taking the offer of comfort, she climbed over him on the narrow bed and rested her head on his shoulder. It wasn't much, but the embrace and the strength in the arm he wound around her was a comfort. A tiny one.

"You're not alone," he murmured, kissing her hair.

They breathed in silence for a few seconds until she shifted the angle of her head. "Why did they put us together?"

"For this," he said. "So we'd talk."

And perhaps reveal something that could be useful to them.

"If you tell them where the keys are, they'll kill you."

"Yes."

"And if you don't…" He didn't say anything. He didn't have to. Her tongue was dry, but she tried to lick her lips. "He'd stand there and watch?"

"Murder was usually my assignment," he said. "But Ares will do his own dirty work."

"He'd never get over it. He'll never be the same."

"Pay attention, he's not the same. He's not who we thought he was. H always knew it. Olympus comes first for Ares. He always said it… It was why H didn't tell him about Zulu. If Ares knew…"

"He'd have told Z," she said.

Except… Pushing up, she supported herself on a straight arm.

"What?"

The Six offered it to him first. Had that been a lie too? Maybe he'd told Zeus and they'd come up with some crazy plan that ended with the Exodus. No, the Exodus might be a part of it, but that wasn't the end goal.

Did Zeus want to know who he could trust? Were they gunning for H? Zeus was, that much was obvious. Daire, on the other hand… H trusted the man he'd raised… No, actually, he didn't, not when it came to a straight choice between individual and institution.

Trust was his religion. That's what Daire said. Harry's lack of trust could've been enough to push his ward to the dark side.

More likely, Daire hadn't told Zeus about the Six's assassination request at all. Just the suggestion would be enough to tear Olympus down, as was playing out in real time. To keep the organization on its feet, he'd have kept the request to himself. More than that, he probably believed his refusal shut the idea down. He hadn't known they'd take it to Harry. Ares's loyalty was to Olympus, not to any one man… she didn't think. Daire would've done what it took to keep the train on the tracks. Zeus being paranoid and vengeful wouldn't benefit anyone.

But she couldn't… Being so confused, and with no way to find the truth, she could convince herself of anything.

Everything they'd been to each other couldn't be a ploy. The Daire who told her about JARR, if that was his true self, would've told her about the plan before Vegas. She wanted him to be real. Desperately. Wanted him to love her.

That zeal gave her both hope and doubt.

She'd forgiven him for Danny because she believed he'd developed real feelings for her. She knew all about starting on a path to one destination and ending up on another to somewhere else.

Did he love her? Was it real?

How could she find out the truth?

Rolling her lips into her mouth, she wet them, turning her attention to the man laid down beneath her.

"What?" he asked again.

Descending, she joined their mouths. For a second, he seemed to freeze. Though his lips parted, they didn't respond to hers. Pushing harder, she ignored the taste of blood and persisted. When her tongue touched a whisper of his, he grabbed her arm to jerk her away.

"You can't make a man who doesn't care jealous."

Her Daire would never watch her kiss another man and do nothing. She needed that proof. That manifestation of emotion to prove her Heart was still hers.

The blurring of her vision could only be tears. Despising them and her own weakness, she didn't know what to hate more, herself or the situation.

"What do you care?"

"Not interested in his seconds, sorry," he said, but scooped an arm around her head to guide it back onto his shoulder. His hold was so strong that she couldn't fight it. Not that she really tried. "I know where that mouth has been… Don't blame you for wanting to clean it out."

If only that had been her motive.

"I hate waiting. Being locked up. Powerless."

"For now… get used to it," he said. "Something will change."

He'd said that to her before and she'd ended up there, a prisoner, hurt, betrayed… condemned.

"They're going to win, aren't they?"

"The deck isn't stacked in our favor, but luck's always on your side, Lady."

Intel was the key to survival. Friend or foe, she and Styx knew a lot about Daire. It might not help that he knew just as much about them. If he could pound on a man he called his brother without compunction and stand by while his father-figure was bound and humiliated, there was no reason to think she'd get a better deal.

Love wasn't enough. Whether their relationship was sincere, or he'd duped her again, love wasn't enough. "*Trust is going to war sure that those with you will give as much as you, fight as hard as you.*" His words. Love needed a great huge dollop of faith to survive. Did she have that or was she holding onto a myth?

FOURTEEN

STYX WAS ASLEEP. He hadn't said anything for a while, so that's what she guessed.

His heartbeat wasn't the same as Daire's. It sounded different. Felt different too. Not as reassuring.

She didn't mean to compare the men. It wasn't so much a comparison of them as it was a measure of her own judgement.

Styx was a good man. Right? She trusted him. Why? Because Daire trusted him. But if Daire wasn't the man she loved, if she'd fallen in love with a figment of her imagination, did that mean her trust in Styx was just as intangible?

A clank at the door. Just like before.

As she sat up, Styx did too. Maybe he wasn't as asleep as she'd thought.

Her radar for everything was way off apparently.

The door swung open, this time without the lights going off. Four goons appeared in the narrow gap, two in front and two behind. All armed. All aiming their way.

"We want the girl," one of the guys in front said.

"Good," Styx said, lowering to lie down again. "She's a pain in the ass. Take her."

"Thanks," she said without making any attempt to

take her weight as she climbed over him. "Way to have my back."

"They won't kill ya."

Gee, what a reassurance.

There was literally nowhere to go except with them. Resisting would only lead to being hurt… or shot. Who knew if the new goons were aware of her value… or her blood's value, to their employer?

Still, she didn't hurry to join them and was in no rush to get wherever they wanted her to go.

More men waited in the hallway. They surrounded her, fingers always on the trigger.

It would be funny if it wasn't so sad.

If Daire was coming to save her, these men would be right to be twitchy. Given he was the instigator of her imprisonment, he wouldn't be coming to save her.

The corridors were like before, pale gray and stark blue.

"Where are we going?" she asked, wondering if these guys knew the route.

No response.

Their trek through the cold halls confirmed Minotaur was back on. If what Daire had said about the single route without it was true.

They took another turn and the passageway opened out. There were a few doors to the side and double doors opposite. Yep, definitely new.

One of the doors opened from the inside, just enough to let her go through.

Humidity hit as darkness enveloped her. It wasn't completely dark, just a different illumination to the previous space.

She paused, absorbing the thick heat. A brilliant white light flickered from somewhere.

"The light's disorienting. Just walk forward."

That voice she knew. Unfortunately.

Anger hit her hard. "Why should I do a damn thing you say, Ulysses?" Ulysses Sherwood was Zeus's real name. Why shouldn't she use it? They'd lived together in London after all. "What did you do to him?"

"I assume you know your father is here."

"Are we pretending that you don't have eyes and ears in my bedroom?" she asked, taking one step toward him. "You've got some sick, twisted sense of humor."

"I've been told that before," he murmured and grabbed her wrist.

"Let me go!"

"You don't want to disturb them," he said, yanking her hard.

The metallic clang under her feet was joined by warm metal under her fingertips. He let her go, which let her get her bearings, a little anyway. They were on a metal walkway, black material hung on the other side of the rail. Curling her fingers around the barrier, she appreciated its stability.

"Where are we? What's going on?"

A break in the material further along the walkway gave way to the light she'd noticed at the door. Her eyes adjusted, Zeus was a few feet ahead, gesturing for her to follow.

Glancing back at the closed doors, she folded her arms. He paused and lowered his chin, just looking at her. Okay, yeah, so it wouldn't get them anywhere if she refused on principle. Curiosity took her in his wake. The light wasn't above them, it seemed to be coming from below and...

Zeus stopped at the gap in the material and actually smiled as he looked down.

Her Heart. Thirty feet beneath them, standing in the center of a huge sawdust circle. What was going on? Something stained the sawdust and smattered the sandbags around the perimeter.

Blood.

Those dark stains were...

She swallowed.

Daire wasn't looking at them, he was just there. Shirtless, in shorts. His hair was wet... maybe that was blood too.

"What's going on?" she asked.

"Shh," Zeus said, opening his arms to take hold of

the railing separating them from a steep drop into that circle. "Just watch."

The light was coming from beneath the walkway, spotlighting the circle, she couldn't see anything in the shadows beyond.

"I don't know what I'm supposed to be..."

Daire moved. His arms rose from his sides. His stance shifted and he began to turn on the spot, like he was measuring something from beyond... monitoring something?

"I missed watching him work," Zeus muttered.

There was someone else. A man. He crossed the sandbag, slowly. Was he reluctant?

Daire's arms dropped, his head angled... what was going on?

Another someone.

A third.

Men creeping into the circle, approaching Daire.

Her heart pounded in her chest. The thump echoed in her ears.

"Oh my God," she whispered.

When the first guy lunged, knife in hand, she gasped. Daire deflected and turned as if sensing the second coming at him from behind. He took the feet out from under a third with a sweeping kick that powered the punch he landed on the second guy while relieving guy number one of his knife.

She wasn't breathing. Adrenaline surged through her system. A fourth. A fifth. How many guys were there?

The first guy was on the deck, tripping another guy who got an elbow to his face, blood spurted in a scattered arc.

Was that her love? Her Heart? Was the dangerous assailant taking these men apart with such ease the same one who'd been so tender with her?

The knife now in Daire's possession, slashed one gut and impaled another man's side before the hilt was slammed into the temple of another.

One by one, the men dropped. Daire moved in his own rhythm, sensing fists and feet before they came close.

The glint of another blade behind her Heart dropped her hands from her open mouth to clench around the rail.

Before she could form words, Daire swung around, grabbed the guy's wrist to twist it up and yank, forcing the blade to fall from his grip into Daire's. Showing no mercy, he stabbed it into the guy's bicep, ringing a howl of pain from his victim.

The strewn casualties all made noise. Whining. Yelping. Sobbing. Fresh blood stained the ground as Daire turned slowly, surveying the damage.

When he was satisfied, he stopped and looked up, opening his mouth to liberate the first blade from his teeth. The way it dropped into his open palm reminded her of the garage in Vegas oh so long ago. He spun each knife in their respective hands.

"I'm bored," he called up, like he'd known they were there the whole time.

Zeus anyway, Daire didn't look at her. And it wasn't blood in his hair, sweat dampened it and his chest. How long had he been doing this? Why was it so hot in the massive space?

"I know," Zeus called back on a sighing snicker.

"Let me have them."

"You think they'll challenge you?" Zeus asked, exuding an impossible to misinterpret pride.

"You haven't found one yet, Sage. You've gotta work harder."

Zeus laughed. She wanted to be sick. Was she really watching them banter? Had she let that man into her bed? Into her heart. And what the hell was Sage?

"Soon," Zeus said. "We have other business first."

As he side-nodded, Daire walked out of view, unwrapping something from his hands.

What business? In the same moment he vanished, someone grabbed her arms and she was jerked back.

"No!" she screamed as she was dragged away from Zeus.

Other men were ready on the other side of the door. They surrounded her, taking hold of her legs, lifting her clear off the floor.

What hope did she have? Little, but she fought anyway. Kicking and writhing, tugging her arms and legs as best she could. Maybe she couldn't prevent it, maybe she wouldn't get free. No. There was no maybe about it.

Sick with anger, with fear and hatred. These men were taking her somewhere under his instruction. They maneuvered her around, passing her from here to there like an object to be shuttled at the will of Olympus.

"Do you want to be sedated?" Zeus roared from somewhere behind them.

"Go to hell!" she screamed, only then realizing his voice was raised because her own wouldn't silence.

Why should she? Her terrorized rage needed an outlet. Her voice was about the only thing she had control of anymore.

"Do it!" Zeus shouted.

Then came the sting and another scream.

It wasn't like before. Whatever was injected into her worked as fast but wasn't the same as the Whist.

Her ears rang, distorting the noise around her. Her vision blurred, her mouth dried. She tried to talk, to shout, everything worked in slow motion. Her mind and body were no longer connected.

Noise. Disorientation. Where was she? Voices broke through as indecipherable mumbles. Who was talking? Why was there pain in her arms and legs? Not pain. Pressure.

A shout… who? What was going on?

The pressure left. She was hoisted higher. There was no pain. No fear. What? Where were they…? They? She?

Someone carried her, cradled her close, then… No, the warmth was gone. Something cold was under her, but what…? She knew that scent. It curled the corners of her lips. Relaxed her. Comforted her.

"She's semi-conscious."

That was close. Clear. Louder.

"Daire," she murmured.

"Good," someone snapped. Her head lolled toward the sensation of a fingertip on her cheek. "Give her the second shot."

Shot? Of what? Where was Daire? Why wasn't he…?

The next pinch was harder, longer than before. A

whine of pain left her throat, but there was little force behind it. Strength withered before it rose. Whatever was happening, she was powerless to stop it.

Daire.

Instinct told her to trust. That so long as he was around, she didn't have to be worried or scared.

"My…" she whispered before, in a flash, her blood became searing hot.

Her eyes opened, her mouth too, in a silent scream. She couldn't breathe. Couldn't feel anything but the burning pain cascading through her.

Then, it stopped. Left in a single second. Gone and she was… Her.

FIFTEEN

EVERYTHING WAS BACK. Her sight. Sound. Awareness. Where was she?

Her eyes scanned the space. Clinical white floor, sterile walls, steel workstations. Glass cabinets held vials and equipment. Was it a hospital? A laboratory.

She wanted to take in more of the space, but her head was fixed in place. Her attempt to touch the restraint was impossible because her hands were immobilized too.

A curtain hung across the wall in front of her. It didn't reach the floor but seemed... ominous.

"What's going on?" she asked, not that she could see anyone.

"What's going on...?"

The drawled question in that arrogant tone. Zeus. Yeah, she wished she didn't recognize it.

"You're sick," she said, unnerved that his voice came from behind.

Anything could be going on back there. Anyone could be there.

"And you're scared."

She smiled, though a laugh escaped her lips too. "Of what? You? Please. We're at the beta site, you have goons to do your work. And you need me. I know that you need me and I know why."

"So you think you're untouchable?" he asked, coming into view.

"Kill me. We both know that's what you want to do," she said, curling her fingers into fists. With the straps across her wrists, escape was unlikely. "Yeah, I lose my life, least I'll know in those final seconds you've screwed yourself too."

Standing in front of her, his eyes narrowed. "How do you do it, Miss Walbeck? You've lost everything. Your freedom. Your mother. Your lover…" His chin rose just a fraction betraying he wanted, or expected, an answer. She didn't indulge him. "We both know your father's obligation to you is tenuous at best… You don't even like each other very much." True? Maybe. That was one warren she wouldn't get lost in. "Perhaps it's your relationship to the other that keeps you going." Who was he talking about? "You and your co-prisoner have grown close… Intimately close."

Styx.

"You can't kill him either," she said. "He knows the location you need."

"Yes, though that information does me no good if he won't share it."

Her smile broadened. "You trained him too well." She licked her lips to hide her delight. No, not to hide it, to give the impression she was laughing at him. Because that's exactly what she wanted to do. "How does it feel to be so completely ineffectual in your own castle? Ooh, the Olympusphere," she mocked him. "The big, scary principal with the world at his fingertips, the coward who—"

He backhanded her face. Yeah, it hurt, more so because her head couldn't move to absorb the blow. The hard restraint across her forehead held her head immobile.

"Guess it's my turn," she said, moving her jaw. "Did you put your hands on my co-prisoner or my father? No, I doubt it. Don't think you're saved from their wrath just because you're too scared to face them."

"You will learn respect," he hissed at her.

Her nails dug into her palms. "For you? I'll respect

you the day you stand in front of my father. Equal. Weaponless. The day you face him like a man for all you've done."

Mirroring her previous amusement, he gave her a taste of his resentment. "Your father will live only a minute longer than you."

So Styx was right, Harry would be kept alive just long enough to watch her die. Styx would be first. As soon as he gave up the location of the keys, which he'd have to eventually, he'd be murdered. They'd retrieve the keys, do whatever was required to release JARR, including using her blood, then she'd be killed in front of her father. Harry would witness the demise of his family, betrayed by the cause he'd dedicated his life to.

"Will you make Ares do that too?" she asked, witnessing his confidence give way to intrigue. "Put him in the ring with the man who made him? You think he'd put up a fight? He'd die for accepting a mission. That's all Harry did. The same thing he's been doing for three, four decades. You'll have your thug murder him to fulfill your own personal vendetta. Let's not call it anything else. You want Harry dead because he threatens you. Because you've always known he could do your job ten times better than you. A hundred times better." His jaw moved when he clenched his teeth. "Olympus doesn't need you. It would get along just fine without you and you can't stand—"

Another slap. This time, she screamed at him in angry response, wishing she could vault from the goddamn chair and claw his eyes out. He wouldn't face her father like a man. Fear? Maybe. His reason for keeping her restrained was a mystery.

"I never thought I'd see the day you'd fight for your father."

"I didn't think I'd live long enough to see you beaten," she said, "but here you are."

He stepped in closer, taking a tissue from somewhere behind her to lean in and wipe, what she assumed was blood, from the corner of her mouth.

"Don't be so sure of that, Miss Walbeck," he

murmured before stepping back and nodding at someone.

The curtain opened. Her father. Styx. Both of them. In a tiny room, no wider than the window between them. They were talking. Shouting. At her. But she couldn't hear anything. They were… Stocks above their heads held their arms in place. The window cut them off at the hip, but she'd guess their feet were restrained too.

God, they were… Styx had fresh blood on his cheek. Harry's eyes were so swollen, she was amazed he could see. Maybe he couldn't. The bruises were… the blood… the… sickness roiled in her stomach.

"What do you want?" she asked, resenting the shit out of the tears that blurred her eyes.

They were trying to tell her something. Trying to communicate. Damnit.

"You know what I want," Zeus said, behind her again.

"I don't!" she screeched. Their hands were in fists too, locked in place, useless, frustrating. Being powerless… Such great men, reduced to… Warm moisture skittered down her cheek. "What the fuck do you want? You want me to bleed? I'll fucking bleed!"

What did she know about JARR? About the process? If this was her end, at least she wouldn't have to see people she cared about in distress anymore.

A door at the side of Styx and Harry's room opened. She hadn't seen it until the two men came in. One had a stick, something she didn't—the spark of electricity flashed just a second before the first guy jabbed Styx with it. Fucker! Styx couldn't protect himself. Couldn't do anything. After absorbing the shock, his nostrils flared as he flashed his gritted teeth at the bastard.

"Give him his hands," she said. The other guy left the small cell, but the guy with the prod stayed put. "If you're so confident in your prized Olympus—"

"Those men aren't Olympus. I wouldn't trust them to discipline a dog."

But he'd sent them in to Styx and Harry. Sent them into the ring with Daire. No wonder he was bored.

"I can't tell you where the keys are," she said, pulling against her own restraints. "If you want me to bleed, just let them go and—"

"They're not going anywhere," he said. "And I don't need a thing from you."

"So this is all just some sick fucking game that you—"

"You talk too much, Miss Walbeck," Zeus said. "You're not the mark. You're the bait."

Before she could say anything else, someone appeared at her side. Daire. Right there next to her, seated on a low stool. He pulled a metal table closer. She heard things being moved but couldn't see what was on it.

"This is wrong," she said, appealing to any part of her Daire that might still be in there. "Whatever he's done to you… whatever he's promised—you can't trust him and you know that."

"He's made his choice," Zeus said. "The right choice."

Her Daire couldn't hurt her. The man loved her. He didn't have it in him.

She ignored Zeus. "We're your family. Not this place. Not this." She swallowed. "You know it's wrong…" More tears skittered from her lashes. "My Heart. You're my security. My somewhere safe. You can stop this. Now. Stand up to him. That's all you have to do. Everything's forgotten. Everything's forgiven. You are my guiding light and I am your something." Even Zeus's laughter couldn't deter her. Maybe this was their last chance. No, it was their last chance. Daire was at her side, busying himself with something. Right there. Why did he feel so far away? Her stomach lurched. Drawing breath got harder. "You told me I was always safe with you." Determination burned hot, but it was hard to hold onto as hope dimmed. "Easy doesn't mean right…"

"It's pathetic," Zeus spat, staying out of view. "You're embarrassing yourself. Ares is a soldier. An elite operative. He is not your cuddle bear. Your sweetums. Whatever the hell else you think. He was raised to be of superior quality. Being anyone's boyfriend is beneath him."

The life he'd lived. Zeus wasn't wrong.

Still, she searched the man sitting by her arm, facing her but never looking at her. "My Heart…" She didn't even care that she was begging. "I love you," she whispered. Still, he didn't respond. In her desperation, she looked to her father and Styx. Both remained in their stocks, solemn, they weren't shouting anymore. Could they hear her? Pleading with the man they'd put their faith in, the man they loved. Her attention swung back to Daire. "Look at me… Baby…" He wouldn't. All those times in the past when he'd avoided her gaze. Those times when their relationship was tested… "Please look at me, baby. Just… Forget everything else… Forget everything else and just be here…" Those were his words. Did he remember? Did any of it mean anything? If she had her hands, if she could just touch him. "You go, I go…" Nothing. "If you won't free us. Kill us. Before he can do whatever he—"

Daire shifted, rolling the stool closer, he raised something… a syringe… with clear liquid in it.

"Let her go!"

Her father. She could hear him.

"I've missed your wit, Harry," Zeus said, sauntering toward the window, on the opposite side to Daire.

"She shouldn't be a part of this. The Accord—"

"Null and void. You did that the minute you started writing to Helen."

Shit. He knew about the letters.

Her father protested. Zeus retorted. Their conversation faded when she saw Daire watching them, listening to what was going on over there, paying no attention to her or their proximity. Gazing at his profile, at his impressive upper body contained in that snug black tee-shirt. He was her love. Had been. She couldn't believe it wasn't real, not when she sat so close to him, breathing him in.

"Ares," she murmured the foreign word.

Obviously, it startled him too because on reflex, his gaze leaped to hers. Before either of them had a chance to process, their eyes were locked. Then in a blink, they were gone. Lowered. He didn't turn away. Even without hearing any words, she knew he'd be beating himself up.

Keeping her volume low, she blocked out the two principals arguing. "It's okay…" Her fingers loosened, aching for his even knowing they'd never be satisfied. "You got your home back. This was what we wanted all along. This was what you wanted. I didn't know it would cost Styx and Harry their lives too, but if mine is what it takes to deliver your happiness. Take it… I'd give it to you for nothing." The words from the last letter he wrote to her. She smiled, though he still wasn't looking at her. "Make it quick. For Harry and Styx. I don't care what you do to me, but for them… If any part of you ever cared for me at all, make it quick for them." His shoulders moved, his chest rose and fell at a deliberate, controlled pace. "I'm in awe of you. I always was… You've proved your resolve. Your love for Olympus. You put everything else aside for the greater good. The world owes you a debt. They'll never know who to pay, but… I thank you. For them. For everyone. You are a true hero."

"Enough!"

The screamed word came from Zeus who whipped around to march away from the window. Oh, something over there had pissed him off. Harry knew how to push his buttons. She smiled again, exhaling her laugh. Her father was made of steel. Anyone else would be diplomatic. Would mediate and broker. Not Harry… She got her mettle from both sides.

"You can't hear the truth," her father spat. "Killing me, all three of us, won't get you what you want."

"Do it!" Zeus barked, marching closer, his arm outstretched toward her. "Ares, do it now!"

Daire raised the needle and she tried to pull away, but it was futile, the restraints held her in place.

"No!" Harry yelled as Daire lowered the needle to her forearm. "Don't! You don't have to do this!"

She didn't know what was in that needle. What scared her father? What should she be scared of? Her heart raced; adrenaline surged.

"Daire," she said on an inhale. "Please…"

"No!" Harry was screaming so loud, his voice became hoarse. "Stop!"

"She's pregnant!"

Styx.

Daire whipped around, going past her and Zeus, probably to focus on his brother. The declaration stilled everyone, even her.

"What?" Zeus eventually asked.

"She's pregnant," Styx said again, calmer. "You sure you want to shoot her up and hurt the baby?"

This had to be some strategic move because it was a flat out lie. The only person who knew about her test was Styx and he'd asked outright. Lying to him wouldn't have prevented their capture, but whatever it was for now, all she could do was trust him.

"Who's the father?" Zeus asked, looking at both Styx and Daire before turning his focus to her.

Licking her lips, she didn't want to look to Styx for direction. The urge was immense, yet she managed to quash it.

"That's none of your goddamn business."

Daire was looking at her. She could feel him. That was as much as she wanted. It was a lie. A lie. And she was letting him believe it.

Zeus growled out frustration and threw an arm out. "Get her out of here!"

Staring at nothing, she missed the guy who came around by Daire until he pushed his stool away, far away from her. The new guy leaned in and another sting of pain went through her arm. Less painful, she was getting used to being put out for transport.

Fighting was difficult when there were so many against her. So many with all their tech and potions to subdue those against them. Let Zeus crow. He'd win this one, but she had faith, in her father, in Styx, in someone, somehow, overcoming his menace. They had to. If they didn't… God help every soul on Earth.

SIXTEEN

WHEN SHE NEXT BECAME AWARE, her head was heavy, throbbing, muddied.

Getting over these drugged out episodes got faster each time. Maybe she was building an immunity.

"You back?"

The male voice opened her eyes. At first, he was just a silhouette looming over her. She raised a hand to try blocking the light behind him. But it didn't last long. Her palm fell to her forehead and descended to cover her closing eyes.

"Styx."

"Do you get that this is serious?"

A lecture? A debate? She wasn't up for either. On a groan, she sat up and dropped back against the concrete wall. Yes, she wanted to get away from his judgment, but getting onto her feet was still a step more than she was capable of.

"What time is it?"

"What does that matter?" he asked, sitting beside her. He pressed two fingers to her wrist and another two under the angle of his own jaw. What was he...?

She snatched her hand back. "Leave my pulse alone." Pregnant. That's what he'd declared to the room, that she was knocked up. "Why did you do that?"

"Tell the world your secret?"

Her own fury bit out in a glare. While he matched it, she also sensed his insistence. Damnit. They were being watched. Listened to. Observed. She couldn't tell the truth. This guy knew Olympus better than she did. Knew Zeus better… Ares too.

"It wasn't your place to say anything."

"You know nothing about the resources they have here. Asclepius may be dead. He may not have written articles and how to guides, but he had decades, and an almost unlimited budget, to play with his theories, his chemicals, his whatever. Make no mistake, there's a bona fide cornucopia of pharmaceuticals stored here. And if there's one person who knows how to use and replicate them, it's your former squeeze."

Because he trained with everyone. In every department. Ares wasn't just useful for his physical skills; he was the closest font of information for Zeus. Styx called his brother an Olympus encyclopedia and he wasn't wrong. If one person had the ability to absorb, process, and repeat taught actions, it was Ares. His whole life had been that.

Spending this time in Olympus, seeing Ares in his natural environment, she was learning so much about his truth. This man was the one the principals vied for. The one the Six trusted. Not because they had to, although they did, but because he was the personification of their collective lives' works. He was Olympus in another skin. The institution built carbon atom on concrete brick. The living, breathing, speaking weapon they'd nurtured from birth, just like the enterprise itself.

"We can't stay here," she said, forcing herself to push off the bed onto her feet. She paused, getting her bearings. Styx steadied her, but the moment she processed the contact, she jerked her arm away. "I don't want anything from you."

"You plan to get out of here on your own?"

What did she plan? If only she could. Walking away from him, she gave her blood a few seconds to warm and flow again. Her head needed the space, the time, the latitude. What was she going to do? If she didn't get out of there, she'd die.

Fine. Maybe that didn't matter, but she didn't want Zeus to win. If he killed her, he'd kill Harry not long after. He could choose to keep Styx alive and hope the grave acts would loosen his lips. Not that it mattered. If she was dead, her blood was dead, so the keys were useless, he'd never be able to rouse his precious JARR.

"You thought they were going to inject me with something lethal."

"No," he said. "Not lethal for you… it would be to the baby."

Spinning around, she wanted to yell, to argue back, but fuck, there was that look in his eyes again. They knew it was a lie. There was no baby. His lie had saved her from something. She didn't know what or why he'd reached for such a desperate and easily disprovable fib. Trusting him could be a mistake, but what choice did she have? It was trust him or acknowledge she was alone and powerless.

Resting a hand on the dresser beside her, she took a breath and turned to lay the other on it. How could they get out of there? Something had to… Damn the futility of it. They couldn't even talk about escape, couldn't form a plan, because they were under constant scrutiny. Damn. Damn. Goddamn! Fuck! Tightening her grip, she growled her frustration in an agonized rumbling screech, pulling the dresser off its back feet a little to slam it back down.

When the hell had she become so powerless?

The same time she fell in love. The moment she trusted him. Handing herself to him had been so subtle, so gradual, that she couldn't identify the single moment it happened. She'd put all of herself into him. Early. Maybe as long ago as her mother's death. Zeus was right. Completely right. She was pathetic. So desperate to mean something to someone, anyone, that she erased herself, and all of her mother's lessons, to grab hold of the first glimmer of affection.

Rolling her lips around her teeth, she bit down, squeezing her eyes closed at the same time. If that was true, if she was facing that reality, shouldn't she also be letting go of what was? Loving him weakened her because she'd handed over her fate. This was easy for him. She'd made it easy by trotting along, following one instruction after another. He'd been kind enough to let her think in certain moments that she was making her own decisions, but she wasn't.

Her life had become Olympus. Not running from it, as she had with her mother. Instead toward it, with him, opening herself to any and all torture if it would ease his journey back to his true love: the company.

Screaming, she pulled the dresser out, slamming it back and tipping it again, over and over, shaking the heavy piece as she wished someone had shaken her.

"Hey. Hey! Hey!" Styx dragged her away, shoving the dresser from her hands as he did. "You need to get a fucking grip."

"I need to get out of here," she growled. A primal need to tear down Olympus darkened her throat. "They took from me. One too many times."

"I know," he said, calm, centered, his eyes remaining on hers as he bent his knees to align their eyes. "I feel it too, okay? But there's nothing we can do. We're here. We're stuck."

"They need me," she said, her voice still low as it passed her dry lips.

"Yes, I—"

"You can't let them have what they need," she said. "They want to live this… want this to be their world, fine. But it's not mine and I will not let them use me to win. I won't do it."

"What do you expect me to do?"

Maybe the guy was dealing with a burden of his own, who knew what was going on in his head? It didn't matter. He'd told her he was one thing…

"Use your bare hands," she murmured, her eyes narrowing. Did he get it? Did he understand the plan was to kill them? Her, him, and Harry. They were going to die. She wouldn't let them take from her to gain for themselves. "Now."

He got it because he was shaking his head as his fingers bit deeper into her upper arms. "No. That's not an option."

"It's the only control we have left," she said. "I need you. I need your help." She didn't want to feel that way any longer. The pain twisted so deep, it was like her heart couldn't beat anymore. Life was a distant memory. Whether Styx ended it or not, she wasn't living in that moment. "Please… finish it."

"You can't be talking like this," he said, his hands dropping to his sides. "You shouldn't be."

"You don't want them to win any more than I do."

"What you're talking about is…?"

"You've done it before. If you can kill your father, you can kill me."

His head turned to the side. "We're not there yet. We have… there are other options."

The exhale that joined her smile was almost a laugh, but her eyes were heating again. "Please, enlighten me… We're stuck here. It won't take long for them to figure out the truth." That the pregnancy was bogus. "Then we'll be right back where we were." With her restrained in a lab and the men watching on. "Don't ask me to be there again… Don't ask me to hate you in my final seconds." Their eyes met. She took his hand in hers, beseeching him with her need. "I need you to do this. It's the only choice we have. It's the only option left."

"No."

If he wanted to join them, he'd have done it already. Telling them the location of the keys, giving them what they needed to access JARR was still a possibility. It would be right up to the moment of her death. Escape? Death was the only way. It had to happen. There. In that room. In that minute.

"Styx…" she whispered, raising his hand to her cheek, rubbing her face against it. "The only way out is the final escape. You have to take me away from them. Put me beyond their reach. Where no one can ever hurt me again."

For the seconds that followed, she prayed with her gaze locked to his that he'd see it was the only route. Was it cowardly? Maybe. She didn't admit that her request was as much about ending her emotional pain as it was about thwarting the evil plot.

She had to die. The only way to ruin Olympus and take back control was to end her life. Now.

SEVENTEEN

"JUST… GIVE ME A SECOND TO THINK…"

Styx turned to walk away, his hand going to the back of his neck as he crossed the room.

The anguish on her shoulders was one thing, it couldn't be a great view from his position either. He and Daire were brothers, had been brothers. They believed in each other, or Styx had believed in him. Just like Harry witnessing the boy he loved as a son betraying him.

None of them were in enviable positions.

Giving her co-prisoner space might help him order his thoughts. Though she'd been out for God knew how long and he'd had all that time to come up with something. Maybe he hadn't expected her to request murder. Who would?

Her attention wandered. Something behind the dresser caught her eye. Color. Brighter than elsewhere. Curious, she went over to put all her weight against the dresser, shifting it a few feet closer to the door.

What she found cleared her head. Handprints. Four. Two larger than the others and a name beneath one. Crouching she touched the first letter, tracing it with a fingertip. Ares. Right there beneath those marked Mommy and Daddy… All these years, the lifetime of an individual, he'd never been Daire and hadn't stood a chance. He'd told her that being with her showed him another side of life. That he hadn't expected love would ever be a part of his world.

He'd never been human. Never fallible. Never a failure. Always living up to expectation. Closing her eyes, she shook her head. Harry adored him, but her Heart hadn't seen it. He'd believed the worst, that no one could value him beyond his importance to the cause.

"If I let you bleed..." Styx's voice came from above her. "They'll have time to get here... to stop it."

"Then don't bleed me," she said, laying a palm on top of the young Ares handprint. "You know how to do it quick." She didn't doubt him and smiled once more at the glimmer of their shared path before standing up. "Strangulation—"

"Takes longer than you think."

"What ways don't—"

"I break your neck."

"Okay," she said, laying a hand on the cold concrete wall. "Then break my neck."

His fingers slid onto her shoulders, slow, taking their time about skimming closer to her neck. It would be over in a heartbeat. In a flash. Wouldn't it?

His progress paused. "I don't—"

"Hesitation gets you killed, Agent," she said, filling her voice with certainty. "The only way I can't be used against others is to take me out of the equation. You know it." And maybe death would be the relief she'd sought after losing her mother. If something came after this life, anything, her mother would be there waiting. "Do it."

His hands dropped and he curled his fingers around her wrist. "We do it in the shower... I'll bleed you after."

Just in case. Good plan. Shit, she didn't give Styx credit for his own skill often enough. When he pulled on her, she let herself be led, trailing just a step behind on their walk to the bathroom. He left her in the middle of the room, turned on the shower, then went to the vanity.

He paused.

What was the delay? All of a sudden, he raised his arm and brought his elbow slamming down on one end of the towel rail, breaking it free from the wall. In a hefty yet slick move, he caught the towel and tossed it over his shoulder while simultaneously ripping the other end of the towel rail out of the bare concrete.

Astounded, she said nothing as he kept going. Swinging the towel rail around with a momentous strength so great that when the steel met the shower screen, it shattered in a clashing crash of sparkling metal and glass. Wow. Maybe his own rage needed an outlet too.

Careless to leave tools for such a man. It didn't appear to be normal glass but didn't stand a chance against Styx's force. He selected a jagged shard from the mess and wrapped the hand towel around the end before looking at her again.

"You're good at this."

"Yeah," he said without pleasure. "Exceptionally."

She smiled. "It'll feel good… looking him in the eye after. You're taking their legs from under them. Destroying their supposed destiny. Obliterating their plan."

"You know with your death, I become useless," he said, creeping closer. "Harry too. You better be waiting on the other side."

She laid a hand on his chest and boosted up to kiss his cheek. "Me and Helen."

He nodded then turned her toward the streaming water. Steam billowed, maybe offering some cover. Her certainty had to be absolute or he might not follow through. No hesitation.

Stepping over the low lip of the shower tray, she laid her hands on the opposite wall. She had to be standing in the spray to ensure her blood disappeared down the drain.

Zeus's people may have time to gather it otherwise, who knew what they could do with their technology. She didn't want her blood to be harvested and somehow reanimated. That would make her sacrifice pointless.

The wrapped glass wasn't in his hands when they slid around the sides of her neck and curled around her jaw, raising it a fraction.

"Brother forgive me," he whispered as her eyes closed and his grip tightened.

A tear left her eye, merging with the spray spattering on her cheeks. The end. Why was she so at peace?

"Major!"

The shout came from the other room. Who would…?

"Shit," Styx said, grabbing her hand, pulling her from the bathroom. "What the hell is—"

"Time to go."

Her father was there. Bruised and battered, but it was definitely him in the open doorway.

"Not a second too soon," Styx said.

God, he was—they were… He dragged her out of the room in her father's wake. Too soon they were moving at a run. This wasn't a clandestine escape; it was a hail Mary pass. Frantic. Desperate… Their only hope.

Running with Styx was less choice and more autopilot. They were free, could be free. This could be it. They could get out. Away. Far away from the beta site. Far from him…

One foot caught the other and she slowed, or tried to, Styx's insistence was difficult to fight while they were connected. Yanking her hand away, she stopped. Shaking her head, her blood vibrated down to its tiniest atom.

Styx turned. She was focused on the floor, processing flashes of her last joining with Daire. That kiss she tried to fight when he wanted to say goodbye. His hands on her body as he carried her to their bed and slid himself into her. The wink he'd offered before she left the Beast. The soldier in the suite of Hugo's hotel. The professional who played her… the efficient fighter in the sawdust ring. The detached operative ready to violate her in the lab… The small handprint next to hers on the wall of her cell. It held her captive… just as the building had held her Heart captive all his life.

"No," she whispered.

"What is it?" Styx demanded. "Come on, goddamnit!" Marching over, he grabbed her upper arm. "Move!"

"I can't," she said, the warmth of her tears skittered down her face. Harry was somewhere up ahead. Her awareness was all over the place. There was noise, maybe it only existed in her head. "I can't leave him."

"My fucking… Are you fucking serious?" Styx snapped and jerked her forward a few steps. "He's fucking gone. He's a snake. You're supposed to fucking hate him."

"I know," she said, her throat narrowing. Shivering, her wet clothes absorbed the frigid air. "I can't do that either."

"Get moving!" Harry hollered from somewhere further along the corridor.

Her eyes locked to Styx's. "I can't leave him. You can go. Both of you. If there's a chance… I can't leave him."

His lips thinned. His chest grew and he swooped down to hoist her over his shoulder. "Yes, you can."

"No!" she screamed, kicking and punching at him. He paid no attention and strode down the passageway, breaking into a run when they got to Harry. "Let me go! Put me down!"

The men kept on going, speeding along the corridor. Tossing her hair aside, she looked back down the long space. He was back there. Her love. Maybe he wasn't her love. Maybe Styx was right. She didn't want to take that chance. Every part of her ached. Driving her fists into Styx's back, she boosted herself up, taking in as much air as she could before manifesting the torturous pain in a loud wail. She couldn't leave him, but she couldn't stay. What was life without him?

With her burning lungs empty, grief weighed on her. She sagged, losing her fight, losing her will. They left the passage, went down stairs. It didn't matter, they were leaving, she didn't need to monitor the route.

Whether the man they'd left behind was her love or not, she'd lost him. They were more than apart. More than just on different sides of a war. The stretched threads of their once secure love were untwining, pulled to their limit, frayed, broken. It was too much. Part of her was with him. Her heart didn't beat in her chest, it beat in his. If he no longer wanted it, if he'd never wanted it, if the whole thing was a ruse… She may as well have laid down with her mother and slipped away.

She didn't want to die alone. He'd told her that she wouldn't. But she was already gone. She'd died in that Vegas hotel room when he walked in and owned his betrayal. Danny was a myth, why shouldn't Daire be? Nothing they'd been through meant what she thought it did. Even if he loved her, even if he'd believed every word, he'd stood by while others imprisoned her. He'd beaten his brother, his father and mentor, if he could hurt them, there was no reason he couldn't hurt her. It came to a choice. Just like Harry had said in the control room on the day they met: Olympus came first for Daire.

Before everything else.

Before her.

Having given him to Olympus, she couldn't whine he'd taken her at her word.

The cool air was the first sign they were outside. It was dark, a door opened and she was tossed into the backseat of a truck. She couldn't move. Her drive to survive was gone. What did it matter? Nothing mattered anymore. The world was gone. Her world. And it had taken her Heart. She didn't exist without him. She was no more. Nothing. Invisible. Hollowed out. Numb.

Olympus was persistent, she had to give it that. It picked and picked at her insides until she was left with nothing. Let it take her. Let it rule her. What was she without all that came before? With nothing and no one to love, she was a shadow. A ghost. Life was over.

EIGHTEEN

"WHAT IN THE ACTUAL HOLY…?"

Her father screamed as he slammed out of the truck. Styx was gone just as fast. Gone, in a flash. Just like that she was alone. Their shouting outside was muffled by the metal and glass shell around her. The haze was shattered when the door at her feet opened. The voices continued as she was flipped to her back by her ankles and dragged toward the cool air.

"It's fucking done," Styx barked. "We forget it and move on."

He bowed over to grab her arms and haul her up, tossing her over his shoulder again, this time to take her out. It was light outside. They'd been driving for… she couldn't even guess how many hours… maybe it had been days… Her head was empty. Her ability to focus, gone.

"She's in shock," Harry said.

Styx dumped her on the compacted dirt. "No kidding, but this truck is Olympus. I need what's under her."

Noise followed his movement, then things were being tossed out of the vehicle.

"Thank Kingsley for the kit," Styx said when boots landed on the ground beside her.

"Everyone strip to nothing," Harry said. "We change

clothes and burn what's left. Everything."

"We camping out?" Styx asked.

"Possibly. We're on the back foot. Ares really fucked us."

"We hoofing it?"

"Yeah. We'll hike to the road and hitch."

"Or stay in the undergrowth."

"We have to put some distance between us and this site," Harry said. "To regroup."

"Do the unexpected."

"He'll expect the unexpected. He'll be ready for anything… I trained him too well."

"You trained him to survive, no matter the cost, that's what he's doing."

"You fucking start—"

"No," Styx said, rearing up, out the back of the truck. "It's finished. We move on, remember?"

"With him as our opposition?"

"You didn't fear Zeus," Styx said.

"I don't fear Ares. Not for me."

The silence raised her head. Both men were looking at her.

"Are you with us?"

Was she? Where was her loyalty? What way was up? She couldn't move. Her fingers were numb, her legs and feet too. Could be the cool dirt beneath her or maybe her heart was slowing. They expected something from her. But what did she have to give? Every part of her worth anything had been given to Daire.

"We left him," she croaked. "We left him behind."

The men looked at each other before her father came over to hunker down.

"We got out to survive. Ares will do what's necessary to survive… We have to do the same."

She couldn't wrap her mind around it. Couldn't believe she and her Heart were so far apart in so many ways.

"No," she said, meeting Styx's eye. "Take me back or pick up where we left off."

"No," he said without contrition. "You go back there

and they win. Wasn't that what you didn't want?"

"I want him. I want my Heart."

"He's gone!" Styx hollered, tossing whatever was in his hand down. "The goddamn motherfucker—"

"Hey!" Harry said, stepping between them. "Both of you calm the fuck down. Tess…" She didn't even try to meet her father's gaze. "You thought it was real. We all did. If I'd known this was his plan… I know what it is to want something more than the air you breathe, but whatever you think it was, whatever promises he made you… He made promises to us too, they mean jackshit. He's with Zeus, which makes him the enemy."

Her Heart the enemy? It just wouldn't sink in.

"She's useless," Styx said. "She'll slow us down."

"Are you suggesting we leave her?"

"I'm suggesting if she wants to be there, if she wants them so bad, who the fuck cares if they pick her up?"

"I fucking care," Harry bit out. "She lost her mother. Was abandoned by the man who claimed to love her. What does she have left but us?"

Her father and Styx. Had each other. Had her. Was that a reason to rely on them?

"That's not enough," Styx said. "Default is not enough."

"Well, how about where she goes, I go. How about you do this alone or with us? Both of us."

"I don't need you, old man," Styx snarled. "Or that fucking devil spawn you raised."

No. It was wrong. Bringing up her knees, she gripped her hair as her elbows met her legs. The men were fighting again. Shouting. Breaking the cool air with their barks and jibes. Daire wouldn't have it. He would never let their ranks descend to this. Where was Harry's cool head? Wasn't her father known for his calm and his reason?

Squeezing her eyes closed again, she opened her mouth to suck in a long breath that came out as a desperate howl. No matter how she screamed, how she cried, the truth was the same. Her Heart was gone. Either by design or default, it didn't matter, he wasn't hers. Why should he be? Why should he give himself to anyone who'd abandoned him? Had he abandoned her, never been hers, or was he relying on her to believe in their love?

"Tess…" Her father's soft voice came in time with a gentle hand sliding onto her shoulder. "We'll get through this."

Raising her chin just enough to peek at him through her forearms, she wasn't sure he meant it. "I can't breathe without him."

Her throat already felt narrow. Her head ached. Every part of her throbbed with the agony of neglect. Her being needed his. Even if it was a lie. Even if he didn't want her. Even with the possibility of ridicule, it didn't matter. She needed him.

The sympathy in her father's expression might have been unexpected. While her head swam, her body drowned, nothing in her could garner any kind of sense.

Harry kept his hand on her shoulder and turned in his crouch to look at the nearby Styx. "There's a rest stop six miles west. I'll take care of things here. Go."

The sound of boots twisting in dry dirt came just before his form flashed behind Harry, sprinting off across the desolate space toward the trees in the distance. She'd seen Daire run like that. Seen that dedicated resolution to complete an objective given by his superior officer. Her Heart. His ward. Zeus's puppet.

She stared at Styx's form as it grew smaller. Her feet were freed from her shoes, her socks taken off, then her sweater raised from her hips. What was her father doing? Loose, she moved as he took it over her head. Not by choice, she didn't have the ability to reject anything in that moment.

"He left us," she murmured.

"He'll be back," Harry said, standing to go over to the truck, taking her shirked things with him to toss them in a foot well.

"How do you know? You were yelling." What they'd actually been saying though was beyond her. "Maybe he's done with us."

"Maybe," he said, coming back with clothes in his

arms. "If he is, we'll figure out another way."

"What other way?"

"There's always another way, Light-Sprite," he said, hunkering down to offer her the clothes. "Can you get changed or do you need my help?"

Her father could strip her naked and dress her, but she'd accused him of treating her like a two-year-old too many times.

Inhaling, she took the apparel. "I can do it."

He nodded once and gave her the things before standing up to turn his back and head for the truck. "Styx will bring back a vehicle, we'll put some miles between us and this site. Keep moving while we come up with a strategy."

"I won't be any use to you."

Undressing herself in such an open space should be uncomfortable. It would be if she wasn't so distracted.

"We don't know that," Harry said, doing something in the truck. "You're my daughter, Tess. Keeping you safe is my primary mission."

She stopped adjusting the sports bra she'd just put on. His primary mission. It was funny. How could she take any person at their word again?

Her hands dropped to her lap. "That's what he used to tell me too."

Harry straightened up, his back still to her. While silence lingered, she chilled, maybe because of her undress or because reality was beginning to sink in.

"I believed it too. I believed that he felt something for you."

"You trained him well," she said, forcing herself to pick up the camisole from the pile.

"If there's any… I'm sorry for my part in this. You wouldn't be here if it wasn't for me."

After putting on the camisole, a tee-shirt went on over the top. "I wouldn't be here if you and mom hadn't slept together." In all the times she and her father butted heads, she put so much on him and never cut him any slack. Yet, there they were, in a desperate situation, again, and he was the only one standing by her. "You loved her…" Her cheeks tingled.

"You loved her for real."

Her father turned without hesitating a moment. Total and complete resolve consumed every inch of him. "There's nothing I wouldn't have done for your mother."

"I'm sorry it wasn't me." Until she said it, the truth hadn't hit her. "If I'd been the one in the car—"

"No," he said, striding over to crouch again. "You were Carrie's world. She wouldn't have survived if anything happened to you."

"But if it had been me, if I'd been the one to die, Daire would've brought mom to you at the beta site. You'd be together." Aching, she didn't feel the tears until they dripped from her chin to her chest. "You'd be together and Daire wouldn't have had the chance to… Mom wouldn't have given him the Scepter. She wouldn't have trusted him like I did. You'd be together and Zeus wouldn't stand a chance."

His fingers curled around hers. "We can't know where we'd be. None of us can predict what will come next."

"Isn't that your job? To cover contingency after contingency?"

A beat passed. "Even I didn't see this coming. I should have. I knew he was angry. That Zulu and the Exodus… I believed Zeus when he told me Ares was his. I should've trusted that belief. It was naïve of me to think he'd get over my betrayal of Olympus."

"You didn't betray it. The Six gave you a mission. It was your job to carry it out."

"Ares never refused a mission. Never one. Until they asked him to betray his home."

"He didn't," she whispered. "He wouldn't betray his home because it's all he knows…" Even if he'd told her different. "I believed in him too. I believed in his love. He told me he loved me, Harry. Made me believe I meant something to him. Zeus was right. I fell for it because I didn't want to be alone."

"You are not alone," Harry said, his grip tightening. "No matter what, you will never be alone."

Attempting a smile, a sob came through her words. "He told me that too."

When her next cry became a gasp, her father rose to wrap her in his arms. Trust. Security. None of it meant anything. She couldn't rely on anyone or anything. Yet, as her father held her and the tears overwhelmed her, she gave into the emotion.

Losing her mother took time to sink in. When it had, Daire was the one there to hold her. Now her father was offering comfort to her grief. Would life always be loss? Was that all she had to look forward to? Pain? Torture? Grief?

When the tears stopped, her energy was wrought and low. It just wasn't possible for her to move. Her father didn't hurry her. He kept her in his embrace, stroking her back, her hair, offering comfort almost like her mother might have.

She'd never be grateful for losing her mother, but at least Carrie hadn't lived to see her ridiculous and naïve daughter be drawn in so deep, all her teachings crumbling to dust.

"You lost him too," she murmured, emotionless, the weight of her head on his shoulder. "He was your son. You loved him. He knew that and still…"

Harry's chest moved, taking a deeper breath and pause before responding. "This is what I taught him to do. I suppose that makes it harder… It's hard to be proud and aggrieved at the same time."

Easing back, she sought his gaze without caring about her bloodshot eyes or puffy, devastated face. "You're proud?"

He shook his head, retreating to sit on the dirt by her legs. "I trained Ares to be the best. The strongest. The toughest. I taught him everything he knows about duty and obligation." Another breath passed his teeth. "I taught him how to eliminate weakness. How to disregard love… to have contempt for anything that wasn't the mission. I was his commander, his leader, his mentor and father. He is what I molded him to be. He is like this, did this, because of me."

Her attention drifted. "I gave him to Olympus. Told him and you that I understood the greater good. That there was nothing more important than the mission… I said all of those things out loud believing I meant them…" Her clenched hands rose toward her heart. "So why does it hurt that he has followed that ethos?"

"Because he wasn't honest." A flicker of anger rose in him. "Because we had a plan. We believed he had enough respect that even if he disagreed with the plan, even if he wanted to walk away, that he'd do it in the open." And he hadn't. He'd done it in the dark. Behind their backs. He'd lied. Her Heart lied to her. "I dread to think what he did to the other agents."

"They trusted him too. They let him get close."

"Yes. They'd have trusted him right up until the moment he slit their throats."

And by then it would be too late. "Do you think they're dead?" She couldn't read whether or not he believed the grave demise of his agents, but his guilt shone like a beacon in the night. For some reason, that renewed her grief. She shuffled closer, taking both his hands. "It wasn't your fault."

"I've lost agents before… never like this. Every time we lost one, I believed we'd done all we could to protect them, that sometimes things were out of our control. And I believed they died for a purpose, that there was a reason… This. Like this… There's no reason for this."

"I can't believe he'd be so cold," she said, her voice little more than a whisper. "The man I lay with in the dark… the man I entrusted my secrets to… The way he looked at me…" Her dry lips wobbled. She pursed them, trying to restrain her hurt. "He wasn't callous… He wasn't cruel."

"I tried to tell you, and him, that knowledge and observation are different things. Daire isn't cruel, I didn't believe he was, never. But Ares… I've never known anyone more capable of compartmentalization. There were times, early in his training, he'd be given an order without more than a minute's notice, and he'd carry it out."

"Murder," she said. "You'd tell him to kill and he would."

"It didn't weigh on Styx. Over time, he became the more suitable assassin. But, yes, I could give Ares a target and he'd eliminate that target without hesitation."

Touching the bruises on her father's brow and cheek,

she tried to be gentle. "I can't believe he did this. He cared about you, he always made me believe that…" Wasn't that the point? That he wasn't the person he'd portrayed himself to be. "They want the keys to obtain JARR. What comes after that?"

"Extracting JARR is less important now that Zeus has control of the beta site again. Don't get me wrong, he'll want the keys and JARR because without them, he has to accept less than complete control. Those objectives come in tandem with our deaths. With them, and us dead, he has the control he wants."

"He'll be out of control," she said. "The Six won't have any hope of overcoming the monster."

"No, they won't. And with Ares recruiting and training new operatives, there will be no obstacle to Zeus achieving his ultimate mission."

"Domination."

"Which he will get with JARR."

"How will Olympus stay secret with him exercising such reach?"

"You'd be surprised how easy it can be to keep a secret. All it takes is a little leverage. If someone has a weakness, they're easily exploited. And everyone has a weakness."

"Not Ares," she said, feeling something new when his code name tripped from her tongue.

"Even Ares." That surprised her. "Olympus is his weakness. If we threaten that, he'll capitulate."

She breathed out a laugh. "We're two people sitting on wasteland with nothing but our lives. Which we have just barely. I doubt he fears us."

"He will," her father said. "When the time is right."

"Because there's always another way."

"And because we know him. Even while playing you, he was giving intel. There are things you know, things I know, things we may not even realize are important, but it all means something in the larger picture."

"I don't know anything," she said, thinking about their sex life. "The only intimate secrets I know are ones I never plan to use again." Because knowing how he liked to be pleasured was not relevant in a war. "It's insane how in love with him I am."

"You're in love with a lie," Harry said. "It will take time; it won't happen overnight. Let yourself accept the truth. That the man you love, the one who still owns your heart, he's dead. Murdered by Ares if that makes it easier. Don't tell yourself it was a lie, just remind yourself it is over, and he no longer exists. You called him your Heart?" She nodded, her chin descending. "Your Heart no longer exists." He grabbed her hand again, the urgency startled her. "It's vital you remember that, Tess. When you come face to face with him again, and you will, he will try to use what you feel for him to get what he wants."

"He'll use what I feel against me. Use what I feel to fix things... for Zeus."

"Yes."

"God, it's a headfuck," she sighed, her forehead dropping to the heel of her hand. "I love him and am devastated. I detest him, yet I crave him."

"He gave you exactly what you wanted, gave you a security you'd never had."

Yes. "He told me I was the first and only person he ever chose for himself... When I was in London, we wrote to each other... I can't... How can it all have been a lie?"

"Maybe it wasn't. Maybe he did feel for you. I was the closest to him when he was six and he still chose Olympus. He sacrificed his connection to me for his home. In his head, for whatever reason, that choice was in front of him again. Only instead of me, you were his alternative. You or Olympus... he chose Olympus." He pulled her closer. "He will always choose Olympus." Something had to give, and she was that something. "Have heart. It's not over yet."

No? If it hadn't been for their escape, she'd be dead, then he'd really be free to follow Olympus to the bitter end.

"How did you get out?" she asked. The timing had been incredibly fortuitous. "How did you find us?"

"Zeus takes pleasure in his taunting. In psychological torture. I knew where you were... The trouble with his doubt of the agents I trained may have led to their deaths, but it also gave me an advantage. Those at the beta site are hired hands, thugs for hire. They don't know he'll never let them live beyond their usefulness. Men like that aren't meticulous, don't have the keen mind required to contain men like me… I'm actually surprised Ares was as careless as to let only three of them escort me. I slipped the cuffs and from there it was easy."

"You killed them?"

"I did what I had to do to get away from them to you and Styx."

"You could've left us."

"Would you have left me?"

Yes, was the simple answer to that. But not in the way he might think. Asking Styx to kill her was her desperate attempt at escape. If her father hadn't appeared when he did, she'd already be gone.

"What do we do now?"

"Specific Olympus vehicles have secret compartments loaded with gear. Styx knew that when he chose this ride. We'll pack up what we need and hit the road in whatever Styx brings back for us."

If he came back. "What can I do to help?"

Her father smiled.

Each second was torture, but the only way to make up for her mistakes was to make her mother proud. Carrie wouldn't want her daughter broken and sullied, she'd want her to stand up, to fight, to run, to survive. Somehow, she would fight to make her mother proud.

NINETEEN

BY THE GRACE OF GOD, Styx arrived just a minute after the Olympus truck grew to a towering inferno that could draw attention. Unwanted attention. Everything that had been, all they took from Olympus, was lost in the blaze that heated her damp cheeks. The time for tears was over. Grief? It meant nothing. With every break came new determination.

Harry tossed everything into their new ride, and they got underway. Doing as her father instructed, they put miles on the clock. Long, slow, quiet miles, but they all needed some time to breathe.

Without instruction, Styx pulled into a motel parking lot. They'd driven through daylight into the night and back to the day again.

"We wash up, eat, and start moving again," Harry said. "I'll get us a room, you clear this."

Her father got out, leaving her and Styx in the truck. In the center seat, it was almost reminiscent of the Vegas parking garage. When she thought Daire was hers. Before his betrayal.

"Did you tell him?"

The parallel was uncanny. "Harry? Tell him what? That the pregnancy was bullshit? No, he never asked."

When Styx gritted his teeth, his lips curled back. Was that anger or… something else?

He got out and pulled open the back door. "Get out."

"You don't want to clear the area?" she asked, sliding to the opposite door to get out.

Marching around the truck, he grabbed her arm and hauled her onto the motel porch. "Stay there. Don't do a fucking thing until Harry gets back."

She had no interest in doing anything and just watched as Styx took the Bergen rucksacks, packed with supplies from the previous truck, and dumped them at her feet. He then went around the vehicle, meticulous in erasing every trace of them from the interior.

Harry came over and gestured for her to follow as he swept the heavy bags from her feet. After passing a few doors, he stopped to unlock the room, dropping the bags with her again. He opened the door an inch and paused, matching his steely eyes to hers. She held up her hands and put her back to the wall. With his first two fingers, he pointed to his eyes, then swept the hand around to point at her eyes and around to Styx, still working. Yes, she got it, she was to keep tabs on Styx, to scream if anything went bad.

Just like Miami, Harry went into the room to clear it. That had been Daire's job in the Sunshine State. They'd trusted him with their lives then. Without giving it much thought or consideration, they'd just believed him when he said it was safe.

Her father came back to pick up the bags again. "We're good."

Going inside, she closed the door and went to the only bed in the room. "How long are we staying?"

"We're not," he said. "I'll go get us something to eat. Have a shower. Get changed."

"Are we going to torch everything again?"

"No. We'll double back on ourselves a little then redirect. We have to keep moving."

Would be useful to have their home on wheels. The Beast. He'd probably let it burn. What other reason was there for him to pack the thing with plastic explosives? Quick exit route. Good plan. She shouldn't grieve an object. Yet it hurt her heart a little more to think of the place she'd thought of as home so easily discarded. It was her fault. She'd told him to take the thing. It would've slowed him down, she'd practically invited him to destroy it.

"He'll expect that," she said, staring at the bags as her dad went for the door.

"Trouble is, he'll expect everything, Light-Sprite."

"Do you think he's coming for us?"

"I think he's doing whatever Zeus tells him to do."

"You said we had intelligence on him… he has it on us too."

"Yeah."

"And we'll come eye to eye again," she said, turning to look at him. "Are you going to kill him?"

Why was that her first question? They'd thought so much about their own lives. What about his?

Instead of answering, her father left the room, pulling the door closed with a harsh thud.

If her father trained Ares to be capable of anything, that meant he had to be capable of anything too. Hadn't the men faced off, gun to gun, in the beta control room, ready to blow each other's heads off?

Heading for the bathroom, she stripped and got under the cool spray wishing to cleanse her memories. It was never that easy. Even as she used the motel shampoo to wash her hair, the spray dampened her face reminding her of before… just before her father came to liberate them. She'd asked Styx to kill her. She'd been ready to die.

They had to be ready to die. All of them. Any minute.

She couldn't linger in the shower. Urgency ate at her guts. Ants danced beneath her skin. She didn't want to stay put. It felt wrong being static.

Wrapping herself in a towel, she used another to dry her hair the best she could and headed into the room, seeking a comb.

Styx was leaning on the wall by the door. With a knee bent and a heavy boot planted on the wall, he could be waiting for a bus, just passing the time anywhere, rather than running for his life.

"Shower's free," she said, opening the closest bag to search inside.

"I see that."

A comb in a pocket of the backpack gave her what she needed. While running it through her hair, she opened the next bag, looking for something to wear.

"Are you going to use it?"

His head shifted angle when she looked at him. "Someone has to protect your ass. I'll shower when Harry gets back."

"Which is why you wanted to leave me behind," she said, pausing in her search to look at him. "I'm surprised you didn't come in there and just finish me off."

"Thought about it."

His cool demeanor betrayed he was pissed. Why? God only knew.

"Why didn't you?"

"Your blood."

"Right," she said on an exhale. "Zeus needs my blood and if he can't have it, you're useless."

"Self-preservation."

"Sure," she said, folding her arms. "Except you didn't care about that in our cell when you agreed to end my life."

"Agreed to what? Don't know what you're talking about."

She frowned. "I was there, Styx. You know it and I know it."

He pushed off the wall to saunter over. "And that's the last time either of us will ever mention it."

"Why?" she asked, her hands moving to her hips. "I know you, Styx. You're never ashamed of anything."

He came to a stop in front of her. "I'm not ashamed. We protect information. Need to know."

"And no one needs to know?"

"No."

"Least of all my father… who might take exception to knowing his student, the only soldier he has left, was so ready to murder his only child."

"You brought it up."

"I have nothing to hide, Styx," she said, sick of the whole thing. "If it comes down to it again, my life or Zeus accessing JARR, I'll expect you to follow through."

"I don't need your permission for anything. If you have to die, you'll die, regardless. I told you in Miami, if you fuck us over, I'll kill you."

Back then, Daire had been quick to make his own threat on the back of his brother's. "And I don't have a protector anymore."

"Don't you?" he asked, raising his chin a curious fraction. "You and my brother were damn close… maybe you still are."

Speechless, she couldn't believe the accusation. No. She could. Styx was reaching the same place as her. With them being so quiet on the journey, everyone had a chance to assess the board. She'd tried to reason Daire's behavior away too, tried to make sense of it. This was obviously the way Styx was making his own sense of the situation.

"If I was in on this, why would I have run away from him?"

"You didn't. I took you away from him."

Oh, so now he thought her reluctance was sinister. "Does it look like I'm in a hurry to go back?"

"Won't hurt him to have someone on the inside of his opposition."

She smiled. "Somehow I don't think he's worried. As the opposition, we're pretty pathetic. No base. No weapons. No money. We're an old timer, a civilian, and a trained, undisciplined hitman. They have a compound, manpower, and all the tech they need." As they had access to all of the Beta stores. "I wouldn't be shaking in my boots."

As she began to turn, he grabbed her arm and pulled her back. "Give me something I can use."

"Use?" she asked, struggling and failing to get free. "What the hell are you talking about?"

"Do you love him?" he demanded, yanking her closer. "Do you still fucking love him?"

"Yes!" she screamed right into his face. "Yes, I

fucking love him!"

His jaw clenched, then he threw her back, tossing her onto the bed next to them. "You're a fucking fool."

"Yeah," she said, holding the edges of her loosening towel as she sat up. "I know."

"He'll kill you, you get that? For JARR, for Olympus, he'll kill you."

"No less than you were going to do."

"No less than you asked me to do," he said, his eyes cutting to hers. "So long as you love him, you're a liability."

"Yes," she admitted, tucking her towel in again. "Because the hardest part of this is… is…"

"Is? Spit it out!"

"If he'd asked me to go with him, I would have." The truth was the truth sometimes, no matter the way it was spun. "If he'd told me Zeus and Olympus were what he wanted… that they needed my blood for JARR…"

"You'd have given it to him."

"I'd have given it to him."

"Shit," he exhaled, grabbing up the nearest backpack to stuff the things she'd taken out back in. "You're fucked up."

"Something else I don't disagree with."

"You don't have principles. You don't have morals. You don't have any damn clue." He pulled the drawstring closed and tossed the flap over the top to clip it back in. "You're going to get everyone killed."

"How am I—"

The door opened and Harry entered. It only took a second for him to size up the mood. "What's going on?" he asked, closing the door. "I can't leave you alone for a fucking second."

Her? Styx? Or both?

"Doesn't matter," Styx said, tossing the pack onto his back. "I'm outta here."

"No," Harry said, throwing the food bag to the bed, remaining by the door to block it. "You're staying right here."

"For what?" Styx asked. "So she can get us all killed? No. Not me, Stratego. You wanna give me orders, I'll follow them, providing they're far from her."

"You're deflecting your anger over his actions onto her."

"She's still in love with him," Styx said. "Which means you're the only hope. Take her far away. Far, far away, lose yourselves, keep running, keep going, don't stop."

"That's delaying the inevitable. We will face Zeus again."

"I'll kill the fucker," Styx said. "First available opportunity."

Harry actually breathed out a scoffing laugh. "Will you? You think your brother will let that happen?"

Styx crowded in even closer, facing off with his mentor. "I think he can't be everywhere all at once. Won't be difficult to divert his attention. I only need a second."

"And if you can't or he spots you? Be smart. We cannot let this rest on the shoulders of one man."

"Think I'll fuck up? That I'll defect just because your prize student did?"

"No," Harry said. "You were always more adaptable than him. Always less reliant. You're independent, a free thinker."

"Undisciplined," she said from her seat at the end of the bed. Styx whirled around to land his anger on her. "You're no Olympus thoroughbred. That was what he said about you. You're rowdy and disruptive… Casual. You accuse me of not understanding that this is serious but want to storm off in a strop because I didn't give you the answer you wanted?" She leaped from the bed. "I was honest. Honest! Isn't that something we can all agree to be with each other?" Harry got her appeal too. "Am I proud of my feelings? No. I'm not. But they are my honest feelings."

"What about now?" Styx demanded, storming back to her. "You said you would've done it before. What about now? Now you know it was bullshit. He never loved you. Never wanted a future with you or to protect you. It was a lie… What would you do if he asked for your compliance now?"

She didn't have to think for long. "You know the

answer to that. I faced reality and the truth of what I needed to do in our cell…" She inched closer. "In those seconds before Harry arrived, I was willing to do the only thing necessary. If he came to me now, right here, in this minute, and asked me…" She took a breath. "I'd tell you, you know what you have to do."

"How do I know that's true?"

"Because I already proved it. You could hear me, right? In that lab, when they had me tied down, I begged him to come back to me, to come back to us. I didn't beg to join him. I didn't submit and ask for acceptance. He's made his choice. And this is mine. I knew it the minute I woke up, Zeus cannot be allowed to prevail, he just can't."

"And if that means turning your back on him or him getting hurt?"

She'd asked her father if he'd murder her ex… but hadn't figured out how she felt about that.

One thing she knew for sure. "Not everyone is getting out of this alive. Someone will lose… and the losers will die."

"It's as simple as that," Harry murmured. "Everyone eat. We're leaving in an hour."

Always giving orders. Now that Harry was back in control, maybe they could fumble their way out or this. Maybe. Somehow.

TWENTY

GETTING OUT OF THERE didn't mean jumping in the car for another long drive. No. They'd picked their spot and only she hadn't known why.

The first hour of walking through wilderness was tiring. Wasn't as strenuous as hour two when the darkness descended. The third hour was a grind. Four turned out to be her limit.

"That's it. I'm done."

The punishing pace had been slowed as she fell behind. They'd made allowances and she appreciated their restraint. Her father could have barked at her. Styx might have taunted her. Yet, they'd walked in silence.

The nearest rock looked like the best option for a rest. Shirking her backpack, she dropped to sit down. Arching her shoulders, stretching her muscles, her relief came out in a groan.

"We'll make camp," Harry said and his second immediately started to set up. "Tess, are you hurt?"

"I'm exhausted and I don't know how you're not. What's the point of this? Putting ourselves through this hell?"

"The point is ensuring they can't pursue us or anticipate our next move. We stay on the move for at least two days.”

“North,” Styx called, still working on the tent. “We head north.”

“For?” she asked.

He straightened up. “We need to build an army of our own.”

“Of the right people,” Harry said. “Styx has a contact he trusts.”

“Gotta start somewhere,” Styx said.

And somehow they’d communicated this information without her knowing it. When? At the motel?

And no one thought to include her in the plan?

“Am I your hostage?” she asked. “Your prisoner?”

“No,” her father said. “We want to protect you.”

“Because you need my blood?”

“Paranoid, Lady?” Styx asked.

Maybe. Some might call it vigilance. Smart vigilance. In truth, the physical exertion wasn’t the only exhausting factor. The questions and possibilities plagued her so much that she’d almost been able to forget her aching limbs.

Turning to him, her own rights flared. “Did he try to recruit you?”

“What?” Styx asked, coming a step closer.

“You heard me. You think you’re the only one allowed to ask questions? I need to know. When did you know? When did you—”

“You think I let him kill my guys?” Offense hardened his anger. “Who the fuck do you think you are? Who the fuck are you to accuse me—”

“Didn’t you accuse me?” she asked, shooting to her feet. “And you haven’t answered my question! When did you know?”

“Ask me that one more time and I’ll follow through right here,” he snarled.

“You don’t have the balls.”

As he started to march over, Harry put himself between them. “What the fuck is wrong with the pair of you? You’re giving them exactly what they want.”

“I don’t trust her.”

"And I have no reason to trust him," she said. "He tossed his accusations at me. Maybe you were right, Harry, maybe he is deflecting, projecting his guilt onto me."

"You're angry, both of you, and you have a right. I'm angry too. Styx, you don't have to trust Tess, just know she's what they want. If that's what it takes, you tell yourself to keep her close to prevent them getting near her." He turned to her. "And, Tess, I told you once Ares was going to be our primary instrument of success, do you remember?" Her fury was still pinned on the steaming Styx. "Do you remember? Tess!"

"Yes! Yes, I remember."

"Being up against that threat, with Ares on the other side, Styx is the only chance you have of survival."

So she was reliant on the man who wanted to use and kill her.

"Why should he keep me alive?" she asked. "One way or another, this could end with me in the JARR control room. Once I've been used, he'll throw me out with the trash." Just as Zeus and his cronies would. "I don't trust him."

"You trusted him in London. You were ready to walk away from Ares in Las Vegas to go to Styx, were you not?"

"He had the keys."

"Yes. You trusted him with those. What has he done in the duration of your relationship that makes you doubt his honesty?"

What had he done? Nothing. The whole Danny fiasco was Daire's precedent. She'd had reason to doubt him and hadn't. What had Styx done to make her doubt him? Nothing.

"I trusted him because Daire did," she said. "If I was wrong about one, who's to say I'm not about the other?"

"You're attacking each other instead of him," Harry said. "Be vigilant, I would always advise all of you to remain suspicious. But until one of us does something to endanger or betray the others, can't we have faith."

"Faith?" Styx spat. "Don't dilute your lies now, old man. You don't tell us to trust until there's reason not to. You taught us to doubt until someone proves themselves."

"And haven't you done that for each other? You

supported each other in London. Tess kept your identity and actions secret from Zeus, from Ares, she took the wrath to protect you."

"To protect Ares."

Harry didn't agree. "Hiding the truth of your meeting and stealing of the keys to Ares didn't protect him. It protected you."

"You talked me out of killing him," Styx said to her, angry frustration moving his jaw. "If you'd let me take Zeus off the board—"

"I apologized for that already," she said, her own guilt dampening some of her rage. "You're right. I should've let you do it. Everything since then has been my fault."

"It's not about fault," Styx said. "My brother was forced to pick a side, to betray us for the goddamn fucking greater good. If Zeus wasn't an option—"

"We wouldn't be in this position." She swallowed. "You don't think I've thought about that. I question every decision I made. Every word I've uttered since I lost my mom… Yet, you're right, I do still love him. I can't just turn that off overnight and I'm sorry for that too."

Styx's focus left her. "My brother is out there on his own. Without protection… Whatever Zeus did to get into his head… the people around Ares are not our people. Not people I know and trust… He's used to a level of deference, a level of respect he won't get with those strangers… He'll feel safe at Beta. He trusts it."

And… "You're worried about him," she whispered. "You're not mad at me, you're… You're mad at you… because you still love him too."

The three of them breathed into the darkness. Caught in their own reflection, they didn't so much as look at each other. All of them were dealing with guilt. The three men had thought Olympus was the glue that held them together. But it was more than that. She'd known it, but it wasn't until now that Styx seemed to be accepting his own love for his brother.

"Ares can look after himself," Harry said.

"You told me you did the dirtiest of jobs, Styx, so Daire didn't have to," she said.

"If anyone should be on that side, the wrong side," Styx muttered, "it should be me."

"He should be the one trying to stop you from making the wrong choice… Maybe you have more integrity than you thought," she said. "Maybe you're doing this because he wasn't strong enough to."

Styx head snapped back around. "He has no love for Zeus. He's following orders."

"Right. Are you making excuses for him? If you wanted to be there, you could've stayed. I told you to tell them what they wanted to know… to save yourself. You didn't do that." Her interest peeked through. "Did he ask you to join him?"

"How could he? If he'd brought it up seriously, I'd have expected betrayal. It only worked because he kept all of us in the dark."

"Tess's point about honesty is valid," Harry said. "All of us have to be honest. The Ares we knew, the man we thought he was, he might be gone, but our connections to him are still strong. He might try to use that against any of us at any time."

Would she be strong enough? If he looked at her, spoke to her, like her Heart, would she see through any ruse to protect herself and those with clearer views? She couldn't swear it. Some part of her justified his actions, felt pity for the boy inside who didn't know any way to be other than dutiful. Ares followed his superior's orders. That's all he was doing. He didn't betray them because he hated them, did he? Not in her justifications. He was lost, searching for his stability.

"Maybe we should just get out of Dodge," she said on an exhale.

"Walk away? Permanently?"

If there was such a thing. "Everyone says whoever has Ares wins. Zeus has Ares. He wins."

"Unless we can break through to Ares ourselves… to get him back."

"You don't believe that's possible, old man," Styx said. "You're as bad as her. Delusional. You heard how she begged him in that place. He didn't flinch."

"Because he doesn't," Harry said. "Not in his commitment to authority. To the task at hand."

"What?" Styx asked, the intrigue in his tone brought her focus to Harry. Her father did look hesitant and… guilty? No, maybe not guilty, but definitely burdened. "What is it, H? What are you not telling us?" One long stride closed some of the distance between the men. "Weren't you the one just lecturing us on honesty?"

"We need to consider the possibility that…"

"That what?" Styx demanded.

Her father's reluctance was ominous. What would put that look on his face? Nothing good.

"There may be chemical involvement."

"Chemical involvement?"

Thank God Styx could ask. Licks of shock paralyzed her again. With everything that had happened and been revealed over the past few days, she wasn't sure she could take any more terrifying revelations.

"It was theory… Asclepius's theory… something he was working on with Garrick…"

"Something what?"

"Coercives." Styx's hand rose to rub his upper lip, covering his mouth. Harry turned more to him. "I was against it; Zeus pushed the agenda. He couldn't connect with our operatives, he didn't have the same link to personnel as I did, as Ares did. He recognized that could be an issue, that if a coup was attempted—"

"Chemical coercives," Styx snapped, his hand jumping from his face as he stormed away a few paces. "You know how fucked up that is?"

"Yes."

"Ares fucking hated it, he said it was unreliable," Styx said, spinning to glare at his father-figure. "He talked about Asclepius messing with that crap… You know how he hated the doc dosing his guys with his fucking potions."

"I know," Harry said, measured.

"But you're fucking telling me, they could be polluting his brain with it?"

"Asclepius didn't have his breakthrough, not while he

was with us… Garrick, he… We didn't discuss it directly, but I always got the impression Zeus hadn't given up on the idea completely."

"So if it's not a drug, it's a chip in his spine?"

"No," Harry said, shaking his head. "It couldn't be… Something like that could be traced, they'd have tracked Ares with it after the Exodus if it was possible."

"And if they got close enough after that? In Vegas or after he left with his detachment?"

"You wanted honesty. This is it," Harry barked. "They were on the table, it's a possibility."

Maybe they hadn't left a man who'd betrayed them. Maybe they'd left a man drugged or held captive by tech that dictated his actions.

"Oh my God," she whispered. "We left him behind."

"Tess," her father's voice softened. "The technology wasn't there yet, the drugs either. Neither would have the power to change the fiber of him. It wouldn't force him to act completely against his will."

"No, but it would make him more open to suggestion," Styx said. "Would allow him to be manipulated."

"Tess's words didn't get through to him, did they? If he had something like that in his system—"

"You have no idea what happened after Asclepius left. What he might have discovered."

"Zeus didn't know Asclepius's location. He wouldn't have any way to use the doctor's work."

"Did Garrick know?" she asked. Silence wasn't encouraging. "Garrick and Asclepius kept their secrets for years. We know that. Both of them knew JARR wasn't locked up right. Their fear of Zeus kept that secret. Why would this be any different?"

"They worked together for years," Styx said. "Had their own shorthand… If Asclepius would trust anyone with his secrets, it would be Garrick."

"Goddamnit," Harry hissed. "Ares wouldn't allow himself to be experimented on."

"That suggests he was asked," Tess said. "I've been under the influence of more Olympus drugs than I can remember and never once were they administered with my consent."

"We have to go to the doc."

"He's dead," she reminded Styx.

"We don't know what he left behind. We can't ask Garrick because we don't know if he's dead or Zeus's bitch." He looked from her to Harry and back. "Can we agree he's one of the two?"

Her father's head dropped in a loose nod.

"Yes," she said without any faith in Garrick's backbone, which implied he'd be more likely the latter. "Garrick's compliance would strengthen Zeus's position."

"Yeah, and give Ares glimmers of normality to hold onto," Harry said.

"Where is the doc's place?" Styx asked.

"Not north."

"Your contact is north," she said. "How long will they wait?"

"They'll be there," he said. "We go there, start recruitment, then down to the doc's."

"He said he didn't write things down."

Styx looked at Harry. "We both know that's not true, don't we?"

Again, Harry shook his head. "I can't read it."

"No," Styx said, returning to pick up the tent material. "Only Ares can do that."

So much stood against them. The wall seemed insurmountable. These men had placed so much faith in Daire that his help was relied upon. More than that, it was presumed to be guaranteed. Being without him. Against him… Could they do it with him as an enemy?

TWENTY-ONE

IN THE MORNING, they trekked to a train station and took a train east. Rather than rent a car, they bought a beat-up jalopy in a cash transaction with a guy at the side of the road. Maybe it was stolen. Didn't matter. They drove with the men taking turns while she watched the country roll by between bouts of sleep.

When they eventually came to a stop near a narrow alley, she tried to figure out what about the quiet city street would attract Styx.

"This it?" she asked. "How the hell did you end up in a place like this?"

"It's not as boring as it looks," Styx said, taking off his seatbelt and opening the door. "One out, all out."

Still confused, Harry glanced back and nodded. She didn't need his permission but got out to follow Styx into a store by the alley.

As the door opened, a bell chimed. Hilarious. Something so… quaint. She wouldn't put Styx there in a million years. From behind her, Harry reached over to hold open the door as Styx went in first.

The cabinets left and right were filled with jewelry. Really? What other surprises did this place hold?

"That all you got for me, Prize?" Styx called out to the empty store.

She wasn't sure who he expected to respond until the curtain behind the register moved. A short brunette peeked around, slipping glasses from her face. The stranger's mouth opened in what appeared to be shock before an excited squeal escaped it. Rushing through the curtain, she tossed the glasses on the counter and picked up her pace to a run. She threw herself up into Styx's arms. He obliged, catching her to return the hug.

"Oh my God," the woman said, squeezing him tighter. "Where the hell have you been?" She pulled back, grinning at him, searching his face. "You look amazing." Running her fingers into his hair, she checked the locks. "Need another haircut?"

"Maybe later," Styx said, putting the woman back on her feet, accepting her hand when she put it in his. "Where's your guy?"

The woman's smile relaxed. "Upstairs," she said, glancing past Styx at her and Harry. "Did you find your brother?"

"Mm hmm," Styx said, raising her hand to his lips to kiss her knuckles. "Got a twenty on Ripp?"

"Getting the old band back together?"

"Something like that," he said, stroking her hair. "Forgot how hot you are."

She laughed. "No, you didn't. I've always been out of your league."

"That and your boyfriend's bigger than me."

The woman laughed again. Seeing someone, anyone, be so open was a wonder. Once upon a time, she might have known people like this stranger. She'd never been one of them. Witnessing such confident trust up close was odd, especially when directed at Styx. Did this woman know what he was capable of?

Maybe that abandon wasn't so foreign. Was that what she'd looked like with Daire? She'd trusted him that much and couldn't deny it, even though it did feel like eons ago.

"Dam called a few days ago," the woman said, "he

said you'd been in the old neighborhood."

"Yeah, 'cause Rook can't keep his beak shut."

"Salt."

"Right. Knew I should've killed that kid."

The brunette jabbed his arm. "If your restraint extended to letting Kieran live, it can extend to anyone."

"Don't remind me of that," Styx said, scanning the store. "Know where the jerkoff is? I could use a little pressure release."

"Rowdy will," she said. "Probably… We don't talk much about him. Needles Wreck."

"Which is never smart. Is your enterprise supporting the family these days?"

Her smile stretched. "Because my guy seems like the kept man type? No, the guys were out last night," she said. "Don't ask, don't tell."

"Good policy."

"Doesn't extend to your friends," the stranger said and nodded past him. "Are you going to introduce me?"

"I was trying to avoid it."

"No kidding. You want my guy, you have to get through me first."

On an exhale, Styx twisted to point at them in turn. "That there's Tess. Sister. The guy is my dad. Harry."

So much for codenames in the field. A smile quirked her lips, Styx trusted this woman. Completely.

"Wow," the woman said, letting him go to pass and smile at them. "I'm Tulsi Tern."

"Nice to meet you," Harry said with a decorum she'd never seen from him.

This would be hilarious if the whole world wasn't falling apart.

"Also known as Patch," Styx said, rounding to make eye contact with her.

Tess's mouth opened in a silent "oh." The pieces were beginning to slide into place.

"Ruin!" Tulsi's unexpected yell startled her, but already the woman was smiling at them again. "You staying over? Have you eaten?"

Unsure what to say, she looked at Harry who was returning the woman's warm smile. Who was that guy? Not the Harry she knew. Everyone was so amiable and polite. How long would that last?

The curtain at the back of the room moved again. The guy who came out was all muscle. Broad. Mean. Didn't look happy or impressed. He paused for a moment, his scowl deepening. Oh, and shit, now he looked angry. Goodbye amiable.

If there was ever a "fuck off" vibe exuded by a person, this guy nailed it. He started to walk again, with purpose, almost annoyance in his stride until he came to an abrupt halt in front of Styx.

She held her breath, bracing for the reunion to go bad.

"'Bout fucking time you dragged your sorry carcass back here, Styx," the stranger growled. "Heard you had some action."

"Not exactly," Styx said, slapping his hand against the new guy's palm to do some mutual shake thing that ended with a one-armed guy hug. A short one. "Rowdy upstairs?"

"Need him?" the guy asked, checking her out. "Who's the babe?"

Tulsi scampered over to the men, coiling the mean guy's arm around her as she nestled in close. "She's Styx's sister. The other guy's his dad."

The stranger's brows rose. "No fucking way."

"Okay, let's get over the shock I wasn't hatched from a defective demon egg and get serious."

The stranger guy frowned again. "Trouble?"

"Plenty," Styx said, fixing on Tulsi. "Get me a line to Dam?" She nodded. He looked at the stranger. "Wanna grab Rowdy and come shake some trees with me?"

The way the stranger's attention sloped to the side, she could tell he was sizing Harry up. "Will he kill to protect her?"

"Not that she needs protection," Styx said, picking up Tulsi's hand again. "But yes. And I didn't bring my trouble here. It's waiting for me elsewhere."

"Have trouble, will travel," Tulsi said, leaving them to go turn over the sign on her door, showing the store was closed. After locking the door, she spun and dropped against it. "Gentlemen, start your engines."

TWENTY-TWO

IT WASN'T POSSIBLE TO DISLIKE TULSI. Not that she wanted to. After going upstairs, the men had their private little huddle, said their goodbyes, and disappeared.

Harry was doing some recce of the building that didn't offend their hostess. Having showered and changed, Tess felt a little more human. The apartment was nice. Compact, but it ticked the necessary boxes. That pretty much meant it was weather-proof and didn't contain people who wanted to bleed her.

Wandering through the living room, she went into the kitchen where Tulsi was chopping something.

"Did you find everything, Tess?" Tulsi asked without turning around.

"Yes, thank you."

"There's wine in the fridge, if you need a pick me up… Bourbon in the cabinet beside it, if you need oblivion."

She breathed out a laugh, turning to lean against the counter next to their hostess. "Either would work… though both are completely impossible right now."

"Don't be so sure. Have faith in your brother."

Wearing a simple smile, she went to the fridge to retrieve the wine. "Glasses?"

Tulsi pointed to the corner with a knife. "You don't have faith in your brother?"

Tess went to retrieve them and began to pour. "Styx isn't exactly my brother," she said, deciding to add a little more alcohol to each glass.

"I wondered. He only spoke about a brother. Do you know him? His brother?" As Tess handed over the drink, the women's eyes met and lingered. "Oh… like that, is it?"

Tess shrugged and rested back on the counter again. "It was." She sighed and tucked an arm under her breasts to support the one taking the wine to her lips. "I don't know what it is now."

"Is his brother in trouble?"

"Someone is," Tess said, drinking more wine. "Maybe everyone."

"Men can be real assholes."

Tess laughed. "You're telling me? Not yours though. Wreck seems like an… interesting guy."

"He doesn't mean to be intense, he's just… cautious."

"He's super hot though."

When Tulsi peeked at her, she smiled, and the hostess laughed. "Thank you… What about this brother? He super hot too?"

"Yeah," she said, curling a finger over the rim of her glass. "Maybe too hot."

"Is there such a thing?" Tulsi asked, taking her board to the stove to scrape the food into the sizzling wok.

"There is if it stops you seeing what's behind it." She shook her head. "You ever had that moment with a guy where they… do something you don't expect and it makes you question everything you thought you knew about them?"

"Yep, I have. With Wreck actually."

That was a surprise. "Really?"

"Yeah."

"And you're still with him?"

Tulsi crossed to the fridge. "I've been about as mad as any person can be with another at Wreck…"

"Can't be easy to be mad at a guy like him."

The fridge closed as Tulsi brought Tupperware to the counter. "Because he's big and scary?" Tess shrugged her confirmation, Tulsi just wrinkled her nose. "He isn't like that… with me. He'd never hurt me… As to what he'd do to anyone else who hurt me…" Still holding her wine, Tess tried to hold up her hands in surrender, which wrought another laugh from Tulsi. "That wasn't a threat. Wreck has a lot of respect for Styx. They worked together for a while. He trusts him… which says a lot because Wreck doesn't trust most people."

"Styx says you got him out of a jam."

"I saved his life," Tulsi said, opening the tub to pour the marinated meat into the wok too. "He saved mine. We know what each other are made of."

"Clarity like that's… enviable."

"You don't trust him?"

"Styx or his brother?" Did it matter? "I don't trust myself right now, I guess that's the problem."

"Love has a way of doing that to us. Making us absolutely sure and completely doubtful at the same time."

"So much has happened," Tess said between sips. "Every time I think I have it figured out, every time I relaxed and let myself believe it was real… I shouldn't have trusted him."

"Why did you?"

"Because my mom died and I was alone… and the sex was amazing." They shared a smile. "He told me he loved me and I wanted to believe him."

Why was she so chatty? Couldn't be the wine, they'd hardly started on that. If her trust in Styx was shaky because her trust in Daire was, then her trust in people Styx trusted should be non-existent. God, it was a headache.

Except what did she have to lose? Everything she said was common knowledge. Daire had shared every detail of them with Zeus, so what the hell?

"They know how to suck us in, don't they?" While stirring the food, Tulsi took a drink. "When did you get together?"

"Few months ago." Though it felt like decades since

her mom had died. "What's the date today?"

"Twenty-ninth."

"Four, today actually." By months. Her Daire would tell her in weeks and days… Had she been so gullible? And why the hell was she even counting? "I thought it was real, which is crazy because he pretty much lied to me or misled me the whole time."

"About what?"

"Everything," Tess said. "Who he was at first. I thought he was a whole other person when we met. Turned out he was just using me to get to my father… Harry. They have a complicated past. After that, he told me he cared about me, told me he loved me, and I believed it. Didn't matter that I was dragged across an ocean away from him, I still believed it. We wrote to each other. Nuts, right? Anyone could've intercepted the letters any time, we weren't exactly explicit, but we weren't… not either."

Closing her eyes, she slid a hand onto her forehead. Everything she was certain of was in doubt. She had no anchor. Was completely adrift. What was there to hold onto? Her mother was gone. Danny. Daire. Everyone she'd used to steady her rudder was dead or someone else.

"Sometimes there are things we just have to say," Tulsi said. "His letters must've given you something."

"False hope," Tess said, her hand dropping to her side. "When I got back to where he was… He left everything for me. Came with me, I thought he wanted to protect me."

"He didn't?"

"He convinced me it wasn't part of his mission when I called him on it. Every time I put up barriers, he battered them down. Everything was a means to an end. He wanted something I had. I had no idea that he was so…" She almost laughed. "All along everyone told me he was a professional, the best of the best. Used to piss me off, but now I see they were right. Styx told me flat out the relationship was part of a bigger play. I ignored him… Yeah, I was desperate, but people were right, he is the best of the best. Amazing. So amazing that I actually thought it was my idea to share the secret with him. He didn't even ask me. Never once. He waited, bided his time, until I surrendered the information of my own freewill. Then it was sayonara."

Her new friend sagged to the side, forgetting about the meal. "Wow, that is good."

"Right?" Tess said, her attention dropping to her glass. "I just don't understand why… There were so many things he didn't have to do. Things he didn't have to say. All of it was designed to draw me in. To make me believe in him. In us."

"And you did," Tulsi said. "You trusted him." She sighed. "I know what that's like. Wreck and I went through our own… I went on the run, alone, believing I'd killed someone powerful." Surprised, Tess blinked up at her. "When Wreck showed up on my doorstep, it didn't occur to me to ask questions. Didn't occur to me for a second to wonder why. I trailed after him like a dutiful little lamb… He led me straight back to the man I thought I killed, a man capable of pure evil."

"Oh my God."

"I know," Tulsi said and shrugged. "I tried to walk away from Wreck, I tried to run, but when he told me the why… Sometimes we just can't walk away from the people we love."

"But that's just it," Tess said, pushing her weight off the counter. "He walked away from me and he didn't have to. I was so sunk, so in love with him that if he'd just told me, if he'd asked me to go with him, I would've gone."

"Maybe he didn't want you with him."

So simple and yet… "Because he didn't love me."

The betrayal was difficult to stomach. Of course it was. Somehow, that wasn't quite as disturbing as accepting the love she thought secure was actually non-existent.

"Maybe," Tulsi said, returning to her stirring. "Men are odd creatures. Sometimes they think they're protecting us, but they're actually just causing damage. I mean don't ask me, I get it. Even when I knew it was Wreck's plan to take me back to the man who wanted to torture and kill me, I went with him."

"Why?"

The hostess side-glanced her way. "Because he was in

trouble. Whether he loved me or it was a play, I was in love with him. And he needed my help… Took a lot of coercion on my part to get him to admit it, but when he did, I was there. I knew it would probably kill me and I went. The man I loved needed me. What was important to him was important to me." A light laugh warmed the air. "I still don't think he gets why. He'd walk to hell to confront the devil himself if I'd been hurt by him, but he still doesn't get why I traded myself for his best friend. His pain was my pain."

She got it. Her honesty with Styx hadn't changed. She loved Daire and couldn't understand why he'd abandon her for Olympus if he truly loved her. He'd asked her to live at Olympus and she'd told him it was impossible. Maybe that was why. His life was the institution, yet… He didn't have to be cold. To be cruel. He could've chosen Olympus and left her behind, that didn't explain his treatment of her, Styx, and Harry. Did Zeus really need that disconnection to trust his precious Ares… or was Harry's warning of these coercives accurate?

After throwing the rest of her wine into her mouth, she returned to the cabinet. "I think it's time for oblivion."

She poured some bourbon into her wine glass, then gestured to Tulsi's with the bottle.

"Not for me," Tulsi said. "My aim's better without it."

"Your aim?"

"Yeah," Tulsi said and drew a knife from the block. "My weapons are weighted just right."

Whirling fast, the hostess threw the knife in one quick motion, sending it across the room into the narrow post at the top of the stairs at the other end of the room.

"Wow," Tess said. "I'm impressed."

Tulsi returned to cooking. "Wreck sleeps better knowing I have a chance of defending myself. Rook taught me." From Fox Den? "I practice because Wreck can't be everywhere at once."

"He really loves you."

"When you've been through something like what we went through—"

"What's going on?" Harry appeared at the top of the stairs. "What's the threat?"

"No threat," Tess said. "We were just messing around."

He zeroed in on the glass in her hand. "What is that?"

"Liquor," she said, holding out the glass when he came striding over. "Want some?"

"No," he snapped, but snatched the glass to toss the liquid down the sink. "What are you thinking? Drinking like that in your condition."

She rolled her eyes as he slammed the glass down. "I'm not pregnant, Harry." Grabbing the bottle, she went to pour some more into the now empty glass. "We'll pay for the waste." Somehow, she didn't own a damn thing. Not one damn thing. Even the clothes on her back weren't hers. "I'm sorry for my father."

"Don't worry about it," Tulsi said. "It's fine."

"You're not pregnant?" Harry asked, crowding in close beside her.

"No, Styx just said that so your protégé wouldn't shoot me up with whatever was in that syringe," she said.

"You can't know for—"

"I took a test before we left camp," she said. "It was negative."

"And since then, how many times have you…"

The question provoked her frown to turn on him. "I'm sorry, did you just ask me if I'm a whore?"

"No!"

"Who the hell was I supposed to have sex with, Dad? Yes, your esteemed Ares fucked me in the Beast when we said goodbye. He did. He fucked me good and hard. No condom. No protection. Just his flesh and mine. Is that what you want to hear? But I guess he fucked all of us the minute he handed the Scepter to Zeus. And, oh, yeah, that was my fault too. Mm hmm. Yeah. Get your judgments in now, don't be shy. I am the fuck up! I trusted him! I gave him all of myself, my secrets, and yours! Yes, congratulations, you were right, I am Pandora! I unleashed the horror! It's all my fault!"

Gulping the bourbon felt good. Oblivion might be a

long way away, but she deserved the pain in her throat. Craved the agony of anything that didn't involve facing her losses.

"You're so angry at yourself that you're taking it out on everyone," Harry hissed. "Styx, me, who's next?"

She slammed the glass back down on the counter. "Who would you like me to take it out on? Him?" She opened her arms. "Bring him to me. Put him in front of me and I promise to take aim at exactly the right man!"

"You're this angry because you don't believe that," her father snapped. "You don't trust yourself to refuse him."

"Would you?"

"For the greater good—"

"Don't you dare throw the goddamn greater good at me one more time! You lived your life! You had your rules and sacrifices, but you had a home, a purpose! You left me and mom out there, running for our lives!" Desperation burned her already raw throat. "We lived in fear! She lived in pure horror! Terrified! Do you get that? Get how desperately petrified she was every minute? The burden that you put on her—that you put on me—neither of you trusted me! Prepared me! You gave her orders and she followed them… She ran because you told her to run! I hid because she told me to! All of it led to this moment!"

"You've been blaming me for everything wrong in your life since the moment we met," he retorted. "Blaming everyone else while failing to see that your choices brought you here! Letting Ares draw you in! Giving him your trust! What the hell were you thinking?"

"That I was alone! Alone! Do you even know what that means? To stand in a world completely invisible? No links. No connections. I was nothing! Scared! Alone! And then he—"

"Coming for you at rock bottom is exactly what your enemy does!"

"I'm pleased you're so smart," she said, swiping up the bourbon bottle. "Does it feel good to be superior to everyone else? You never made a mistake in your whole goddamn life, did you? Oh, wait, I was your mistake, wasn't I?"

"What do you want from me, Tess? What do you think the world owes you?"

"Nothing," she said, pouring alcohol into her glass. "I don't think it owes me anything." She took a drink as she turned to meet his eye. "But I don't owe it anything either. Your expectation of me is unrealistic. I am not Ares. I will disappoint you. I have disappointed you, again and again. Maybe I could live with that…" Her next inhale was ragged. "Knowing I disappointed mom isn't as easy to accept."

"No one is perfect, Tess," Harry said. "Even Ares." Always back to Ares. "You knew him about as well as any of us and how he hated to disappoint anyone. This was a no-win situation. Choosing us meant disappointing Zeus and Olympus. Choosing them disappointed us."

Looking into the dark liquid, her melancholy swirled again. "I think of how he was, who he was, and can't believe it wasn't real, that he'd ever hurt me… and I only had him for a short time compared to you and Styx." Expressing grief was easier for her than the men. "I can't imagine how you feel."

"You had him in a way no other person ever did. Deeper, closer than anyone else ever got."

"Doesn't mean it was real."

"No, it doesn't." Maybe her father's pity was the hardest to stomach. "The man you thought loved you… he doesn't exist. Because if he did, love you, completely, in the way I loved your mother, he wouldn't have had the strength to do this to you."

"I would've gone with him."

"I know," Harry said. "The only thing I can be grateful for now is that he didn't take you. That had to be a conscious choice on his part."

Did that mean he did feel something or that he just couldn't stand to be near her?

"He lied to me."

"Yes."

He'd promised they would be together again, that he'd come back to her.

"And he lied to you."

"Yes," Harry said, loosening. "And that lie cost lives."

The lives of the other Olympus agents. Daire could've somehow convinced Harry to send him alone. He could've told the other agents to run for their lives before Zeus got close. He hadn't. People had died. If Ares was willing to kill, or at least witness the killing, of his own people, those he'd trained and nurtured, the transition to Zeus's side was definitely complete.

"Stopping them won't be easy," she said, "him and Zeus."

"No," Harry said, putting an arm around her shoulders. "But as long as we stick together, there's a chance."

Trusting her father hadn't come easy and she couldn't claim to be all the way there. Once upon a time she'd pondered whether he could be trusted with JARR or to take care of Olympus. She should've looked closer to home, like in her own bed, for the real threat.

TWENTY-THREE

ASLEEP IN THE BED Tulsi identified as Rowdy's, Tess was deep in slumber when a whisper of pressure on her cheek roused her.

Her eyes opened a little, turning toward the contact, it took a second to focus. "Styx?" she mumbled, just making him out. "What time is it?"

"After three. Go back to sleep."

"Are you just getting back?"

"Yeah."

"Where are your friends?"

"Wreck went in to Tuls, Rowdy's keeping watch. Harry's getting some shut eye."

Did someone have to keep watch if he was so sure the trouble wouldn't follow them?

"You need to get some sleep too," she said, wriggling across the bed. "You haven't slept in a real bed since Vegas."

She wasn't counting the bed in their prison.

Without a word, he sat on the edge of the bed to unlace his boots then lay down. Opening his arm to her, it was automatic for her to tuck her head on his shoulder and lie in close.

Lying there, in the dark, free, the burden should be a

million miles away.

It wasn't.

"I'm sorry if I've been a jerk," she said, resting a hand on his chest.

He tugged on a tendril of her hair. "Me too."

"He gave me his word."

"I figured that's what your last thing was about."

"What did he say after?" she asked, fixating on her fingers in the darkness. "I left the trailer and you stayed behind. What did he say?"

"Told me to keep you safe. To put your life before mine… That asking forgiveness was riskier than asking for permission."

She frowned. "What permission?"

"I don't know. I disagreed. We always haggle over details before missions. Just one of those things."

"Do you think he went to the beta site and summoned Zeus or went to him?"

"The second. Quickest and easiest way to get H and his team out of the running."

With shock subsiding, things were becoming clearer, and their emotions weren't so raw.

"I miss him."

"I know. Me too," he said, raising his head to kiss her hair. "Where's that sleep you promised?"

She hadn't promised but took his point. They needed rest. Progress would come tomorrow… it had to.

***

FROM SLEEP, AWARENESS BECAME INSTANT when the man beneath her sat up with a sharp gasp.

It took her another second to register daylight. Styx's straight arm, that had been around her, supported her semi-upright weight.

"Never know what I'm going to get with you two."

Harry stood at the end of the bed, frowning at them. That Harry was more familiar than the one she'd seen downstairs the previous day.

"Ares wouldn't have let an intruder get so close," she said while stretching.

When Styx showed his cool eyes over his shoulder, she smiled and shuffled off the bed.

"Harry isn't an intruder."

"And I guess you knew that when sensing him in your sleep."

"Miss your boyfriend?" Styx asked, sinking onto his back again. "I can give you the codes to get back in."

"I know the code, thank you very much. And I don't miss him, you should be more vigilant."

"You were sleeping too, Lady."

"I'm not the super-agent."

"Oh, I see, you thought I'd be your new bodyguard? We're different animals, honey, I want my targets to get close. The closer the better. That way I don't even have to get up to kill them, they come right to me."

"The point is to protect, not to kill."

Styx snorted a laugh and looked to Harry. "You hear that shit? Yeah, she didn't know him at all. Maybe if we heard them in private, we'd have been able to tell he was playing her like a cheap banjo."

"You two ready to cut it out?" Harry asked. "You're rested, it's time to go."

"Copy," Styx said, vaulting off the bed to stick his feet in his boots.

"Where are we going?" she asked taking a step in time with the men when they went for the door.

Harry glared at his second. "You didn't talk to her."

"I'm not really the talking type, Stratego. Different animals, you know?"

Her father's frustrated exhale didn't bode well. "You're staying here, Tess. These people will protect you, Styx trusts them. We'll come back—"

"Think about leaving me anywhere and I guarantee I won't be there when you come back for me," she recited words she'd said before. "Remember?"

"Still?" her father asked. Was he disappointed or pissed? "You won't let us protect you."

"Sticking me with strangers isn't protecting me," she said. "Ditch me if you want. But weren't you the one telling Styx that you need me? If you lose me, they could find me first."

"Devious little thing, isn't she?" Styx asked before turning to her. "Who'd you get that from? Mom or dad?"

"Experience," she said. "You think I'm going to sit around and wait to be found? That's not what I do." They assessed her. "You said the doctor is next. Is that still the plan? No reason I can't join you. We all know he's dead. Site should be easy to secure."

"You'll slow us down."

"You said that already, Prince. Make your choice. Take me or lose me."

They couldn't afford to lose any more allies at that stage, surely they realized that. She didn't need them, not exactly, not until her blood was needed. Then she would need allies of her own.

Much as she hadn't admitted it, Styx had proved himself at the beta site. He took the beating rather than the easy way. His own brother ensured he was extended an invitation to Zeus's side, and he'd told them to go to hell. Easy didn't mean right. Styx embodied that.

Her father was her father. And he'd come for them. He could've escaped Beta without taking the detour to her room. But he had. He'd saved her life. Again. These men were her best bet and they needed her.

***

"SEE YOU IN MIAMI."

Those were the words she'd heard Rowdy say to Styx as they said their farewells. Why Miami? Was that next? What could be in Miami that would take them back to that city?

On the drive, she tried to think it out. Only squeezing between the seats of their new ride to put on the radio succeeded in clearing her head.

Miami would be the last place Daire would think to find them. Which would probably make it the first place he'd look. Or would he? One fake out could be two, a turn this way and that. The complex life of a spy with strategy upon strategy wasn't easy to navigate.

Did she want to go back to Miami? With its memories and its failures? Its triumphs and happiness? Its heartache and disappointment?

No, it wouldn't be good for her wounded heart. But she wasn't going to cower and hide. If Miami was the goal, she'd keep her head up, no matter what.

Her father turned the radio off. "We don't need him," he said without preface.

"We do," Styx said from the driver's seat, picking up the conversation without missing a beat. "I know you don't like him—"

"I don't trust him. Neither should you."

"He's more my wavelength than yours."

"He cannot be bought."

"No."

"He values nothing but himself, nothing but the game."

Styx drew in a breath, his hands slid to the top of the wheel. "'Cept Kero. If you believe the stories."

"She's volatile."

"More than him?" Styx asked like he didn't believe it.

"If you're suggesting we use her—"

"Getting near her would be easy… if we could find them."

"Swift's the only hope of that," Harry said.

"Yeah."

"And if we engage the Kindred," her father said. "We'll have their resources and won't need him too."

"Except you know he'll go further… and he has access to the Laird."

"I'm surprised you think the Laird's necessary… Ares was our link to him. You don't usually advocate taking prisoners."

"And if I get my chance, Zeus will be toast."

"We may need him. He'll be locking up Beta, setting up God knows what kind of security at Gamma. If he switches sites—"

"Ares set up Gamma," Styx said. "Why the fuck was he the point guy?"

"Because he's Ares," Harry said. "Garrick was working on his own shit. I was drilling the troops. Ares has autonomy, we trust Ares with the authority to work freely for Olympus's best interest."

"Huh," Styx exhaled, his fingers moving to hook just inside the bottom of the steering wheel. "He was given command of Gamma."

"Technically, yes. You could look at it that way."

"Which means he's rigged it to his spec."

"I had no reason to mistrust him then," Harry said. Unless he counted what he'd said to her about being more vigilant in trusting Ares's acceptance of his apology… or not trusting it. "We don't know he planned to betray us at that stage. Allying himself with Zeus may have been impulse… or opportunistic."

Styx was looking at her in the rearview. "What?" she asked when she got sick of his scrutiny.

"Nothing."

"Planning to accuse me of duplicity again? He told me nothing about the setup of Gamma." That wasn't entirely true. "Almost nothing."

"Which is it?" Styx asked. "Nothing or almost nothing."

"You're a real asshole," she said. "Anyone ever tell you that?"

"No one who's still alive."

"Enough with the bickering," Harry said. "We can't breach **Beta** alone."

"Yes, we can," Styx said. "We'd just die a few yards over the perimeter wall."

"Less than ideal," she muttered.

"We have no reason to think Gamma will be easier to annex."

"Would give us a base of operations," Styx said. "Though I'm going to guess our access codes won't have been activated there. No point standing there staring at it with our thumbs up our asses."

"If Minotaur has our access codes…" Harry said, "they'll be active across the network. Getting in isn't the problem. Stopping others from coming in after us would be impossible. Even if Minotaur was in place, it takes authorization from all three principals to lock a building down. I don't think Zeus would be interested in sharing his authorization codes."

"No, but it was a nice dream. If we could go into lockdown… we'd get some breathing room. Gamma's worth a look though, at some point. See what supplies might be there… if you're sure we'd get in. Somehow I doubt Zeus left our access codes active."

"He might," she said. "We were prisoners and he's that arrogant."

"Erasing an agent requires at least two principals and a third person of the same rank or higher than the operative you're erasing," Harry said. "Zeus would need Garrick's and Ares's authorization to take you from the system, Styx. No one's erased a principal before. I'm not sure how that would work."

"Ares will know," Styx said. "If there's anyone who could do it, it's him."

Silence fell again. All were angry and offended by what had gone down. But their troupe felt incomplete. Without Ares. Whenever there was a reminder of that, they all confronted their private grief again.

Undoing her seatbelt, she lay on the backseat. "Can you turn on the radio? Please?"

Though it probably pissed her father off, someone did put the music back on. Her eyes were closed, she didn't care who did it.

Obviously, Harry wasn't a fan. "If we must…"

The stations began to change. One tune, another, talking, a commercial, sports commentary, more music.

"…President Byron—" The station changed but quickly went back. "…tomorrow night. The impromptu gala for the former First Lady's birthday has become the must have invitation of the year in the power-hungry city."

"Raising money for such a worthy cause is admirable," a female speaker took over. "The question is why such short notice? What's caused this sudden crisis of conscience?"

"Us," Harry said and the radio went off.

When she pushed onto her elbows, her father was doing something on a cellphone.

"Since when do you carry a cellphone?" she asked.

"Since Ares took his base unit," Styx said.

"What are you doing?" she asked, sitting up to grab the shoulders of the chairs in front to pull herself between them. "Why would Byron be having a party now? Are we buying the birthday party line?"

"No," Harry said, turning the phone to Styx to show him the screen. "Detour?"

"Yes, sir," Styx said with a little too much zeal.

"Whoa, hey, wait," she said. "You can't really mean we're going to the party? How do we do that? Security will… What's to stop them taking us again?"

"We'll be prepared this time," Styx said.

"It's a summit," Harry said. "This is how it happens, Tess."

"How what happens?"

"What is the greatest threat to Olympus?" Styx asked, glancing at her in the mirror. "My brother teach you anything between fuck sessions?"

"Exposure," she said, unimpressed by his teasing reminder.

"Yeah. Principals meet with the Six at events filled with the public. Ensures if anyone tries anything, the threat of exposure keeps them in line."

"All of them?" she asked. "The Six and the three principals?"

She couldn't trust it. Somehow, it made sense, yet roused her suspicions.

"One last gasp of diplomacy," Harry said, making eye contact with Styx when his attention left the road. "Divert to D.C."

"Yes, sir," Styx said, optimistic in his delight.

If it got Styx excited, a body count may follow.

"You want to go to D.C.? What about the doctor's, how far is that? Shouldn't we go there first? Indiana to D.C. isn't a quick detour."

"Would help if we were in Indiana," Styx said. "Which we're not… Even diverting now, it'll be just shy of twelve hours straight driving to D.C."

"And you'll need to sleep before the meet," Harry said. "Our ranks are thin."

"Our ranks are you and me, old man," Styx said, "and I still rate our odds."

"You don't have your brother's caution," her father said, weight in the words. "You take your brother's prudence for granted. Don't forget you're working without it. Without the safety net he provides."

"You think he's losing sleep over working without me?"

"I do," Harry said, surprising her and Styx. "He was your caution and you his impetus. This is the kind of mission I'd never allow either of you to take on alone."

"We worked alone all the time."

"Even then, both of you would pore over the details and brainstorm contingencies until the last moment… and you'd always be on comms if required."

Something about Styx's sullen silence saddened her. They were each other's safety net. How many times had they put their lives in the other's hands? Maybe too many to count. Now there they were, going into the field, not just alone, but on opposing sides.

"Good thing we have each other then," she said, sliding between the front seats again. "Tell me how I can help."

TWENTY-FOUR

USING A FINGERTIP, she brushed more of the concealer across Styx's brow.

"Hey," he said, jerking away.

"Don't be a baby," she said, grabbing his shoulder to pull him closer again.

The men's bruises may be fading, cuts healing, but they weren't all the way there yet. They wouldn't care about the principals or Six seeing Harry's. It had been her suggestion Styx perhaps shouldn't draw attention to himself looking like he got the better end of a brawl. Especially when he'd been the one on the receiving end of a beating.

"You remember your role," Harry said, approaching them. "Tess? You must follow orders."

"I know," she said, concentrating on covering up as much of Styx's injuries as possible. "I stay with you. I say nothing."

"It's too risky for all of us to walk in there together. We need someone outside. Someone on overwatch."

"I was there for the conversation, Dad. You want me with you and Styx will do his best not to double figure his body count."

Styx got up and walked away from her mid-swipe. "I

made no promises," he said, opening the closet.

He took out two black cases and brought them to the bed.

"What is that?" she asked, though her father seemed as accepting as Styx. "Where did they come from?"

"Styx retrieved them while you were in the shower," Harry said, giving his boy the nod.

Opening the smaller of the two first, Styx revealed a foam interior with custom spaces carved for what was inside. He took one small transparent piece out to hand it to Harry.

"What is th—"

"Earpiece," Styx said, handing her one. "We'll keep you off the primary channel. You won't hear me unless there's a problem. I need the option of talking to you."

"Talking to me," she said, looking at the tiny object. "Suddenly this whole spy thing is much more real."

"Put it in your ear." Reaching behind himself, Styx snagged something from beneath his jacket in the back waistband of his pants. A gun. The moment she saw the heavy black metal, her mouth opened and she took a step back. "I still say you go armed."

"I don't need to go armed," Harry said, slapping a hand to Styx's upper arm. "I have you covering our asses. They'll only take it from me anyway."

"And we don't need to increase our enemy's yield," Styx muttered, tucking the handgun away again.

"What's in the other one?" she asked, sort of to distract them from their thoughts.

"M200."

Though it was said with confidence, she still shook her head, clueless. He unclicked the case locks and tossed off the lid.

A gun. More than a gun. A rifle… and a sight. It could only be designed for sharpshooting.

"You know he'll likely have an M82," Harry said, apparently neither of them noticed her shock. "You won't see him."

"I'm not worried."

"You never are," Harry said. "Don't forget he won't

be covering your ass."

"He won't kill me," Styx said. "Even if he had the perfect shot at maximum range, he wouldn't kill me."

"Because of the keys?" she asked, staring at the rifle.

"Because when he kills me," Styx said, closing up the case again, "he'll want to be at minimum range."

Her father wasn't as confident. "Unless you make a move." Harry put a hand on Styx's shoulder to turn him his way. "You are under explicit orders: do not take a shot. Any shot. Without a go order."

She couldn't see Styx's face but wasn't sure he'd be happy to follow that request.

"So you keep saying, old man. But I will not let them take either of you down."

Harry's huff was definitely annoyed. "I wonder how I ever kept you in line without Ares on your ass."

"Yeah, that's it," Styx said. "Even when he defects to your enemy, you still value him over all others." Whipping the handgun from his waistband, he stepped back, extending an arm to point the weapon, point blank, at her temple. "You want to end this here? We end it now."

Frozen, not even a hair twitched. Her father, though he was less than five feet away didn't show any sign of concern.

"Yes," Harry said. "Because that's not exactly what Zeus wants."

He chambered a round. "The three of us can be dead in less than five seconds. They'll find our bodies before check out. You want to hit 'em where it hurts? This is exposure max., old man."

"You better show me you can keep this anger restrained or you'll be benched."

"And then what would you do?" Styx asked. "We need each other."

"We follow the hierarchy!"

Her father's authority was bold, certain, and apparently enough to reach his pupil.

Styx grumbled and stuffed the gun back into his pants. "This is a wasted opportunity."

"Not a wasted opportunity," Harry said, consoling in his reassurance. "We will learn the Six's position. Do they wish us to stand down? To rebuild?"

"And if they want us to rebuild… with Zeus?"

"That's impossible without the keys."

"You can't give them something you don't have," Styx said.

"Right."

"So the plan is to make Styx the hold out?" she asked. "No. That's incredibly dangerous. What's to prevent them—"

"They can't kill me," Styx said.

"Until they have the keys…" She still didn't like it. "And if you're ordered to give them up?" Both her and Styx turned to Harry. Styx had rejected Zeus's authority; would he be put in the position of having to deny Harry's too? "You can't… All of this would've been for nothing."

If Styx gave Harry the location, he'd be deemed useless. The only way to survive at that point would be to fall back into line. Somehow, she just couldn't imagine Harry and Zeus trusting each other ever again. But if all that happened, she'd be their only enemy. The enemy of them all. It would be impossible to prevent them taking her blood and then she'd be eliminated. Suicide or homicide?

Thinking like that wouldn't get them anywhere. Confidence. She had to find confidence. To trust the men who'd brought her this far with them.

"We're nowhere near that yet," Harry said and nodded to the side. "Go setup, Major."

Ready to follow orders, Styx picked up the case, but she grabbed his sleeve to stall him. When he looked at her, she couldn't think of what to say with Harry listening in.

Her ally's brow raise prompted her to speak. "I need to talk to you."

Styx glanced at Harry but slipped an arm around her to take them into the bathroom where he locked the door.

"What is it?" he asked, his volume low.

"Orders or no orders, if they try to take me, trade me—"

"You want me to take the shot?" She nodded, absolutely sure death was a better option than being captured again. "There are other options."

"No," she said, linking their fingers. "You need to take the shot."

"Okay."

"If Harry… if he agrees to any plans to rebuild, if you think he'll surrender…"

"You want me to take him out too?"

"No," she said, licking her lips. "Take me down and then you run. Go. Far away. Fast. Get the hell away from this."

His eyes narrowed. "What are you more afraid of? That they'll get JARR or—"

"They'll torture you, Styx. There's no gray area here. I see that now. You have what they want. It's easy for me to deny them what they want from me, I just have to take it away before they can get to it." Meaning her. "You can survive with your knowledge… if you get away from them. Don't come back here. If this goes south, move out, immediately."

He smiled. "You think I need you to give me instructions?"

"No," she said. "I know you're smarter about all of this, but… Without Ares and Hades… if I'm gone…"

"I'll be alone."

"And hunted," she said. "I know what that's like… Sometimes you need a second opinion, a push, reassurance, and I'm telling you: run."

"'Kay," he said. "That all?"

She nodded. "Good luck."

"It's not luck, it's skill," he said, hooking his finger beneath her chin to raise it. "I won't leave you standing cold and alone in the world, Lady."

She smiled at the memory of their first meeting. As he turned to stride out of the room, London felt like a long time ago. Thinking of the city always reminded her of how she'd screwed everything up by failing to allow Styx to follow through.

Wandering to the bathroom threshold, she watched Styx leave the hotel room, the door closing with a click and a snap. Would they see each other again? Maybe. Maybe not. It was a toss-up whether either of them would ever see daylight again.

"Having you with me is the safest course," Harry said after she'd been standing there for God knew how long. "Otherwise, I would leave you here in the room. Now do you understand why you'd have been safer with Styx's friends?"

"No," she said, rejecting the assumption. "The last time you left me alone in a hotel room, your men tranquilized and abducted me. This is me learning from that mistake. If I'd stayed behind, I wouldn't have known any of this was going on. Even if I heard about Byron's party—"

"It's not necessary for you to know everything all the time."

The man must enjoy aggravating her. "Why does it upset you so much to include me?"

"This isn't the life I wanted for you."

"And you think you're protecting me," she said. "If the last week has shown us anything, it's that knowledge is power. Keeping me in the dark is dangerous."

"You can't reveal what you don't know."

"Is that your problem? You still think I'm a liability."

"I know you're a liability, Tess."

Turning her back, she couldn't believe the déjà vu. "Oh my God."

"It's not your fault."

"What happened to the guy telling me I would never be alone, that there would always be another way? What happened to the father who consoled me after losing the love of my life?" she asked, whipping around to glare at him again. "Or was that all bullshit to keep me on your side?"

"My primary mission is to keep you safe. That hasn't changed."

"Maybe I don't need to be kept safe," she said. "Maybe I need to be treated as an equal. Treated with some respect."

"Tess," he said, firm as he approached. "You cannot act out at this meeting. You mustn't say a word."

Was it just a lack of faith in her father or was watching

Styx walk out more traumatic than she'd given it credit for? Maybe instead of lashing out and fighting all the time, she should try facing the truth, giving some of that honesty they kept harping on about.

"I'm scared," she said, registering the surprise on her father's face. "I have already lost so much. You and Styx are all I have left."

"And we will not leave you," he said, his eyes darkening. "You are my daughter."

"He was your son," she whispered. "He was my world."

"You are strong." He took her hand. "You can do this." A breath passed. "Have heart and take it from a man who's lost more than most. You feel numb. Hollow. Like a shell without purpose or hope. But you can keep going. Any time you think you can't. You think you're finished and there's nothing left… Remember your happiest moment. Remind yourself what you're fighting for."

"I don't know what I'm fighting for."

He traced his thumb over the apple of her cheek, possibly brushing away a tear. "You're fighting for your mother. Just like me. One day…" he smiled, "we'll see her again. I promise you, Tess. You will. It's your duty to do everything in your power to make her proud… She won't judge your mistakes. Won't judge how you fall down." He looked deeper. "She judges us on how we get back up. On how we keep going. On how we say her name and treasure our love for her, safe in the knowledge we will be able to look her in the eye again. We will have her embrace."

It was too much to hope for. Too much to believe there could ever be such a reward. "She'd be so ashamed of me."

He smiled. "No. I am not ashamed of you. I am proud, Tess. Of your strength… your resolve, your certainty."

"I was certain of him."

"What he did was on him. That's his shame. Not yours. Your mother would never tell you not to love. It took so much from us but gave us a bounty in return. I have no regrets, Tess. None except giving him the choice… If I'd taken him against his will…"

Figuring out what he was talking about, she almost couldn't believe the root of his guilt. "He was six years old."

"I don't blame him for that moment. I never have. Both of you, all of you, would've had such a different life, if I'd taken his choice away."

Which could possibly be why her father kept her in the dark now. By taking away her choice, he thought he was doing what was best.

"It is my choice to be here," she said, tilting her face into the caress of his hand. "With you. At your side. Under your command." Even if she did speak out against it at times. "This is my choice and Styx's. We are with you and want to protect you as much as you want to protect us."

"You're an incredible woman, Tess. Your mother's daughter."

"My word is steel. I'm my father's daughter too." From the way he sealed his lips and his throat bobbed, she got the impression his emotion may be closer to the surface than he'd like. "We're going to beat this. Beat them… Together."

"Yes. We are."

She didn't want to be left alone in the room. But wasn't looking forward to facing Zeus again either. Especially if Ares might be at his side.

"If they take us back there—"

"I will not allow that to happen," Harry said. "Trust me, Tess. Please, Light-Sprite, trust me."

While she doubted every decision she'd made over the past four months, it wasn't easy to trust anyone, least of all herself. Being out of control was no comfort. Even if it was false, she had to tell herself that her resolve meant something, that she was more than a pawn and had the ability to influence her own fate.

"I trust you."

And her own pride bloomed when his rose. Coming together, in these horrific circumstances, might be swift. But it didn't feel rushed. Danger lurked around the corner. They were going to be in the lion's den, by choice, in blind faith. Her father's faith that honor would prevail was their only reassurance and that was hardly concrete.

Alone, Zeus may not be trustworthy. She didn't know the Six well. Except maybe Three, Hugo Balfour, and he was no leader. Not among his peers. All they relied on was her father's belief in his former comrades.

It may be a mistake. One that could lead to all their demises. What would Harry do if Zeus tried to take them prisoner again? What would he do if Styx was forced to take the shot and her blood was spilled in front of him?

Every person had their limit. Would they reach that on this night?

TWENTY-FIVE

THE TIME WAS UPON THEM. They couldn't linger any longer. Harry checked his wristwatch, something else retrieved during Styx's supply run.

Her father nodded at the door and opened an arm toward her. "It's time to go."

Inhaling, she steeled her courage and moved the silk of her floor-length midnight-blue dress that shimmered whenever it caught the light. Styx must have collected the V-neck garment with its side-split while he was out. Tuxes had appeared too. Just going with it, she didn't ask questions about exactly where everything had come from.

"Do you remember the rendezvous point?"

That she'd been shown before they came to the hotel. The place they had to meet if it all went wrong. "Yes," she said.

Her father touched her lower back to guide her toward the door. She didn't have a purse or anything. No key. No money. But it wasn't a night out on the town. They weren't even leaving the building… weren't supposed to be anyway.

Harry reached around her to open the door and there in the corridor, standing by the opposite wall was Ares. Tall. Proud. Upright. Rigid, he didn't lounge on the wall. There was nothing casual about him, this man was militaristic.

"Ares," Harry said, sliding his hand to her waist, guiding her half a step backwards as he looked left and right down the hallway. "Do we need an escort?"

"We're going to wait here a minute," Ares said. "Step out of the doorway."

"Or what?" she snapped.

Her father stroked her arm, putting his around her as he moved forward to let the door close. If they were taken from there, the back-up plan would fail. Styx couldn't shoot her if he didn't have a line of sight. Beyond the fact that the hallway didn't have windows, his position wasn't optimized for this level… she didn't think.

It aggravated her how Ares could be so cool, so aloof and still avoid her eyes. Unlike before, when it felt like he was ashamed of his actions or that he couldn't handle disappointing her, this came off different. Here and at the beta site, it was like she was so insignificant that he just didn't bother to acknowledge her. Even her question went unanswered. Or what? Or he'd kill them? Force them? Hurt them? There were two of them and one of him, yet the guy wasn't concerned. Why should he be? She'd seen him fight and being outnumbered was little more than an inconvenience. It sure wasn't a worry.

"You should be in position already," Harry said.

Although he was looking down the corridor, one side of Ares's mouth tipped higher. "You think I need a rifle to take you out, old man?"

"I think if your leader is being reckless, it's up to you to predict the unforeseen. I taught you better than that."

Something Ares had said to her.

His cool eyes came around to her father's. "You think my leader is being reckless?"

"My guess is he seduced you with authority… An authority you had before even if you didn't have the title. Olympus is your primary mission. Protecting it your cause. You need this summit to be smooth to ensure the organization's future."

"Yet, you expect me to perch myself on a roof ready

to take out anyone who spills their champagne?" His shoulders went back another inch while his attention returned to the corridor. "If Styx touches that trigger, he'll be signing his death warrant… and yours."

In Olympus, at the beta site, she'd been desperate to reach the man inside. The one she loved. There he was, right in front of her, the man she'd shared her body and her secrets with… She'd seen him carefree and at ease. Seen him be a soldier. Tough. Detached. Lie or not, that man had once been hers.

He slipped a hand into his pocket. When he pulled it back out, he held something toward Harry: his base unit.

Harry did a double take and she wasn't surprised. To be given back the link to the other principals was unexpected.

"Answer the call," Ares said.

Letting her go, Harry took the base unit and raised it to his ear. "Hades."

The hallway was a good choice of location for a call. It protected all of them. Styx couldn't get a shot. But neither would anyone else, anyone from the other side who may want to disrupt the cause.

Her father walked down the empty hallway, not fast, but enough that his lowered volume kept his words from the ears of those not meant to hear them.

Without any idea how long the call would take or if they'd be going to a meeting after, she relaxed. She didn't even intend to look at him, not really, but he was there, on the opposite side of the hallway that couldn't be more than four feet wide.

"Look at me," she said for some unknown reason. He didn't react, which only served to piss her off more. She took one long step toward him. Getting close probably wasn't smart. If he wanted to hurt her, going to him provided all the opportunity he needed. "The big, bad wolf isn't afraid of anything… Look me in the eye." Because she needed to know it was true and may never get the chance again. If he could look her in the eye, disdain her, show that she was nothing, then at least she could reassure Styx his brother wasn't under any chemical influence. "I might take your reluctance as a sign of something."

"What?" he asked, still without meeting her eye. "That I don't take your orders?"

Once upon a time, he'd said the opposite. "That you're ashamed. How true is your love for Olympus? As true as your love for me?" Because that had turned out to be a crock of shit. "Is it possible for a man without morals to feel true love for anything? Anyone? Other than himself?"

"You're angry," he said on an indifferent sigh.

"I am angry. And you don't have a damn clue why," she said, checking her father was still talking on his base unit more than a dozen yards away.

"I think I have a good idea." It didn't feel good to hear him mocking her. "Something to do with the sex and the double-cross."

"I don't care about that. About your recent choices. I gave you to Olympus, this comes with the territory, I get that." And she'd said the same at the beta site. "I'm angry you're still not happy. You'd really fuck me, your father, and your brother, for a man you can't even bring yourself to respect." Until that moment, she hadn't figured out the true source of her resentment. He didn't even like Zeus and yet there he was, taking on the man's mantle like it was his own. "You are better than this. Than me, Styx, Harry, Zeus, the Six, all of us combined. Why are you running his errands?"

That brought his focus to hers. "Excuse me?"

"You heard me," she said, getting closer. "You want the keys? Go find them. He's your brother. If anyone can figure it out, it's you." A glimmer of a memory from Miami came back to her, though she pushed it aside. "You want to hurt Harry? Done. Mission accomplished. And me? If you wanted my blood, let's not either of us pretend you had to do more than ask." He blinked in surprise. "All this charade is doing is giving me time to take it from you."

His lips hardly moved. "What does that mean?"

"You know how stubborn I am. Even if everything you were to me was a lie, you saw the real me. The true me. I didn't have a guard with you. Maybe I should care more about that, but I can't while you pander and yield to such an inferior commander. You are better than this, Daire Canon, better than him."

"I lied to you," he hissed, edging nearer. "I had to get my hands on the Scepter."

Calm crept over her. "You didn't even know I had the Scepter until after London."

Why was she only just putting those pieces together?

"You think I didn't know?"

Maybe he had. Or he'd suspected. Was that key really his sole motivation?

"I think if you wanted Olympus, you'd have had it long ago. Before London. After the beta site… Sticking close to me and Harry was one thing, a great way to know your enemy. Zeus had the keys. You knew he had the keys…" Damnit, she wasn't doing herself any favors. Talking to him, using him as a sounding board. Everything just made more sense when she said it aloud to him. "God, I'm so sick of this bullshit."

"Welcome to the Olympusphere, Miss Walbeck," he said and started to step backward.

She snagged his pinky with hers. "I believed it. You know I did. How many times have I said that to you before?" Too many. Her head was almost as heavy as her heart. "You pride yourself on being the greatest Olympus asset. Your sense of identity, your validation, comes from how valuable you are to the organization."

"You should be more guarded," he said, taking his hand and focus away from hers. "You're showing the enemy weakness."

"Like you did," she said, thinking of the intelligence Harry said Ares had given them. "Olympus is your weakness. You are willing to go through anyone you have to, to do anything, literally anything…" He didn't look at her. He didn't even flinch. Yes, this was Ares the soldier, she recognized him. Harsh and unwavering. The elite operative didn't disguise himself in any form other than the one she saw. True. Enduring. Elite. Kowtowed. "What were we? For months… what was that? If I don't know, how can anyone else? You can talk about us all you like, tell my enemies every secret. But I was the one in the dark with you all those nights. You… and me… alone. You can talk about it, but no one else will ever understand it…" She licked her lips, her concentration trained on him. "I guess only we know the truth."

Again, his eyes came to hers. They looked for a second before narrowing. Was he trying to tell if she was delusional or something else? Figuring him out was impossible while she didn't even know what she herself was doing.

"I know how to hurt you," she murmured, restraining the words as much as possible, getting closer again. "I can hurt the man I thought you were and the man you are now with the same act. Whether you meant what we were or not, I can take the Olympus you want from you… I can disappoint your superiors."

He smirked. "By sharing our secrets? They know we fucked."

"Hurting you has nothing to do with sex. Damaging Olympus is not about love either. I can't deny I did that too."

"So what is the big secret, Pandora?"

She leaned closer. "You ended us. Murdered the man I love. I don't owe you a damn thing. I am free to walk my own path."

"You're not free while Olympus needs you. We may not be holding you, but we can get to you. Anywhere. Anytime."

"Not anywhere," she said. "You showed your hand too soon. Once, I'd have given you the Scepter and my blood without question. Not anymore."

"When I want it, I'll take it."

"No, you won't," she said, calm, yet optimistic. "Your brother will make sure of it."

"Will he?" he asked. "How much love did you have for me if you've moved on already?"

Was he reciting Zeus's poison or really making an accusation? Though, how could it be an accusation if they were free agents?

Stepping in, she found her confidence in sliding a hand up his torso. "Jealous?" she purred, moistening her lips. "Maybe I've decided I like my men a little more…

murderous." Pouting, she raised her chin. "I'll add you executing every agent under you to your application…" Angling her head, her smile was perhaps a little mocking itself. "But I wouldn't expect success with me to come before you grow a set. I prefer my men a little more… dominant."

Before the word was all the way out, he grabbed her upper arms and spun them around, slamming her hard against the wall. As he lunged down, he got so close, his breath rushed against her lips.

"Hey!" her father yelled.

She couldn't breathe fast enough. Oxygen was thin. She needed more about as much as the mouth hanging just an inch from hers. But it was their transfixed eyes that sought satisfaction. They'd never been so close without following through. Without wanting each other. Without doing what felt good. What came naturally.

Was it natural to want him now? This man knew how to arouse her, how to pleasure her, what her body felt like around his as she climaxed beneath him.

Her Heart.

Her love.

The traitor.

Betrayer.

Turncoat.

"Baby," she inhaled, a tremble in her breath.

"Back-up, Lieutenant," Harry demanded, grabbing Ares's arm to put himself between them. "Put your hands on my daughter again and I'll relieve you of them."

Ares retreated one stride. "Meet's upstairs," he said without responding to Harry. "I'll escort you."

"We don't need an escort," Harry said, putting an arm around her. "Go take your position. Babysitting is below your paygrade. Conduct yourself with dignity, Lieutenant. That's something I taught you too."

Her father turned her away from Ares to guide her down the hallway. She'd said the same thing. Would the observations filter through or was the great Ares really happy being nothing more than an errand boy?

TWENTY-SIX

THE ELEVATOR OPENED to a foyer area filled with goons. Guess that was to be expected given how many rich, influential people were in the building. But it was no glamorous party. No, that was downstairs in the fancy ballroom. The real work was done in an upper floor suite… apparently. Not the penthouse, just a standard suite. Was there a reason for the downgrade? These people couldn't be used to anything less than premium attention.

The goons in black weren't in formation. They just loitered, watching as Harry took her across the foyer into the open suite. If it was a setup, they'd have a fight getting back to the elevator.

Hopefully, Styx had checked it out and given Harry the go. Now she sort of regretted not being on the primary frequency.

A woman just inside the door held a tray of drinks. All different. Maybe to individual specification. It didn't matter. Without acknowledgement or interaction, her father took her past the woman to the gathering of men in the lower-level seating area.

"Hades," Garrick said, approaching to offer a hand.

They'd learned something already: Poseidon was

alive… and he wasn't damaged like Harry and Styx. He must've flipped fast.

After a handshake, her father eased aside enough that she and Garrick could make eye contact.

"You look well, Pandora," Garrick said, hazarding a smile.

She couldn't blame the man for being spineless. Judge him? Yes, but if it was in his nature to yield, he was always going to be under Zeus.

"No thanks to certain parties," she said, edging closer to her father to show solidarity. "I suppose this clarifies who stands on each side."

"Now, Young Tess," Byron said, rising from his armchair perpendicular to where Zeus sat to come striding over. "This meeting is to put paid to that. We are one side, all of us." The former President smiled and slapped a hand between Garrick's shoulder blades, startling the man. "Let's sit down and talk this out."

Like a family meeting around the kitchen table.

Byron and Garrick went to sit. Everyone was settling. Zeus was seated, Balfour too, she was counting. Harry nearby… a middle-aged man, a woman maybe in her forties, and an older guy. Ages and genders were less important than numbers. Her, three principals and… five others. Five? Her first thought was Daire. He'd explain what was going on without her even needing to ask.

The drinks woman departed, and the door was closed.

"We're one short," she said.

"With you in the room, our numbers are correct," Zeus said.

"Where's Four?" Harry asked.

"In the wind," Three, also known as Hugo Balfour, said.

"How do you know who we are?" the woman asked. "We could be Four."

"He's met Four," Balfour said.

"Hades is known for his skills in the field," Byron said, lighting a cigar. "I wouldn't be surprised if he's gathered intelligence on all of us."

"His won't match what JARR knows," Zeus drawled.

And that was the kicker.

Her father guided her to a free couch, the one nearest the door. Daire would've chosen that vantage point too.

"Straight to the agenda," Byron said, rolling his cigar between his thumb and forefinger. "That's what I love about you. No foreplay."

"I suppose that's why you're here, Tess," Balfour said.

No foreplay or the agenda? JARR, that's what he meant. Her rolling over and surrendering wasn't on her agenda. Not even close.

"I'm here because your buddy there has a habit of abducting and beating people," she said. "Do you see my father's face?"

"You don't have to concern yourself with that today."

"I think I do," she said. "Either he's working on your authority or he's gone rogue and you're too much of a pussy to put him back in his place."

"Tess," Harry said, taking her hand. Though there was plenty more she wanted to say, she sealed her lips and dropped against the couch. "What is the point of this summit?"

"I would think that was obvious," Byron said, his lowered brow aimed at her, though he wasn't talking to her. After another couple of seconds, he switched to her father. "We need to put this back together."

Her father exhaled a disbelieving laugh. "You think that's possible, Philip? Do you honestly believe it?"

"We have to. What's the alternative?"

"Follow through on Zulu, then put something new together," she said, without caring about Zeus's sneer. "He's a cancer."

"He's led Olympus for decades," Byron said. "His experience is invaluable."

"You didn't believe that while putting Zulu to Ares or Hades."

"All of that is in the past," Byron said, seizing control.

"We need to move forward. We have all relevant parties here, it's time to make a plan."

"Beta is done," Garrick said. "The move to Gamma must be completed."

"Meaning we need to relocate Minotaur," Byron said. "And JARR."

The room may have expected a response from her, she gave none.

"You need to produce the keys," Zeus said. "Now."

"I don't have the keys," her father said. His note of smugness was apt… and amusing.

"Your assassin has them," Byron said. "Am I correct?"

"His assassin?" she interjected, offended. "You better be damn pleased that assassin is not here to show just how fitting your offensive description is. If he's going to be accused and sentenced for the crime anyway, he'll damn well commit it to maximum effect."

Zeus laughed, a snide, condescending sound. "And we believed Ares was your favorite."

"I couldn't care less what you believe about me, Ulysses," she said. "I don't believe you want to put this back together. For the life of me, I can't figure out why you resent Hades so much for the mission issued by your so-called allies."

"Again, all in the past," Byron said. "We must move forward."

The guy really didn't want Zeus to contemplate that truth too much. Especially if Ares really was out there positioned to watch the room, probably with Zeus in his ear. A chill went through her. She'd whispered in that ear too. Thinking of Zeus doing it now, even through an earpiece, was a little nauseating.

"You didn't come here without a plan," Harry said, fixed on Zeus. "What's the offer?"

"We want Tess," Zeus said to which Harry exhaled his disbelief. "We'll give you five days to hand her over. Make your choice."

"You want me because you want my blood," she said.

"But it's useless without the keys."

"Garrick is working on that. In the interim, we would like you at the beta site."

She didn't get it. "As your prisoner?"

"Were you a prisoner in London?" Byron asked. "No, you'll be invited to reside at Beta. A guest. With access to wander the building, you'll eat with others, reside with them, you'll be a part of the fabric of Olympus."

Not something she'd ever wanted.

"And while we have you close…" Zeus started, "your father and his assassin can complete the setup of Gamma."

So while they had her on hand at Beta for the removal of JARR when it became necessary, she'd also be a leash for her father and Styx.

"No," she said, shaking her head. "No deal."

"How could I be assured of her safety?" Harry asked.

Incredulous, she couldn't believe he'd even consider it. "Dad?"

"You will retain control of two keys," Zeus said, ignoring her. "We will both have part of the puzzle. We will need each other." Which was the fragile foundation Olympus had been surviving on for a long time. "As a sweetener…" Zeus glanced at the older gentleman, he had to be Lowell, Six, their tattletale. "I will release two of your men."

Shock loosened her jaw.

Even Harry shifted, his hand tightening slightly around hers. "You have my people?"

"Yes," Zeus said and snickered. "Did you think I'd murder such useful assets?"

Now she really did feel sick. They weren't assets. They were people. "Not like there's no precedent," she said, her lip curling in disgust. "Maybe we should ask Albany his opinion."

"Our people are valuable to Olympus," Zeus said without addressing her. "While their loyalty is uncertain and we work to find others, it was important they be kept close… and safe."

Ugh, he didn't care about safe. He cared about control. He hadn't kept them alive just because they were assets, they were tools of control, something else that could be leveraged against Harry.

"Who do you have?" Harry asked.

Zeus taunted him. "Do you value one more than another?"

"I have no proof of life. No reason to believe you."

"Would you believe Ares?" Zeus asked. "We created quite the strategist."

Did that mean keeping them alive was Ares's idea? She could believe that more readily than Zeus being the one to show mercy. Though he had screwed her, Styx, and Harry over, so it wasn't like he believed in compassion or sentimentality.

"I'll believe they're alive when I see it for myself."

"That's acceptable," Zeus said, picking up his own base unit from the end table next to him. He pressed the screen a few times then nodded at Harry. Her father took his base unit from his belt to look at it. "You have access to the security net. Look for yourself. All is as it should be."

"And it will be better when we can get back to what's important," Byron said. "Do we have an agreement?"

"She's my daughter."

"All you're doing is ensuring her safety," Zeus said. "How do you hope to do that without the resources of Olympus?"

What a way to tell a man he was useless.

"She cannot be harmed," Harry said. "And she has to agree herself."

That was a helluva moment to start giving her a say. Though, she appreciated it. If her father agreed to a deal that treated her as an object, she'd rebel on principle.

"If it's what our faction believes to be best, I will do whatever's necessary," Tess said. "But we will need time to discuss our options. I'm not signing anything tonight."

A ripple of laughter crossed the men. "We don't commit anything to paper," Zeus said. "A man's word is his steel." Was that an Olympus thing or was he mocking her father? "As we said, you will be given five days. On the fifth day, we'll make the exchange. If you're not at the exchange point, we will take that as proof of your defection. At that point, you forfeit all Olympus fidelity and action will be taken."

If anyone had asked her, she'd say they were past that point, but what did she know about Olympus rules?

"Understood," Harry said. "We'll take that under advisement. The exchange point?"

Zeus smiled. "I think that goes without saying, old friend." She didn't have a clue what that meant. From the looks passing between others, she assumed they were in the dark too. Her father's chin rose, he knew what Zeus meant and she'd guess it wasn't a happy memory. The lead principal's smug satisfaction dwindled just a fraction. "Leave the base unit."

Suddenly, Zeus stood up, glanced at each person, except her, and then departed. Just like that, he crossed the room and walked out. No consideration for whether anyone else may have business to address.

"I have to get back to my wife," Byron said, stubbing out his cigar. "Hades, you—"

"Yes."

"Good man," Byron said, coming over to wait for Harry to stand and shake his hand. "We'll put this back together."

Others stood as Byron left.

She wanted to know what was going on, so got up beside her father. "What's happening?"

"It's over," he said, tossing the base unit to the couch. "Done."

"So we can leave?"

"Not yet," he said. "Principals never leave at the same time."

"Because?"

"Two reasons, we're afforded time to put space between each other and if any threat tries to take the previous down…"

"Seriously?" she asked. "You'd be expected to go out there and save Zeus's ass?" She scoffed and folded her arms. "Good luck with that."

"Ms. Walbeck?"

She didn't expect the older guy to be talking to her, but he was. The others were chatting among themselves.

"Yeah?" she asked, suspicious.

"Lowell Parr," he said, offering a hand.

She drew her eyes off it. "I know who you are."

His silent plea to her father went unanswered. She couldn't imagine him being any happier at having the man who'd caused the mess approaching them.

"I was hoping we could talk," Lowell said. "Alone."

"Why should I trust you with my daughter?" Harry asked, though she was curious about what the man wanted to say.

"I thought we could step outside," Lowell Parr said, gesturing to the external terrace beyond the closed glass doors. "We won't go far."

The terrace ran along the width of the suite, as far as she could see. Another section jutted out in the central portion. No doubt extending the view.

Styx was out there. Nothing would happen to her so long as he was there to protect her. And, as far as she knew, there was no other way to exit from the terrace. Something Harry would know for sure.

"Okay," she said and glanced at her father to reassure him she was okay.

His frown was concerned, but he gave her the nod. Maybe he was curious too.

Garrick seemed to be saying his goodbyes, though Balfour was trying to take him aside. Obviously, after the summit was when the plotting and politicking went on.

She opened the door and held it for Lowell who passed her. Staying put while the door swung shut again, she watched him walk to the edge of the terrace, just next to where the projected area began to stick out.

"You wonder why I did what I did," he said.

"I don't wonder anything," she said, walking toward him though his back was to her. "I don't spend that much time thinking about you, Mr. Parr." Sometimes honesty was the best policy. She went onto the extended section to stand at the glass barrier perpendicular to his. Didn't seem like much to save them from the fall, but smarter men than her built the structure, so she trusted it. "Does it matter to you what people think?"

"You and I have never met," he said, clasping his hands together as his elbows took his weight on the glass. "I wouldn't want you to form a negative opinion without fully understanding my reasons."

"Fear was your reason," she said. "I've lived with Zeus, I know what he thinks of himself. Sometimes believing yourself to be intimidating is enough. I also know he doesn't shy from violence. That said, I'm not going to console or placate you. I'm pissed that you did what you did. You endangered my father, people I care about, and sent this whole thing into a tailspin. It's on you. Anyone who says different is lying."

His shock came in a blink. "You are your father's daughter."

"Thank you," she said, choosing to take that as a compliment. "What do you want from me, Mr. Parr?"

"It would be… useful for us to develop a relationship."

"Would it?"

"The rest of the Six, as they are, struggle to trust me."

"I wonder why," she said, maintaining her rigid, unimpressed veneer.

"Miss Walbeck, you cannot be this judgmental if you wish to maintain a place in—"

"I don't wish to do anything and I can be anything I want. Who are you to tell me otherwise?"

"I have been with this organization longer than anyone."

Good for him. "Yet it's taught you nothing. You can't play both sides in this game and you need a serious set of balls to survive it," she said. "I've been a part of this for less than a year and already I know enough about the maneuvering and plotting to make me sick. You have an allegiance to yourself, which totally misses the point. This isn't about you or me. It's not about one person. It's about one goal. Know your objective. Whatever it takes, you achieve that goal. No deviation. Stay on the path. No wavering."

If Styx could hear her, he'd no doubt laugh at her for using his words. They were fitting.

Lowell grabbed her wrist. "You need to respect those superior to you."

The sound of displaced air didn't really register until the burst of blood appeared on his forehead. She was still trying to figure out what was happening when his body flopped forward and flipped over the glass barrier. He was... was that...?

"Bail." The word in her ear came from Styx. "Lady! Now."

Shit. Shit...

Oh God.

Harry was there at the door and grabbed her hand to pull her across the suite. There were fewer people present, but she couldn't count. Couldn't register.

Her father took her into the elevator and stabbed the button for the parking garage. They weren't even going back to the room. They were...

Cold. Stiff. She couldn't... He was dead. She'd just seen... Six was dead.

TWENTY-SEVEN

HARRY WAS YELLING.

What he was saying…? She had no idea.

Her ears were still ringing.

Thank God Styx was driving. In her father's current mood, with his current level of wrath, they'd probably be pulled over for speeding and reckless driving. Which wouldn't be good for whoever stopped them. Yes, Styx was the bare-handed killer, but who taught him how to be that way? The man gesturing and shouting, conveying his point without any finesse.

Tuning back in, she couldn't process what was going on or what would happen next.

"What were you thinking?" her father yelled at Styx. "I said not without direct orders. I did not give you orders."

"I saw the chance, I took it," Styx retorted. "It's done now. What do you want me to say? I can't take it back! It's done!"

Her father's jaw worked as he considered his ward's profile. His anger wasn't going anywhere fast, but Styx had a point. What was yelling going to achieve?

With her sitting straight, perched on the edge of the back seat, she clung to the shoulders of the front seats, holding on for dear life. She checked Styx in the rearview. His brow was pulled down showing he had some anger of his own. Lowell had screwed them. Getting to him, taking the chance, was worth it… maybe. It did seem like super inopportune timing, especially with her being the one alone with him at the moment of his death.

"What happened to your eye, Styx?" she asked, having noticed the redness and bruising around a previously uninjured part of his face.

Quite an achievement because there wasn't much of him that wasn't injured in some way.

"Not everyone loves me as much as you do, Lady," he said, still snappy. "Look, it doesn't matter…" Styx was done talking to her and seemed to be addressing his superior. "You heard the news, they're treating it as a suicide. That was his suite. We know he has no family. No one will come looking for him."

"Will they or will they not find a bullet in his head?"

"We don't know if there was an exit wound," Styx said.

She couldn't begin to guess and hadn't been aware enough to check as his body dropped from the terrace.

"If we hadn't left when we did, they'd never have let us go," her father said. "Zeus will not take kindly to this."

"I don't give a shit," Styx said. "I don't take kindly to a lot of shit he's done. Want us to compare lists?"

"Byron will take the heat for this. With the First Lady's party—"

"We don't know how this will pan out. It's done. We accept it's done and don't invite shit. Zeus can't take this as a declaration of war."

"Oh, he can," Harry said, then sighed. "But he won't. Not so long as he wants Olympus to continue. Lowell was a good set of ears to have on the inside, he'll find another way."

"Are we going to talk about his invitation?" Styx asked. "You really want to hand Tess over after this?"

"I wasn't sure I wanted to hand her over before this. If we want Olympus to continue, we won't have a choice."

"If we don't, we need Zeus off the board."

"Haven't you done enough killing for one night?" Harry snapped.

"Not even close, old man," Styx said, his hands sliding up the wheel. "We won't be at a disadvantage if we're the ones setting up Gamma. With or without Zeus, we could continue beyond him. We take our time setting up Gamma, extract Minotaur, JARR, then we take Zeus off the board."

"We use him until everything is done."

Styx shrugged. "What's the problem? Seems perfect to me."

"Except for the part where we use my daughter to extract JARR."

"There's literally no other way to do it. If you want it, we have to use her."

"Uh, her is here," she said, waving between them.

"And what do you want to do? Leave it where it is?" Styx asked. "You help us, we keep you alive. You help Zeus, he bleeds you dry. You think he cares about keeping you alive?"

No. And with Asclepius saying it wouldn't be possible for the bleeder to steal JARR because they'd be too weak, she had an idea just how much blood they'd need.

If she could opt out completely, that would be the most advantageous for her. Seemed unlikely though. Zeus would make it happen with or without her consent. Harry and Styx were her only hope.

"At least we know he won't kill me before he has JARR."

"Right," Styx said. "So we play along. Exchange you for a couple of guys who can help us with Gamma. We make it a fortress. Fill it with backdoors." Not literally, right? "So we have the advantage. It's our home turf." Harry was pondering. "What do we have to lose? We could try to kill Zeus now—"

"He'll be on hyperalert after tonight."

"Right, so we won't get close… What else can we do?"

So many avenues were closed to them. She'd question what Styx was thinking by pulling the trigger on Six, except, like he'd said, it was done. Harry underestimated how much his soldiers resented Lowell for his lack of a backbone.

"We go to the doctor's," Harry said. "Find what we can there."

"Then proceed to the exchange point?"

Harry nodded once.

"Where is the exchange point?" she asked. "He said you'd know."

Her father's focus moved to the windshield. "I do know. I know exactly where it is."

"Where is it?" she asked.

"Yeah," Styx added. "Or is this one of those places you only shared with Ares?"

"This is one of those places I shared with my daughter and her mother."

"Me?" she asked.

"Yes," he said. "We'll talk about it later. Now we have to get to the doctor's before they track us."

"You think they will?"

"Why do you think we're in a different vehicle?" Styx asked.

Earlier, the black cases with the guns and earpieces had come from nowhere. The clothes for the meet too. Turned out he'd switched their ride while she was in the shower as well. She wouldn't have said Styx was gone for that long. Apparently, she underestimated him.

Shaking her head, she loosened her grip to sink into the backseat. "I'm glad he didn't kill your agents."

He who? Ares or Zeus? Even she didn't know what she meant.

"What happened in the hall?" Harry asked. Watching the world go by, the darkness matched what she felt inside. "Tess?"

"What do you mean?" she asked, her head loose on the backrest.

"You know what I mean. What happened with you and Ares?"

"You left them alone?" Styx asked like he was mad.

"I was ten feet away."

"What happened?"

Was Styx asking her or Harry? With the lengthy silence, she guessed both men were waiting for an explanation.

She sighed. "Nothing happened. He was just… We… Nothing happened."

"Didn't look that way when he was slamming you against the wall," Harry said.

Styx barked, "What?"

"It's nothing. I pushed his buttons is all."

"Tess," Harry said without disguising his impatient disappointment. "You think you know him—"

"Didn't you tell me I did? That all that time alone with him gave me valuable intelligence?"

"Yes," her father said. "But you must acknowledge he is not the man you thought he was. At one time, you may have felt safe with him. We all did. We all trusted him."

"He's dangerous," Styx said, taking a harder line. "Your mouth gets you into trouble all the damn time. Ares is serious trouble."

"He could kill you in seconds."

"He's smarter than that," she said. "He needs JARR as much as Zeus."

"That didn't give you the right to take risks," Harry said. "Just because he won't kill you doesn't mean he can't hurt you."

Would he? It seemed so foreign to her brain that Ares, Daire, her Daire could be dangerous to her, that he'd ever hurt her. Just like she'd told them she couldn't switch off her love overnight, she couldn't switch on her caution with him either. Yes, it was crazy, after what he'd done, but… She hadn't feared him, not for a single second. Even when he grabbed her, she wasn't afraid.

"He didn't beat me."

"Doesn't mean he won't or that he couldn't."

"No, I know, I…" She sat up straight again. "I mean it's harder for me to fear him like you both do or—"

"We don't fear him," Harry said, both men scoffing at the suggestion. "Not ourselves. Whatever he does to us, he could do to you too. You're not as strong as us. You haven't endured what we have."

Which she couldn't argue.

"I can't imagine him hitting me," she said. "I can't imagine him physically hurting me in any way." Her father twisted to look at her over the shoulder of his chair. "I know it's madness. I know he's capable. I do know that. And I'm not saying I won't be more careful, I will, I'll try, but I..." She exhaled. "I was the one alone in the dark with him... that man couldn't hurt me if his life depended on it."

Sympathy colored her father's gaze. "He's trained his whole life to make others believe he's someone he's not... I can't say it was all a lie. Turns out I don't know him as well as I thought. But you have to be careful. Don't rely on the man he was to trounce the man he is now. Olympus is his mission."

She nodded.

Her father was right. She should be afraid. Honesty was just the best thing to offer. Ares was not her Daire. He wasn't her heart. But the man who'd pushed her against that wall, he came in so close that... Her eyes closed as her fingertips drifted to her lips... for a second there, she'd wanted her Daire to take what he wanted. What still belonged to him.

Damnit. She had to forget him. To get over their love. He'd hurt her heart. It ached for and craved him. No. No more. Done. They were done. Finished. Forever.

TWENTY-EIGHT

THE CAR JOLTED, startling her awake. She half sat up, bracing her elbows against the backseat. Had she been asleep? Obviously. Blinking bleary eyes, she peeked out of the side window and saw nothing but sky. Out the windshield, in full, glorious panoramic view was the doctor's house. They hadn't parked so close the last time they were there, no need to be so cautious with the owner deceased.

Rising into a seated position, her attention was drawn to the dark stain on the flat ground near the abandoned home.

"Styx is checking things out," Harry said without turning around. "In case the doctor left any surprises."

Still fixated on the stain and what it represented, one obvious thing was missing. "Where's the body?"

"Animals do our work in a place like this," he said. "He's been dragged off, picked apart."

Wincing, she was thankful her father couldn't see her. "Nice." She wasn't sorry that the doctor was dead but wasn't gleeful about being an accessory to murder either. "It seems so long ago. Funny how time plays with our heads like that." Men did that too. "Won't Styx need backup? What if there's a problem?"

"If there's a problem, better one dead than all of us.

But there won't be a problem."

Could her father be that cold about the man he'd raised? Yes, he could. He could be as cold as he liked and could be warm too. Which was real? Sometimes his mood dictated which he was. Other times, she was reminded he could be a calculating super-agent too. He'd taught Daire and Styx all they knew.

"Should we empty the trunk?"

Of the rather inconvenient rifle. That should be the first thing to go. They'd parked at a rest stop to change into the clothes they'd left in the car. At the time, she hadn't thought much about them leaving luggage in the vehicle… rather the previous vehicle. Now she was grateful for it. Had the men known their departure would be so hasty?

"We're not staying. This will be a quick in and out. We'll grab what we can and hit the road again."

Smash and grab. She'd never been party to one of those either, but her experience had broadened since Olympus revealed itself in her life.

Didn't feel right to just sit there, waiting, doing nothing while Styx was inside, or God knew where, taking the heat.

"How long was the doctor here?" she asked. "On his own?"

"Here specifically? I moved him a couple of times."

She didn't miss his lack of an answer to her question. "Did Zeus know he was alive?"

"As Zeus proves time and again, he gets intelligence from more than just me."

Which, she supposed, was her father's way of saying he didn't know. Why couldn't he just say that?

The side door opened. She gasped as she jerked around. Styx. Shit. Where had he come from? She hadn't seen him approach.

Styx bent down to lean in and address his superior. "All clear."

"Good," Harry said, unfastening his seatbelt.

She slid down the seat toward Styx who switched his frown to her. "Where are you going?" he asked. "You can't wander around out here."

"I'm not your prisoner. I've been in that house before and this involves me as much as it does you two."

Daire came to mind again. Why did he keep doing that? Whenever she repeated things he'd said or shared a sentiment he'd voiced, her thoughts zeroed in on him. It was a bad habit. A bad, nasty habit. She'd had original thoughts before he came along and expressed opinions they shared. Sometimes just in her own mind, sure, but before he'd said them aloud. Still they felt like his, not hers. Maybe it was just her body's way of driving her insane. Reminding her how her ex hadn't loved her at all.

Harry got out and Styx closed the door. They were talking as they moseyed in the direction of the house. Her boots hit the dirt a second later. Yes, Styx could close a door in her face, but she was capable of opening it right back up.

"You can't just leave me here. That wasn't the point. Either you take me with you and make sure I don't walk myself into trouble or I'll wait until you're inside and just follow you anyway." Daire would include her. He'd let her join the expedition. "It's only an empty house."

Okay, so maybe it's booby trapped, but sitting in the driveway, waiting to see if they'd been followed or if anyone was going to sneak up behind them, didn't strike her as the smartest plan either. Was it about power? Was it her father's decision? Did Styx think he was protecting her? After their mission in London, he should know better. She took risks. Smart or not, she was willing to put herself on the line when something was important.

He should know that. Above anyone else, Styx should know that because he'd met her like she met him. Isolated. Alone. Forced to rely on a practical stranger. They'd been there for each other and followed through, which was more than she could say about Daire or her father.

"Fine," her father said and they started walking again.

They'd made her paranoid enough that she feared some sniper would take her out as they crossed to enter the house. It was ridiculous, no buildings overlooked them. No one knew they were there. Someone could be loitering in the trees, as she and Harry had when they first arrived there. But she trusted Styx was thorough.

Going inside, the stale smell of pipe smoke reminded her of the man her father had killed. Memories of him by the fireplace didn't last long when Styx tried the round handle on the door to the left of the entrance.

Nothing. It didn't budge.

He and Harry made eye contact. The younger man shrugged once, stepped back and smashed the door open with the heel of his boot in one swift kick.

"Subtle," Harry said.

Styx entered to descend the dark stairs. "I reserve subtle for when it's needed."

Which, obviously, he felt like it wasn't in that moment.

Surrounded by blackness, if she didn't have Styx in front of her and her father behind, she'd feel more afraid. Sandwiched between them, she was sure the men would sense a threat before it got anywhere near her. Trust. They'd come a long way in just a few days. Running for your life did that to a person.

At the bottom of the stairs, something metallic twanged and light flooded the space.

Avoiding the swinging cord hanging from the light fixture, she turned to look into the basement. There were no walls dividing the large immaculate space. How did the doctor keep it so clean? It reminded her of his lab at the beta site, so she shouldn't be surprised. Still, it seemed sort of incredible that Asclepius could have a room so sterile in such a shabby home.

Seamless white floors and walls were the cradle for the counters flanking the perimeter and the fixed steel table in the middle. A couple of steps later, she noticed the perpendicular table further along, in front of a curtain that shrouded something at the far end.

"What's that?" she asked, pointing at it.

"It's an autopsy table," Styx said.

Harry corrected him. "An examination table."

"Which is better?" Styx asked. "Dead or alive?"

That thought would linger for a while. How could the doctor have anyone to examine or anyone to dissect? She didn't want to obsess about it.

Her father hung back with her, keeping a hand on her shoulder to ensure she didn't go too deep into the room Styx was exploring. Without touching, he glanced to the left, probably reading labels, inspecting the bottles and boxes in the glass, wall-mounted cabinets above the counters laden with scientific equipment. At the end stood two full-height metal cabinets.

Solid cabinets she discovered when Styx rapped a single knuckle against one of the doors. "Bet the good stuff's in here," he said.

"We'll get to that."

The men looked at each other again. She guessed Styx got the nod from her father when he turned to the curtain at the end.

"Time for the big reveal?" Styx asked.

"Get it over with." Harry squeezed her shoulder and leaned in to murmur in her ear, "This is why I didn't want you here."

"'Cause you don't know what you'll find," she said, her chin moving toward her shoulder. "I'm prepared for it to be horrific. Horror movie material. You're not shattering any illusions. I didn't think he was Florence Nightingale, an angel caring for the sick and weary. I have him pegged as more of a Mengele. I'm ready for anything."

"You think you're ready for anything," Styx said from the other end of the room.

"I like that you're strong, need you to be strong," her father said. "But every time you comment on Olympus's past, it reminds me that you and your mother were pure. I never wanted you to be part of this."

"You think I judge you for the things you've done?" she asked. "I try not to think about the cruelty or suffering you left in your wake."

Because if she thought about her father committing those acts, she'd have to think about Daire committing them too. That had been her subconscious justification while her

Heart had been her Heart. Now she didn't know what to think. Opening those doors and letting the horror in might help her process and accept the truth of who Daire was. But as her regard for her father grew, the less she wanted to think about his ability to be cold and murderous.

"It has to be done," Styx said, reaching for another cord, pulling it hard to open both drapes at the same time.

She didn't know what she expected despite saying she'd been prepared. What she saw was so disturbing that an icy frost settled over her.

"Bulletproof," Styx said, knocking on the transparent wall.

Three doors, two separating walls inside making three separate spaces. Each contained a metal toilet and sink reminding her of prison documentaries and movies.

"They're cells," she said. Much smaller than the one she and Styx had occupied at Beta. Bedroom or not, both meant the same thing. "He was holding people here." She whipped around fast. "Did you check? Did we strand anyone?"

"If you stranded anyone, we'd be looking at bodies," Styx said, crouching to study the lock. "This is smart tech." He twisted to Harry. "Olympus supplied?"

The question mark was ambiguous, but she definitely heard it. Knowing that Styx wasn't involved in any of this was some consolation.

"You can get in."

"Could if I needed to." Styx stood to full height. "I don't care about what he didn't do." He returned to the tall cabinets. "I care about intel that could be valuable. We need to find his bible."

His bible? The doctor had a bible? How could someone willing to imprison innocent people be devout? No benevolent God would accept experimentation on people as necessary for any reason. None that she wanted to consider anyway.

Opening drawers beneath the counter, Styx was looking for something unknown. Eventually, he produced a couple of items that he bent and contorted, concentrating on his work as he returned to the cabinet and hunkered down.

He slipped metal into the keyhole.

"You're picking the lock," she said, but got no response.

Less than five seconds later, he turned the handle and the double doors on the first cabinet swung open.

"Behold the motherlode," Styx said, standing up, hands on hips.

Had Daire picked the lock at the Rotunda that quickly? Maybe. She'd been distracted by his kiss. Her body's need to return to times with him she'd rather forget was all-consuming. Her sanity needed her to forget, but her heart still yearned for what was. What he wasn't. The lie.

Approaching, she wanted to see what was inside. Boxes. Papers. Files. Folders. Didn't look like they belonged to a man who didn't write things down that was for sure. There were vials too. Bottles in mini-crates, metal and cardboard.

"And there's another one of these," she said, riveted on the contents.

"Yep," Styx responded, slipping out one of the notebooks to flick through it

Harry came up behind her, looking over her shoulder to see the symbols and diagrams inside. "It's in Greek."

Styx bobbed his head in agreement. "Literally."

"What else is there?"

Styx handed the notebook off to Harry and chose a folder next. Resting it on his forearm, he flicked through the plastic wrapped pages. "Not Greek."

"Not English either," Harry said, easing her aside to get a closer look. "Not any of the European languages… or Middle Eastern."

"It's Asclepius. Him and his stupid codes."

"Codes protect the knowledge, which protected him," Harry said. "Smart."

"You know only one person ever cracked his cipher," Styx said, shoving the folder back into its space, then picking up a thicker notebook. "This is it." He flicked through the pages. "Asclepius's bible."

It didn't look like any bible she knew. The cover was blank. Bruised and faded. Black. Blank. Featureless.

"I don't understand," she said. "What is that?"

"The doc kept everything important in one place," Styx said, reading through the pages. "All this other stuff is important, it's ongoing work, notes from previous projects, but this…" He snapped the book shut fast and held it up. "It's his gospel."

"You don't have to—"

"So if anything went wrong," she said, cutting off her father. "He could grab that and run."

Styx bobbed his head. "Except the problem is, it's encoded. With the doctor dead, only one other person can read it."

"Ares," Harry said. "At least he said he decrypted the code."

"You didn't believe him?" she asked.

Styx answered. "We believed him when he said he was loyal to us too."

Fair point and one she couldn't argue. She'd believed him when he said he was in love with her. That made her the biggest dummy of the group.

"If Ares can do it, that means it can be done," Harry said. "That's good."

"And how long will it take?" Styx wasn't so optimistic. "Days? Weeks? Months? How long did it take him?"

"From when he set his mind to it…?"

Harry paused. She anticipated a response.

From the way Styx's eyes widened, she guessed he did too. "Yeah?"

"About six weeks if I remember right."

"Shit," Styx exhaled the word through his teeth. "You know it will take me twice as long, I'm not as patient as him. And we don't even know if it's worth it. Breaking the cipher was his focus. He had nothing but time and no distractions. We don't have time."

"What do you want me to do?" Harry asked. "We pack it up, we take everything, and worry about making sense of it later."

"And if Ares takes it from us? Not only will he have it, but he'll have the information too. For all we know, he already knows this shit. Did he have the doc's location?" Harry didn't respond, which wasn't encouraging. "Seriously? Was there anything you didn't tell him?"

"I didn't have to tell him. I never had to tell him. I didn't tell him anything. He's observant. Smart. Keen. He knows what he's doing and can't stand a puzzle. Tell him he doesn't know something and he'll go to any lengths to find it out. It's just his way."

"He's what you trained him to be," she murmured.

How many times had they justified his actions because he was simply following his training?

Styx was adamant. "We need to read this. We need to know what we're facing." He pointed at the bottles. "We need to know if we can use any of this to our advantage. We can't just drag it around forever."

"We'll store it. Put it somewhere only we know."

"You don't get it. Some of this could be useful. We might need it."

"You want to go around dosing people? Administering drugs you know nothing about?"

"Do I want to?" Styx asked. "No. But I don't want to be standing on the opposite side from my brother either. I don't want to be worried about who's gonna destroy the world first, Zeus's hubris or Byron's blind, terrified loyalty."

Giving up, surrendering, wasn't an option either. Someone had to have faith there was a chance of winning.

"What about me?" Tess asked. "What can I do?"

"Can you read Greek?" Styx retrieved the first notepad again and held it toward her. "Ancient Greek."

"No," she said, not appreciating the snide question. "Can you?"

"We need an Ares," Harry said, breaking their glare-off.

"An Ares? Like there's more than one of him?" Styx put the notepad on the autopsy table and began to pull out boxes to dump them there too. "There isn't more than one.

Ares is one of a kind."

"To make sense of this…" Harry said. "We need Ares."

"Then I guess we get Ares," Styx said, dumping another box.

"We'll fill the car. It should take everything."

Get Ares? What did that mean? She stood there trying to figure it out while Styx and her father started taking boxes up the stairs. Get Ares. Was he suggesting that they kidnap him? That they somehow force him to work for them? Even if they did manage to take him by surprise, restrain, and confine him, he wouldn't do what they wanted. He wouldn't just give up and start reading aloud.

She didn't want a prisoner. They wouldn't be able to move with a prisoner. Especially a prisoner like Ares who would see every moment in the open air as an opportunity for escape. What was the alternative? They lock themselves away somewhere until they cracked the code? She'd be useless. What did she know about deciphering secret symbols and messages? Styx said he wasn't patient enough. That left them with Harry. They needed him in control. Leading. Having her father with them, on their side, holding everything together was the only glimmer of hope she and Styx had.

"Planning on helping or are you just gonna stand there all day?" Styx asked, startling her from her thoughts.

"Wasn't sure you wanted me to touch anything."

"Dig in," he said. "There's no chance we'll leave evidence behind." Hefting out a stack of folders, he dumped them into her arms. "Give them to Hades. Don't touch anything glass."

Because it was valuable and he didn't trust her not to break it? Because the drugs were potentially the most dangerous thing there and he was worried she'd be exposed to them? More likely the former. Styx could expect a lot from her but often assumed the worst.

Traipsing up the stairs with the folders, she handed them off to Harry who was packing the car, optimizing the space they had. Was there enough room? With the trunk, backseat, and footwells, they might make it work. Worrying about that wasn't her department.

She went up and down the stairs, taking things from Styx, doing as he said, until all the cabinets, including the glass ones on the wall, were empty and the vehicle full.

Styx went back for one last check. They'd stripped it as bare as they could, but apparently, he wanted to be sure. When he came back, he dumped a lidded Banker's Box on her lap and then got in the driver's seat to turn them away. He drove to the edge of the trees and stopped.

"What are we waiting for?" she asked when they just sat there in silence.

"Just checking it takes…" Styx said, focused on the mirror. He smiled. "We're good."

The vehicle started moving again as she twisted around to see out the back window. "Checking what…?"

Smoke poured from the open windows and door, flames flickered up the wood. No evidence, huh? This fire thing was becoming a habit.

They'd done their job. Thoroughly. And were on the road again. The road to where? She wasn't sure and didn't even want to ask.

Five days. One was already gone. The countdown was on.

How many prisoners got forewarning of their captivity? In these circumstances? Not many.

In four days, she'd be in the enemy's hands. Alone. With only a glimmer of hope that her allies would succeed.

TWENTY-NINE

THE MUSCLES OF HER BACK and shoulders were objecting to sitting cramped up in the backseat next to a bunch of frustrating junk. "It feels like we've been driving for days," she said, stretching out.

"We have been driving for days," Styx said, exiting the highway.

Two to be exact. With the men switching out. Not equally like Styx would with Daire, but he at least got a couple of hours sleep here and there. Way less than she and Harry.

The doctor's writings offered some distraction. She'd explored the odd symbols in his so-called bible, traced the lines of the diagrams with a fingertip. But it meant nothing without a key.

Every time she picked it up with hope of a breakthrough, she was disappointed.

Tension made her antsy. "And you still won't tell me where we're going?"

"We're going to a meeting."

"With who?" she asked Styx, sliding to the edge of the seat. "You said it wasn't the Zeus meet and I believe you because it feels like we're driving in circles."

His calm infuriated her. "Maybe that's what we have

to do."

"To descend into hell? That's where Zeus belongs."

"The underworld's ours, Lady. You forget who your daddy is?"

Hades. Head of the underworld.

"As long as it has central air and regular beds, I'll stay anywhere."

"Does your Beast have central air?"

The Beast. She missed it. In some ways, she was grateful not to be faced with her previous life every day.

Being there would be worse. It would. Was it the Beast she missed or the man?

"We don't need him," Harry said from nowhere.

Styx flipped the conversation without missing a beat. "You keep saying that, Stratego."

This wasn't a new disagreement. Propping her elbow on the box at her side, her head fell to her hand.

"He's leading us on a wild goose chase," Harry said. "He could be working for Z."

"Could be," Styx said, rolling his shoulders.

"Why else would he keep changing the coordinates?"

"Kero likes to be on the road."

"They live on the road."

"And off the grid," Styx said. "It'll be worth it. You're not sure we need him. I'm not sure we want him working for Zeus."

"Is that what this is? We contract him so Zeus can't? Exile doesn't know loyalty. He'd take money from both sides and still do his own thing. You can't trust him."

"Pandora..." Styx announced, drawing her into their cryptic conversation, "what's the key to survival?"

"Intel," she droned and might resent being asked to perform like a parrot... if she had anything better to do.

"That's right," Styx said and tapped the side of his nose. "My in with Exile is foolproof."

"Doesn't give me much confidence if it's in your hands," she said. "You'll find a way to screw it up."

"Only if you're anywhere near it, Lady."

"Quit the squabbling," Harry said. "You are taking

Pandora to the meet."

They objected in unison. "Why would I—"

"I don't want—"

"Enough," Harry said. "While I deal with stashing the cargo, you two will be each other's shadows."

"I don't think so," she said. "I'm no super-agent."

"No shit," Styx muttered.

"You're going to stay together and look after each other."

"You're taking the doctor's stuff to a secret hidey hole without us?"

"You don't trust me?" her father asked.

Raising her chin, she feigned pondering. "Let me divine your reasoning… you don't trust me not to give up the location." She sighed. "Deja vu."

"Tess—"

"It's okay. I get it." Running a hand through her hair, she dropped back in the seat. "I don't want to be tortured for information." And after living under lock and key at Beta, that possibility was more real than ever. "I don't want to know. I don't want to know anything."

"Write down the date and time she said that," Styx said.

Except she did want to finish trying to figure out the bible. Okay, so she wasn't exactly making headway, but at least it was becoming familiar. She slipped it into her Bergen backpack, figuring it didn't matter if the notebook was with everything else. Maybe breaking the hoard up, even a little, would be smart.

Hmm… their surroundings were curious. Had they seen another car since leaving the highway? It was quiet. Maybe too quiet. No people. No homes. Just rundown roads, wasteland, broken down buildings. No one was hanging out, no one lived or worked there.

As they continued, even the dilapidation thinned until they were driving down a hill in the middle of nowhere.

"Where is this?" she asked. "Where are we going?"

If they wanted to kill her, she'd be dead, so it wasn't like she feared murder… Though they'd all been in close quarters for so long that there were times even she considered throttling them.

"To the meet," Styx said. "Didn't we just cover this?"

Yep, snide was his go-to when he was tense… better than murder.

"The meet is here?"

He turned a corner, entering an old factory site. The chain link fence was busted and rusty, offering no security. If there had ever been gates, they were long gone. The single-story structure was a sorry site. Broken gutters, smashed windows, no one had been around there for a long time.

"We've got less than forty hours," Styx said, pulling in around the back of the building, presumably so they weren't immediately visible. Though it wasn't like the cops would happen to be passing. "How long to the rendezvous?"

"Twenty hours on the road without stops," Harry said.

Styx took the keys from the ignition and dangled them over Harry's palm for a second until letting go. As her father's fingers curled around them, her lips dried. He was going to leave her and Styx there.

The men were already out of the vehicle retrieving their packs from the trunk. There was some food in there, water, essentials. If they had to hike out, they'd make it.

Saying goodbye to her father wouldn't cause such anxiety if it wasn't for her last goodbye. When she and Daire parted, she told him it wasn't goodbye, that she didn't want a goodbye. Would her father be standing on the other side the next time they saw him? Was it really possible to trust anyone?

Styx opened the door and grabbed her arm to pull her out.

"Hey!" she said, but the men were talking to each other.

"Start heading east," Harry was saying. "I'll find you."

"No, you won't," Styx said, pushing her toward the hood where their packs were dumped. "Talla post?"

"Yeah," Harry said, heading around the car again, looking at her over the roof. "Behave yourself."

"Yeah, right," she said, yanking her arm from Styx.

"Try not to change sides before we meet again, Dad."

"That's guaranteed, Light-Sprite," he said, seeming to enjoy the notion. She didn't. That wasn't a joke. Not even close. "I came back for you at Beta, didn't I?"

Yes, that gave a smidge of consolation. Styx took her arm and swiped a strap of each Bergen into his other hand to carry both to the corner of the building. Staggering along, she watched over her shoulder as Harry got in the car, turned in a wide arc and disappeared, leaving a cloud of dust in his wake.

"You do know he took our only mode of transportation," she said, forced to trot along with Styx as he kicked open a door to drag her inside. "Next time, you could try the handle first."

"Think they'll come after us for property damage?" he asked. "Wish someone would. I could sorta use the fight right now."

Tension was par for the course. Staying on the go at least didn't give them a chance to emotionally process what they'd been through. The strain was getting to them all, and she was no exception.

He swung her around into a room that was little more than a concrete shell with debris scattered on the floor.

She exhaled, tossing her hair from her face. "Tell me about it. I need to get laid."

Styx crooked a brow. "Good luck with that."

"I suppose a shower is out of the question," she said, glancing around. "What is this place?"

"What we need," he said. "Out of the way. Somewhere no one is looking for us. Back in the corridor, go down half a dozen doorways and swing a right."

"Okay," she said, taking the backpack he offered her. "Why?"

"You want a shower?"

Confused, she swept the bag around onto her shoulder. "There's water here?"

"Might even be hot."

Her eyes narrowed. "You've been here before?

"I've been everywhere before," he said. "Let's just say this is a sort of… community safehouse."

"Olympus?"

He laughed. "Definitely not Olympus."

"You know you're weird," she said, hefting the bag higher on her shoulder. "Different."

"To your ex?" he asked, tossing the other bag toward the corner. "Thanks for the compliment."

"No, I mean… everyone else talks about Olympus like it's their world. Like there's nothing else, never has been, never will be. You don't talk like that."

"I told you why I did it. Why I was a part of it."

Daire. And without him… "Would you give it up? I mean, will you? When this is done?"

"Done means dead, Lady," he said. "You think Zeus will stop until everyone else has been wiped off the board?"

"If we get there first… What if we take Zeus down?"

"He'd have to be cold in the ground before we could be sure he was done. If he's down, Hades takes over."

And what would happen to the great Ares? Would they have to take him down too? Would he switch back to his father's side? Would Harry and Styx ever be able to trust him again?

She backed away. "I'm going to explore."

"You go where I tell you to go and nowhere else."

"Why?" she asked, pausing at the door. "Because this Exile person knows where we are? Shouldn't we set up traps of our own for him or something?"

The tilt of his lips betrayed his amusement. "Can tell you've never met him. If Exile wants to hurt you, he'll code a drone strike to your location." Her mouth dropped open. "Or he'll have the feds surround you and take you alive."

"The feds? He works for the—"

"He avoids them. Hates them. But he's not against them doing the heavy lifting. They'll bring their army, capture you… then he gets his prize."

"They'd hand him a prisoner?"

He laughed. "Exile doesn't need anyone to hand him anything. His woman's been in chains, surrounded by law enforcement, and they've unlocked those cuffs to let her stroll right out. Everything's digital these days, Lady. Exile owns the world. Literally."

She still didn't get it but slipped out of the room to go on the hunt. Whoever this Exile was, Styx respected him, or what he was capable of anyway. Trusting the guy was out of the question, but there was something refreshing about someone who didn't hide what they were. Exile apparently suited himself, lived his way, and said "*fuck you*" to anyone with a problem.

THIRTY

SHE STAYED IN THE SHOWER until the water cooled. Styx would have to wait for it to heat up if he wanted one… unless he'd showered somewhere else in the building at the same time.

Clean clothes felt good. They'd stopped at one of those gas station laundry places the previous day… maybe it was the previous previous day. One became another when they were all spent the same way.

Her stomach rumbled. The shower had been refreshing, real food was probably a pipe dream. They'd camped out before, but a fire to cook anything could draw unwanted attention. And what did they have to eat anyway?

Hunting was out of the question. They were out of the way, but not that out of the way. She sure didn't want rat for dinner.

After towel drying her hair and getting dressed, she went back down the corridor expecting to rejoin Styx. As she drew closer, male voices slowed her to an eventual stop.

"…prototype of the Titan chip for a while," a stranger said.

"A while?" Styx asked, amused. "Torres just handed it over?"

"Not to me," the stranger said.

"Kero?" Styx asked. She didn't hear a response. "I'm sorry you didn't bring her."

"Why?"

"Heard she's nicer than you," Styx said.

"Yeah, she's not your type."

"She's more my type than you are."

"I'm lower maintenance."

Styx laughed. "I don't know how you do it, man."

"Do what?"

"Live on the road with a woman. They can be a pain in the ass. Sex must take the edge off."

"Sometimes," the stranger said.

"I have a feeling if she was here, you'd be on board already."

"You've got my attention and I have no love for your former leader."

"Right."

"It's the Point on crack. My girl will be happy to hear it has a younger cousin… Whoever slid the AI in there is a crazy mother…"

"You're interested," Styx said. "I got you on the tech. Admit it."

"Point's nothing. Already had my hands on that… The other part…"

"Right. Hence why I'm coming to you. There's no one else who'd have even a chance of—"

"You want me to take this thing apart, you'll have to get me inside… or make sure the building's empty. But you don't need me for that. Why not just blow the whole place to hell?"

"Appealing," Styx said on a semi-snicker. "There's no telling what JARR will do if it's damaged. And Z will have contingencies for any attempts at a direct strike… Anyway, forgetting for a second it's not an easy building to approach on the QT, I have people inside."

"Sherwood's people? You trust them?"

"He's holding some of my guys," Styx said. "Can't carpet bomb the place until I get them out."

"Can they get close to Sherwood? Get intel on those contingencies?"

"They can't, but I've got that covered too. My guy on the inside is as close as anyone could get. And Z trusts him."

"A double agent?"

"That I'd trust with my life and yours."

His guy on the …? What? Everything stopped. Her brain began to clack like a needle stuck at the end of a record. Clack, clack, clack. A double agent. What did that mean? They had someone on the inside… an ally? She couldn't…

"Least you've done one thing right."

"Gee, thanks," Styx said.

"Keep me in the loop."

"That doesn't tell me you're in."

"Whatever I say doesn't matter," the stranger said. "My word means shit."

"Yeah, but you live in this world too."

"Kero lives in it, that matters more to me," the stranger said. "I'd let it burn for spite… if it didn't mean letting her burn too."

"Which works out for the rest of us." Movement came as what sounded like chair legs scraped on the floor. "Thanks for showing up."

"Thank Kero." The stranger's voice was louder, shit, were they… No, she wasn't going to run and hide. Didn't matter anyway. The men came into the corridor, stranger first. Without so much as looking at her, he acknowledged her. "Pandora."

Styx stopped a couple of yards away, his back to her. The stranger exited the same way they'd come in. A second later, the roar of a motorbike engine sprang to life and skidded out of there.

When the sound dwindled, her focus narrowed on the man just in front of her. "A double agent on the inside?"

"Yeah."

He went back into the meeting room. Rather than a shell, a table and a couple of metal-legged chairs stood in the middle. She didn't care about the furniture. She did care that as her heartrate soared, Styx didn't even have the decency to look at her.

"Tell me I'm wrong, that you weren't talking about… The only person close to Z we ever trusted is Daire," she said. "You didn't mean Garrick… did you?"

"No, I didn't."

But he wasn't denying her mention of the previous man. "Is it wishful thinking? You wish something of the brother you knew is still in there… Tell me this isn't some deeper plot hatched by the two of you—the three of you."

"Harry knew nothing about it."

She stopped. The whole world lurched on its axis. That meant… was he saying…

"He is in there. He is my Daire…" she whispered. "And we left him behind!"

"Yes."

Rage smacked her. "Why the hell wouldn't you tell me that?"

"Because if you'd known, you never would've left him."

"Damn right," she declared, fuming in the mire of fury. "How dare you! How dare you make the choice—"

"It was his choice," Styx snapped, whirling to show his scowl. "His choice! We need someone on the inside. Someone listening, watching. An ally infiltrated at the highest level. He is the only one Zeus would take the risk of trusting. You couldn't have known the truth, you had to believe it."

It was galling. Unbelievable. Wrong. Horrifying. Incredible and completely terrifying.

"But I don't need to believe it anymore?" she asked without hiding her affront.

"Vegas, the pick up, beatings, imprisonment, D.C., he's proved himself. That's what he had to do. Prove to Zeus that no one meant anything to him. Nothing… Except Olympus."

"Zeus is Olympus," she murmured, disappearing into a trance.

That's what he'd told her. Daire. That Six would argue Zeus is Olympus.

He loved her. Or did he? How could he love her and

do this to her? Put her through such… He was still there. They'd left him. Abandoned him. Just like Harry had done when he was a scared kid. His family existed in Olympus. But that wasn't the building. Harry was Olympus. Styx. His memories, good and bad. His mother died for it. Love it or hate it, it had brought them together.

Was his loyalty with Olympus? Zeus or Harry? Was his love for her true?

Her mouth parched. Something sour touched the back of her throat. She couldn't… wouldn't… Searing pain hit her so hard she couldn't tell if it started in her head or in her chest. A man on the inside. Her man…

The past wasn't done tormenting her. "I won't put you in the position of choosing between me and your integrity."

Those had been her words. They poisoned her. Them. So much time had passed. So many things had happened. Had she really stood in the Beast proud of how they'd come through? Of how they were still together. This plan must have been cooked up by the brothers at some point. How else would Styx know about it? They couldn't have figured it out in Olympus while they were prisoners. No. So much made sense now. Vegas. His cool certainty… All that time… In the cell… the things he'd said…

Closing her eyes, she tried to turn away from the memories, but they weren't going anywhere.

"Lady—"

"Don't," she said, shunning his pious pity.

Yes, they were better than her. All of them. These men. These capable men. Reasoned. Composed. Able to sacrifice everything for the greater good. She wasn't like that. Wasn't righteous and honorable. She wanted truth to mean something. Wanted things to be simple. They never would be. Not in this world.

Sniffing, she pulled herself together and wiped the moisture from her lashes. Standing around crying wasn't going to change anything, so she started for the door.

"Where are you going?" Styx asked.

"None of your business," she said a second before he

appeared in her path.

"We need you," Styx said.

"Yeah? I don't give a damn what you need."

"Where would you go?"

Shit, he was right. Daire had learned everything he knew about women from his mentor. Apparently, Styx had too.

"The where doesn't matter. As long as it's far away from here, it's fine by me."

The only way she knew how to go forward, how to progress beyond that single tormenting moment was to run. Just like her mother taught her. Maybe her mom hadn't only been running from Olympus all those years. Maybe she'd been running from Harry. From the truth that the man she loved would be the death of her.

Going back to the changing space connected to the shower room, she began filling her backpack with what she'd collected since leaving Olympus with nothing. Nothing. That's what she was. That's what she meant to the world.

How could he do it? Daire. Her love. Her Heart. How could he…? It wasn't the pain. The beatings. The torture. It wasn't even the anguish. Thrusting more things inside, she stuffed them down, paying little attention. It meant nothing. Everything meant nothing.

Grabbing the bag in both hands, she whirled around, hurtling the damn thing across the room. An angry, bereaved howl of torturous pain leaped from her desperate lungs. The bag hit the wall, scattering its contents across the floor. But she didn't care. Driving her fingers up into her hair, she pulled at it, finding comfort in the physical pain.

What the fuck was she going to do?

Dropping to her haunches, she screamed again, her tears burning hot as they flooded from her eyes.

She'd lost everything.

Zeus was right.

Completely and utterly.

Her life was over. It had been the moment her mother died. Everything had been taken from her. She'd been born without freedom. Born without reason or purpose except to run and hide. To be a pawn. Manipulated as a device in a men's war. She wasn't a person. Wasn't human. She was an object. Not one meant to live an existence of freewill. Her will was nothing. She had no rights. No options. No choice… What was there to live for? What could she hope for the future? Nothing.

The only thing she had was her blood. They needed that for nefarious purpose. Wasn't it the responsible thing to take it from them before they could damage each other with it…? Before they could damage the world?

That was it.

The searing pain didn't leave her gut. It grew in mass, becoming heavy with the realization of her purpose.

Her mother was right. She couldn't let it catch her. Couldn't let Olympus win. It had taken everything and everyone she cared about. Olympus would not win. Zeus would not win. No matter the cost.

The greater good.

Daire had given himself to it. She had given him to it. Sacrificed any chance of a life beyond Olympus for either of them. If it was the world and everyone in it, or her life… the choice was a no brainer.

Drying her tears, only one course of action was available. Only one place to end her wretched existence. And one person who needed to see her demise.

Rising to her feet, she didn't even bother to wipe her tears. Deadline be damned. One thing ruled her. Starting in a determined march, she went to the bag and its strewn contents. Grabbing the small khaki messenger bag from its pouch on the back of the Bergen, she stuffed a few essentials inside. Power bars, water, notebook, pen, underwear, ball cap, hair ties, compass. Just enough to get her through the journey of the next few days.

She lengthened the strap to toss it over her head as she left the room. To use their original entry point, she'd have to go past the meeting room. Past Styx. Rather than run that gauntlet, she went the other way. She didn't want to talk. Didn't want to argue. Didn't want to deal with their petty war anymore.

Being petite and short, getting out of the building was easy enough. She climbed out the window at the end of the corridor. That gave her a straight line to the perimeter and through the rusted old fence into the brush. The freeway couldn't be more than four or five miles in a straight shot, not far, easy to traverse, and there would be at least two hours until sunset. Heated by her need, her pace quickened until she was running.

Olympus.

She'd see it again.

One last time.

It would be the last thing she'd ever see. The place she died would be the same one she met her love. Fitting. Her love and her life would end in time with her sacrifice. He'd be proud. He would be. The greater good was his driving force. He gave himself to it every minute and had given their love to it too. Why should he expect anything less from her?

THIRTY-ONE

RUNNING DIDN'T LAST. Between her bouts of grief, the grating pain in her chest slowed her down. But it didn't matter. She hadn't gotten more than a mile when Styx's voice rose behind her.

"You gonna carry your own shit?"

Had she known he was so close? No. Being honest, he didn't feature in her melancholy. In such an open space, there was nowhere to run. Not that she'd be able to lose him anyway.

Stopping, fixated on the glimmer of civilization in the darkening sky, she let him come around and dump the Bergen at her feet.

"That all you have to say?" she asked.

"What do you want me to say?" he asked, still scowling. "I won't apologize, if that's what you're waiting for. He would. But he's not here."

"Why him?"

"He was the only one Zeus would let get close. His loyalty to Olympus has always been…" He inhaled, his expression relaxing. "Truth is, if it wasn't for you, he'd have been there sooner."

"Don't. Don't make it seem like… I didn't stop him doing anything."

He snickered. "Course you did. Even you know that. He was always going to be in the middle of this, you just gave him another factor to consider."

"Why wouldn't he tell me? I don't understand why—"

"You've got a lousy poker face and…" His eyes cut to the side. "I wouldn't let him."

Another shock. "You wouldn't… What the hell?"

"You can scream at me. I'll tell you everything… But we need to get off this path. We're sitting ducks."

"I have to get to the freeway," she said, grabbing up her Bergen to return to her purpose. "I have to go."

"Go where?" he asked, staying at her side.

They were moving, which was what he wanted anyway. "Beta."

"Beta?"

"They want my blood so bad, they can have it, all of it."

"Right. So you're going to commit suicide," he said, almost like he was fed up. "Good. That's a really good plan."

"I don't need your approval."

He grabbed her arm to whirl her around. "You really think he'll let you do that?" He Zeus or he Daire? "You can't… you… Look, you want to kill yourself, go ahead, I'm not gonna stop you. Don't you think you should understand the why first?"

"It doesn't matter. I don't care about the why. If he's given himself to the greater good, I can to."

"Right, and you think that's what this is? That he's gone back to Olympus because he wants to be there? Because he thinks its purpose is righteous? Please, seriously, if that was his reason, you'd be there with him. I'd be there with him. You have to understand before you can decide what you want to do next."

"He didn't want me to decide. You didn't want me to decide."

Tightening his grip, he shook her. "Would you fucking listen to me? You want to be on the inside of this, you better stop thinking with your heart and start using your head.

Your boyfriend lied to you, boo-hoo, the fucking human race is at stake, don't you think that's a damn good excuse?"

She swallowed. "The human race?"

"Yeah," he said, his hand loosening. "Are you going to listen to me?" She nodded. "Okay…" He seemed to relax. "We need to lay down some miles first. You with me?"

She nodded again and followed when he started moving. The human race? Daire had made his decision to stand with his brother, not Zeus. Whatever the brothers had cooked up, Styx said Harry hadn't been part of it. Was that at the time or was he still in the dark? She wouldn't know unless she trusted in the man leading her. Questions could only be answered if she gave him the time to explain.

Trudging along at his side without a word, her Heart was the only thing she could focus on. Beta. The D.C. hallway. He wasn't a stranger who didn't love her, he was a man on a mission. The things she'd said… the things he'd done… Would they ever be able to forgive each other?

***

HUMANS HAD AMAZING CAPACITY.

The freeway wasn't Styx's goal. He walked them right into the city and to a tall motel building that rented rooms by the hour. They paid for the night and went up the stairs. It wasn't until they were inside that she dumped her things and broke the silence.

"When did it happen? When did you decide to send him back there?"

"I didn't decide any damn thing," Styx said, putting his own bag on the floor to go to the only dresser in the room. From the top drawer, he produced takeout menus. "Want to order a pizza or something? We should eat."

Not so long ago, she'd been starved. Eating was lower priority than finding out why they'd abandoned the man she loved. "How can you be okay with him being there alone?" She spat out her exasperation. "All the fucking shit you gave me when—"

"I was pissed, okay?" he said, slamming the drawer.

"Running out of there the way we did was… spur of the moment."

"I don't understand."

"No, and you won't," he said, holding up the menus. "Until I go downstairs to call out for food. I'll be back in two minutes."

She stepped out of his path, so he could leave the room. Food. Yes, maybe that would help her make sense of things. Sitting on the end of the bed, she unlaced her boots to fold her legs under her. Her open hands caught her forehead as her elbows met her knees. Daire. Her Daire. Her Heart… Styx had been the one to tell her he was gone, that she had to come to terms with it all meaning nothing. He'd made her believe the relationship was a sham. All the time he'd known…

When the door opened, she didn't move. Her head hurt. It pulsed. Cradling it was the only relief. She didn't know whether to be mad or devastated… or both.

"You remember when we came back to camp…" Styx started. "Ares was guarding the trailer. It was just the three of us."

She felt the bed move but still didn't look up. "Yes… And do we have to call him Ares?"

"Yes," Styx said. "Because he is Ares right now. He has to be."

On an exhale, she tipped her head to the side to see him. "It was something I said. You said JARR and marched us back to him. When I repeated what I'd said, he got it too. Both of you figured something out that I missed."

"You've heard of Pandora's Box?"

"Yeah."

"Few people realize, it wasn't a box at all. It was mistranslated. Pandora had a jar, not a box."

Her head rose slowly from her hands. "Pandora's jar? JARR."

"Right."

"That's what you figured out, but I don't understand what—"

"What was in the jar?"

"Death. Evil. Misery."

"Right," he said, shifting up the bed to rest his back on the headboard. "I don't think it was a fuck up at all that you're the key to this. I think you were always supposed to be." She didn't get it. "It doesn't matter. JARR is what we think it is. We think it is… We don't really know… What we do know is it's not a matter of accessing JARR to get at the information. The procedure, the one that involves your blood, it won't only give us access to information…"

"It's on me if it gets out there," she said, recalling the conversation. "My blood will unleash something too."

"Right."

"Unleash what?"

"That we don't know. We suspected as much, that there was something more sinister going on, that's why we needed someone in there. Someone to get close to Zeus… and to Garrick… Garrick will trust Ares even more than Zeus. Neither of them would trust me. I'm not an Olympus thoroughbred."

And now she felt bad for saying that. "You needed to know what JARR really was. Har—Hades was with me and mom when it was applied. He could never tell you or Ares what we were facing."

"Right. And tying you to it was just another fuck you to Hades."

The information hoard they found at the doctor's proved the man was a liar. It wasn't exactly a stretch that he didn't tell Harry they'd tied his daughter to the possible apocalypse. Though Asclepius had said he didn't know exactly what went wrong with the setup, that somehow, they didn't do a test, they finalized the process. She couldn't exclude the possibility Zeus had set them up. That he'd orchestrated the mess in some way the doctor didn't know about.

"You and Ares suspected it," she said. "When I was talking about being responsible for unleashing temptation… you knew it was a jar, not a box and—"

"We knew there was more to it."

"That's how you cooked this up."

"Hades sending us out with our own detachments

was too good a chance to miss."

"You never intended to follow the plan," she said, leaning closer. "Either of you."

"No."

"All that stuff in Vegas about… You knew he was going to Zeus."

"Yeah," Styx said. While there was a faint note of contrition in his voice, it wasn't in his expression. "I didn't know the when."

"You could've told me," she said, but he was already shaking his head. "I don't know why he wouldn't tell me. Why he'd keep me in the dark about—"

"Because I told him to."

"Because I have a lousy poker face?"

"And because it would be easier on you," he said, then paused. "All that shit you said at Beta… would you have said it if you knew he was a double agent?"

Would she? She didn't know. "My pain was real."

"You laid it on thick." Which Zeus had loved. "I was worried for a second." Her drifting eyes blinked back to his. "I was always worried he wouldn't be able to do it… Me and Hades, fine, he can screw with us, but you… I thought for a second you had him… Ares… when you said that name…"

He'd been as surprised as her. Guilt over her words, the way she'd doubted him. "I doubted him… You made me doubt him."

"I'm good at my job too, Lady. I had to make you believe it. Zeus was always going to give the great Ares a chance, but he's still in there alone and will have a limit. I don't know where it is, at some point, my brother will have to step in."

"How did you know Zeus wouldn't order him to kill the Olympus agents? Even if it wasn't him, Zeus could've demanded the execution—"

"Ares is good at his job too," Styx said. "I don't know how he did it exactly but shit like that doesn't worry me. He knows how to manipulate a situation; I knew our guys were okay."

Which was the opposite of what he'd said to her.

"Kingsley wasn't okay. You're not okay."

"Our people know how to take a beating," he said. "The first part of his mission, after tracking Z down, was making him believe Ares's fidelity to Olympus was unchanged."

Her sickness tumbled again. "Which was why he handed over the Scepter."

"You know, it's funny. I sit here telling you I had complete faith Ares could do his job and keep our people alive. He had complete faith in you. A faith I didn't share."

"He knew I'd give him the Scepter."

"Yep," he said and became more somber. "He's also aware you'll never be what you were… together. He knew this would cost him your relationship." A tear tumbled from her lashes. "He loves you. But everything he's done… Everything he'll have to do… You can never be together again." Holding her breath, she was afraid to breathe without him. "It's what Olympus means."

"To sacrifice ourselves to doing what's right," she croaked through dry lips. "No matter the cost… It's why he didn't want to give me his word."

"Yeah," he said with a head bob.

So much was beginning to make sense.

On a groan, her forehead sank into her hand again. "Before anyone else, you trust him."

"What?"

"He told me to trust you. Before anyone else, I was to trust you."

"Because I'm the only one who knows he's playing Zeus. The only one… except you."

"And you should know I would never say anything to endanger him. But I don't understand why you didn't tell Hades."

"Ares didn't want to go ten rounds. And the betrayal had to be real. To everyone. We didn't know if any of our agents were playing both sides or if they wanted revenge of their own. There is so much we don't know about JARR and Zeus's plans. Ares had to get in deep, win his trust, gather intel."

"The key to survival."

"Everyone's survival," Styx said. "We still don't know the particulars, but Zeus is trigger happy. He wants JARR… and all it brings."

"Could you guess what's going to be released when they access JARR?"

"Could be anything. Chaos and anarchy are the best bets. Might wipe world debt or infect every system on the planet with a virus that brings humanity to a halt. Maybe it has the nuclear codes and will hit global targets triggering nuclear winter. Whatever it is, it's a doomsday event, Ares knows that much."

That piqued her. "How do you know that? You can't have talked at Beta."

"Are you kidding? Zeus brought in his merc minions to watch that shit like they should've brought popcorn. No, we didn't talk at Beta. Once he's in, when he's there, it's important to keep his head where it needs to be. He's Ares. He needs to be Olympus faithful Ares. He can't show mercy. He can't soften. He can't give Zeus even a glimmer of reason to doubt. He can't show any hesitation."

"Hesitation gets you killed."

Her love was her love. Her Heart was trapped in Zeus's web, too close to run if it all went wrong. She needed to know more. She needed to know everything.

THIRTY-TWO

STYX GAVE HER A SECOND to process before continuing. "Me and Hades, we took the brunt of him proving himself loyal to Zeus. Ares is capable of anything in the name of a mission. In the name of doing what's right."

"I know that... I just wish he'd trusted me to—"

"It was easier for you to hate him... but you couldn't even get that right." When he hazarded a smile, she offered a feeble one in return. "I wouldn't let him tell you. It was a trade-off. He didn't want Hades to know."

"And you thought he should."

"To be in that mind, to go to the place he needed to be at to succeed in this, Ares had to switch off everything that wasn't the mission. A good way of proving who you are to someone else is to become that person."

"I have experience of that," she said, sinking onto her side, lying the width of the bed, hand in her hair. "He was Danny right up until the moment he wasn't... You wanted to tell Hades but said you wouldn't if Ares didn't tell me."

"It's been a while since we've run an op like this."

"Together maybe," she said. "But in his mission to put me in front of H, Ares played me right up to the second we walked into the Beta control room. That wasn't so long ago."

"The damage… with you. He's never had to deal with it before. Usually on a mission, he goes above and beyond to make everyone proud."

"He doesn't deal well with disappointing anyone."

"Hades is more likely to forgive… it's not guaranteed, but it's possible… Not that it will matter if we're all dead."

"He'll succeed."

"How can you be sure?"

She smiled. "I live in this world too." Her optimism vanished and she sat up again. "My blood… JARR needs my blood… At Beta, in that lab, he was going to stick me with—"

"Luckily, he had me at his six," Styx said. "He would've had to comply with Zeus's orders, I had to say something."

"You were helping him," she breathed out the words. "Saving him from hurting me."

"Wouldn't have killed you, I meant that. He put his fist through my face more times than I could count. But one little needle stick…"

He was smiling, she didn't think it was so funny. "He was going to hurt me. He didn't hesitate."

"Didn't he? How fucking long did he sit there next to you? I've never known him to drag out simple processes for so long. Thank fuck Hades was there to distract Zeus."

"But he didn't know that's what he was doing?" Her father had helped without even being part of the plan. "Oh my God… in the shower… you were going to… Why didn't you?"

"Took his sweet time about that," Styx said, then became serious. "If we end up at the wire and it's the only course out, I will follow through."

"I know. This doesn't change that. Doomsday or my death… it'll be your responsibility."

"Yeah, but the only thing keeping him straight in there is you. Others called you his weakness, but he was right in Miami. You are the fire in his belly. You'd be victim number one of this doomsday event, which saves the rest of humanity's asses. If he loses you, he's lost the war. Those are his words. He needs you to live. So you can't go rushing off to kill yourself thinking you're doing the world a favor. If you end up dead… he'll trigger a doomsday event of his own. Screw codes. He'll go nuclear on his own."

How could Styx talk about her having such influence while at the same time telling her they could never again be together?

"Why are you telling me this now? You knew I was listening to your conversation with Exile."

"Yeah, you're not subtle. Even when you think you're being quiet, you're really not."

"From a super-agent's point of view, I'm not sure anyone is. Not if you're anything like my…"

"Listen to me…" Boosting himself away from the headboard, he leaned over to scoop up one of her hands. "You are safer at Beta. Whether you were on the road with me and Hades or stuck at Beta, it will be a fight to stop the countdown. To find out Zeus's plan because it will involve more than just destroying humanity. He'll want to control whoever's left. If he has contacts at high levels of government—"

"Which we know he does. Explains why he and Byron are so close."

"Maybe. But the merc army is a sign he has big plans."

"Merc army?"

"The first wave we met, he has ten guys brought in to do his dirty work, to be the muscle. They're just the start."

"And easily eliminated if they step out of line."

"Right. It doesn't stop with them."

"How do you know—"

"Ares has seen plans for something much bigger," Styx said. "Zeus has talked about him commanding them. Being General to his army. Zeus has kicked something into motion, we just don't know the details yet. We need the intel before we can stop it."

"Is that why you need Exile? You're out here trying to build a counter force…" she said. "If you tell Hades— you're telling me, why shouldn't he know too?"

"Good thing about our situation, Stratego knows Zeus better than all of us. He already knows Zeus has a plan and it's something we have to stop. Hades is helping without knowing a tiny part of the overall picture."

"I didn't know it either. Believe me, it's not so tiny."

"We argued about it…" Styx said. "Almost blew the op before it began."

"Argued with who?"

"My brother. I was mad he didn't want Hades on the inside. We went toe to toe." That she could believe. "I thought he'd back down after my ultimatum. If I wasn't to tell Hades, he wasn't to tell you. It wasn't until after, when I saw the fire the betrayal put in Hades's belly… You're Ares's something. You are… But Ares is Hades's."

Another tear slipped free. "He feels so much guilt."

"Yeah," Styx agreed. "And doesn't blame Ares for being where he is."

"H sees it as his fault that Zeus is ruining the good man he raised."

"We need Hades to have that fire in his belly. You are Ares's fire whether you know the mission details or not."

"Is that why you're telling me now?"

"Ares instigated this, bringing you back to Beta. Somehow, maybe it was Zeus's idea, I don't know, but you're safer in one place. Safer not being Zeus's enemy."

"I am Zeus's enemy," she said. "I know which side I'm on."

"Right. Except my brother doesn't want you on a side. You're a neutral party. Stuck in the middle of a man's war." That would be offensive if Styx wasn't so insistent. "*I* am the enemy."

"You?" Searching his eyes, she couldn't believe he was so calm about being setup as the obstacle preventing Olympus from achieving its goal. "You're the enemy because you have the keys. Zeus has the Scepter. When I go back to Beta, he'll have me too. As far as he's concerned, I'm just a pawn in the middle, needed for something I don't have to be conscious to give. All he needs are the other two keys."

"And time. Whatever he's planning, he still needs

time to put it in place.”

“You have the keys…” Just like they’d talked about in the D.C. hotel room. “You’re the hold out.” She snatched her hand back and jumped off the bed. “No! That’s not fair! You are not taking the full force of Zeus’s fury.”

He shrugged and leaned back on the headboard. “He’ll aim some at Hades, just because, that was always a given.”

Marching to the end of the bed, her fists jumped to her hips. “Zeus will hate you.”

“He was never a fan.”

“How can you be so glib about this? We’re talking about armies and doomsday events. These are life and death stakes.”

“He won’t kill me. Not until he has the keys.”

Flash frost dropped her temperature. “He’ll take you apart, piece by piece. He’ll torture you.”

“No, he won’t,” Styx said and actually smiled. “He’ll make Ares do it.”

The heat that came with that reality scared away the frost to replace it with grief. “And you won’t break.”

“Nope.”

So casual. So at ease. Completely nonchalant.

What had she said to Ares in the hotel hallway? “He’s your brother.”

“And we both knew this would end only one way.”

“No,” she said, shaking her head, trying to rid it of the chilling prospect of losing either brother. “I mean… I said to him in the hotel… in that hallway… He’s your brother. If he wanted the keys, he’d be the only one capable of finding them.” He didn’t say anything though his measured gaze cooled. “In Miami—”

“Don’t,” he said, sitting up straight.

“You said if—”

“Don’t.” He vaulted off the bed and stormed over to grab her shoulder. “You cannot put that on him. If you tell Zeus—”

“I wouldn’t tell Zeus anything. Ever. I don’t trust the man for a second. If I wasn’t of use, if you weren’t, and he didn't have such a sick obsession with hurting Hades, we'd all be dead ten times over. You. Me. And Hades."

"Don't forget that. Not for one second. Not to stop anyone's suffering. No price is too steep. You understand? No matter the sacrifice."

"I don't want to sacrifice," she whispered, the warmth of her wet eyes gathered again. "I don't want to sacrifice either of you."

His grip on her shoulder loosened as his hand slid to the back of her neck. "You'll be safe at Beta. So long as you don't blow his cover, you'll both be safe."

"In a prison."

"You'll be given latitude. No more locked doors. You'll be treated as a guest."

Like London. When she'd taken advantage of the liberty and turned on her host. "He won't trust me."

"No, he won't. Not for a second. But he doesn't have to. On the compound, with Ares watching over you, he won't have anything to worry about. For one thing, he still has H's agents to use against you. If you act out or try to run, chances are he'll kill someone."

That was a responsibility she didn't want on her shoulders. She shuddered. They were talking about one potential victim while at the same time discussing her Heart being responsible for every soul on the planet. It was a burden too big for one person. Styx had his back… from a distance. He'd prevented his brother hurting her, for his brother's sake more than hers.

"How did we get out of Beta?" she asked, peering closer. "In the shower, we were about to…"

"He orchestrated it," Styx said. "We needed to witness the betrayal and he needed to show Zeus we were nothing to him. Being captured was necessary. The imprisonment was necessary to prove his loyalty."

"He always planned to break us out?"

"Me and H, yes, at some point. The plan was never for him to break us out himself. That would blow his cover and we need him inside as long as possible… I'd guess he gave Hades the tools he needed to do it."

And Harry was the patsy who'd followed their plan thinking it was his own.

"Did you know about D.C. before we got there?"

"Mission like this is less about knowing and more about banking in time to their breeze." Her clueless expression wrought a snicker from him. "Following the clues. The breadcrumbs. Going with the flow keeping the objective in mind. We couldn't firm up every part of the plan. Situations like this change and you have to trust your opposite to support you without supporting you." He pointed to his brow. "And thanks for this by the way."

"Your new bruise." The one she'd asked about in the car on the way out of there. "Why thank me?"

"Whatever you said to him in that hallway pissed him off."

Curling her lips into her mouth, she hid her wince. "I didn't know you were working together."

"You know it now. It can't change anything, but at Beta… this could happen fast or drag on for years." Years? "Communicating directly could be difficult. Impossible maybe. We might need a conduit—"

"For information." That was the reason for his revelation. "I'll be at Beta. You'll be at Gamma. The only way you can talk to each other is through me."

"We'll need regular proof of life. They'll argue they can't kill you because they need you for JARR, which is true. We'll want to know you're being treated right." Giving them the excuse to talk to each other. "You have to assume you're being listened to at all times. That communications are being monitored."

"I understand."

"Any odd words. Anything that seems important. Ares will give them to you. You give them to me."

"I can do that."

"You cannot talk to him like he's your… yours. He's Ares. You're on opposite sides. He betrayed you and broke your heart."

"I know."

"Anything familiar. Anything you think… You're

never alone at Beta. Even when you think you are."

"I don't want him to get hurt… or to ruin your plan."

"I was there to help him out before, so he didn't have to stick you with that needle. I won't be there the next time. If he has to hurt you…"

She nodded and blew out a breath. "He's really still in there."

"When you go undercover, you have to be that cover, in every way. Every single way. You'll have to watch him prove his loyalty to Zeus. Hurting you is one thing, if Ares hesitates or refuses to do it, that could screw everything up. Remember, you're under Zeus's control. If he finds out the truth, that Ares's loyalty is a lie, or that my brother values you more than the organization… You'll be trapped in there. Both of you… Never forget Zeus is a sadist. He enjoys other people's suffering. Yours. Ares's. Whoever's. It's about power. He gets a kick out of it."

"We'll be okay," she said. "You're worried about him using us against each other, but he can't order Ares to hurt me too much. If I can communicate with you and Hades, I could tell you he's being an asshole and blow the deal."

"Right, but that doesn't stop Zeus ordering Ares to hurt other people in front of you."

Shock was cold. "Other people? I'd have to watch…"

"I don't know and we don't have much time to prep you."

Was it better to know the man committing the heinous acts was doing it against his will or not?

"You're telling me I have to be prepared for anything."

"Be strong. But no one expects you to be anything other than yourself. Don't subdue your natural responses. Don't assume Ares will do anything except follow Zeus's orders."

A knock at the door startled her.

"It's the pizza," Styx said, pulling her close to kiss her hairline before going to his pack for money. Another knock. "Yeah, we're coming!" With the money in one hand, she watched blindly as he also retrieved a gun from the Bergen for his other hand. "Go sit over there…"

He gestured at a chair by the dresser, out of line of fire. Paranoia or good sense? Life got more complicated by the second.

THIRTY-THREE

HOOKING UP WITH HARRY went without incident.

At the motel, Styx woke her before sunrise to start their drive to the rendezvous point. He'd gotten another vehicle from somewhere. She hadn't asked.

Being on the inside of the secret came with its own struggles.

Her Heart.

With her arm folded against the window, numbness crept in when the familiar Miami streets passed her windows. It all came back to this city. Why was that? It meant so much to her parents, they'd met there. Their letters brought her to the city with Danny. They brought her back when her father sought the Scepter he'd left for her mother. For the first time, it almost felt like she had something resembling a home. Not a specific site, but a city. It was a start.

Another motel allowed the three of them to get some sleep. They'd need it. The meet was just a matter of hours away.

It was while in the shower that the idea snuck in. Once it was there, she couldn't shake it.

Styx was the only one present in the room when she came out of the bathroom.

"Where's H?"

"Went to scout the site," he said, laying an arm along the back of the couch.

"Did he tell you where it was?"

"Nope."

"Doesn't it bother you to go in blind?"

"Why would it bother me?" he asked. "I'm not going in blind. Didn't I just say Hades is scouting the site?"

"Yeah, but—"

"And I'm betting Zeus won't take the risk of coming here himself. If we wanted to, it would be a prime opportunity to take him off the board."

No press. No party… Though she didn't know that for sure because she didn't know where it was happening.

"You think it'll just be…" Like he anticipated she'd been about to use his real name, Styx's brows rose. She swallowed before saying the word that once again caused nausea. "Ares."

"He won't be alone. But, yeah, he'll be in charge."

Did he know that for sure or was he assuming? Either way, with Daire secretly on their side, they didn't have to worry as much about being hoodwinked. Could it happen? Sure. But if they were in real danger, her Heart would get a message to them… wouldn't he?

It was so difficult to figure everything out. If only she could talk to him. Styx's explanation about JARR and Zeus's plans for it made sense. Her Heart was the only one Zeus would trust, that had been said numerous times, so he was the only real candidate for the mission.

But what did it mean?

Would he have told her if it wasn't for the bargain with Styx? And the certainty they couldn't ever be together again, what did that mean? That he planned to die for this mission? That Olympus was his true love and even stopping Zeus couldn't change that? Would there be an Olympus after this mission was complete? Was he her choice? Could they get past all that had happened?

"Hades not being here makes this easier," she said, grabbing her canvas purse as she crossed the room.

"What easier?"

"I have to go do something."

"Uh…" He leaped up from the couch to get between her and the door. "I don't think so."

"It won't take long. I'll be back in an hour. Two max."

"Again. No."

She shook her head. "You can't just say no… And I need some money."

His chin tilted. "Oh, do you?"

"If you don't give me money, I'll find a way to steal it or break in. That means I'll be less likely to make the meet given, you know, I'll be arrested."

"Did you just threaten me?" he asked, his lips twisting in a tight smile.

"If that's how you choose to take it."

"You're…" he started and paused to show her a finger. "Stand there and wait. No games, right?"

That's what Daire told her before they parted. No games. Trust Styx.

She stayed put while he went to open his pack to retrieve cash. He stuffed it into his own pocket and grabbed a gun from another part of the bag.

"Why do you need a gun?"

"I'm coming with you," he said, approaching.

"I don't need a babysitter," she said. "Even if I did, we don't need a weapon."

Taking her shoulder, he turned her around to push her out the door. "You annoy people. Never know when someone might take offense and start shooting."

"How ironic would that be," she said. "All this planning, politicking, super sleuthing, and we get taken out in a random drive by."

"Hilarious," he said, deadpan. "What a hoot for Hades and Ares."

"Okay. But you probably won't get in with a gun… Do you have a license for it?"

"Anyone tries to take it, they'll see it in action. Where are we going?"

"Nowhere we need to start shooting. We need a cab."

"A cab or a car?"

"Cab," she said, trying to see his determined face that was set on the street ahead and didn't budge. "Are you going for the record of most crimes committed in a day? Concealed weapon. Kidnap. Grand theft auto."

"I'm a guy without limits."

"Don't think Exile would be busting you out."

"I don't have the same relationship with him as Kero."

That almost sounded like a joke, yet he wasn't smiling. With an arm around her, he took her from the curb to hail a cab. Once they were inside, it was up to her to give their destination.

"The Rotunda, please."

Sinking into the seat, she didn't look at Styx. Did he know the place? Had he been before? She had... a lifetime ago.

When they arrived, Styx paid the driver, then they were standing outside. She'd been so sure in the shower that she at least had to check. Was it insane? Probably. But she had to know. If her future would be spent under lock and key, she had to take this chance while she had it.

"What's wrong?" he asked after they'd been standing there a minute.

"Nothing. Nothing's wrong." Taking his hand, they went inside, paid their entrance fee, then she was looking up. "The Glitter."

Styx glanced up. "What?"

"It's what my mom called it," she said, setting her sights on the skate desk. "I might need your lockpicking skills."

"Oh yeah? And what would you have done without me?"

Something. The closer they got, the more her determination grew. At least until the moment she stopped in front of the lockers. It was empty. Nothing inside. No need to pick the lock. All she had to do was slide her hand inside and... she couldn't touch it... not until she was alone.

"God," she breathed.

"What is it?"

"Nothing," she said again and turned to pat his chest. "There's a milkshake bar on the other wall… Get us something to eat."

"If you sneak out of here—"

"Why would I do that?" Her Heart was waiting at the end of that day. Some form of him anyway. "I don't want to miss the meet, I just… I need a minute."

His curious eyes narrowed as they scanned the lockers before he retreated. He wouldn't go far. Maybe wouldn't even go to the milkshake bar.

"You can do this," she whispered.

She didn't know what would be worse, there being a letter or not. If there was, what would it say? Would it explain his thinking? Would he break her heart? If there wasn't, she'd built herself up, some iota of hope brought her to that spot in that moment. She needed to know.

It was crazy to think he'd have time and he wouldn't be alone. How would he explain to his new colleagues, Z's mercs, that he needed to make a stop at a roller rink? He wouldn't, would he? He wouldn't tell them. That would reveal the exchange point. He was smarter than that.

All her thoughts were procrastination. Stepping forward, she moistened her lips, taking a deep breath at the same time. Her eyes closed when her hand swerved around the door to slip her fingertips onto the roof of the locker. Memories of his hand guiding hers were so vivid that she almost leaned back into his strength. He wasn't there to hold her up, not this time.

The seam was there, all she had to do was push and—

The moment the metal fell, the crease of paper hit her hand. Her breath came out in a puff as her eyes sprang open. There was something… Her father had been there since she and Daire were last there. But why would he leave something? He knew his love was dead.

With her heart thumping against her ribs, she withdrew the paper, using the other hand to push the flap back up and lock the door, taking the key.

An envelope. Blank. Just like the letter from her

mother to Harry that she'd discovered. It couldn't be from her mom. Harry had no reason to leave anything…

Glancing here and there, suddenly aware anyone could be watching, she turned to walk along the wall, past the roller rink and into the darkest corner.

The noise around her dwindled to nothing. There were no others. It was her. Alone in the seat at the small corner table. She wasn't there to have fun. To watch her friends or family on the rink. She was alone…

Opening the flap with trembling fingers, she slid the paper free. Closing her eyes one more time before putting the envelope on the table and sliding her thumb into the crease, opening out the sheets.

Immediately, she recognized his handwriting. Last time she'd opened a letter from there, she'd recognized her mother's. That was a shock impossible to eclipse, at least that's what she'd thought.

Her Heart. She was alone with her Heart…

THIRTY-FOUR

If you're reading this, it means you know. Or maybe blind faith brought you to these words. If it was, I don't deserve it. Also, if H is picking this up. Stop reading. None of this is meant for you.

I don't know where we are. What happened… or even why I'm writing this. Maybe I'm dead. Maybe you hate me. I wouldn't blame you. You were supposed to. That was the point. No, it wasn't the point, I just couldn't… This was cooked up by me and S. No one else. Just us. I wanted to include you, I thought it was right that I tell you the truth. I couldn't do it in person, so I'm doing it here, knowing if you ever read these words, it's likely I'm already gone and this is over.

Swiping a tear from her cheek, she brought his words closer to her eyes.

I love you. That's one truth that will never change. Before this started, some selfish part of me wanted to believe you'd always know that. That you wouldn't doubt it. After what you said in the lab, I... You're an amazing person. You meant every word. You did. You didn't plead for your life, you didn't scream hatred. You loved me so much that... You kept your word to give me to Olympus. You appealed for a swift end to others' lives and dismissed your own. You are the strongest person I have ever known.

"Baby," she whispered, running a fingertip across his words.

I'm in awe of you, LR. How do you do it? Keep getting up? Keep standing strong? You never waver and I... Some nights I get up ready to leave it all behind just to get back to you. Just to look at you one more time, to watch you like I used to, I took those nights for granted.

"We both did," she murmured to no one.

Sleeping without your heart beating near

mine, it wounds me. Like, somehow, I can't get enough oxygen to my muscles. There's pain, baby. Pain being without you.

It's a burden I'll bear for a long time. The rest of my life… which I guess could already be over.

This, us, is too broken to fix. I know. Finally, I found something to prove me wrong. Unfortunately, it meant losing you. Losing us. I lied to you. Hurt you. Betrayed you. I'm sorry. There aren't enough words to express how sorry I am. I could give you excuses. Write words to appease you. Tell you I was forced into it. I wasn't. I'm here of my choosing. Doing what I choose to do. I wish I could tell you it was for some lofty reason. S will probably give you a list of them. Yeah, they're all true. The threat is real and someone has to stand against it. But I care less about saving the world than I do saving you in it.

I don't know how this will or has played out. Could be we're all dead. Could be we failed. I have to take the chance, baby. I can't be there, at your side at the end, unless I'm allied with Z. That was it. The thought that shattered any doubts and set me on this course.

Your blood is needed. He'll want to use you for it. If it gets to that, if we get to that point, the only way I can ensure you keep your life is to be there. Maybe it doesn't make sense to you, or it sounds like I'm trying to justify my actions. I make no defense and don't expect forgiveness.

I've also thought about what I'll do if we get to that point and fail. If H and S fail. If they're killed. If Z follows through with his plan to unleash JARR... Someone has to be there for you. If I have to maintain this façade of allegiance and work for him for the rest of my life, I will. I will do whatever he asks, whatever he commands, the only payment I'll demand is your life.

There are bunkers under Beta. Stores to survive a siege for years. We'll survive there, baby. Even if I fail to protect the population, I'll protect your life.

Pushing her lips together, it wasn't possible to contain her tears anymore. Sniffing, she threw her head back, breathing through the torture of experiencing his. This man, her man, was doing what was right and still beat himself up for it.

Zeus didn't deserve his loyalty. She wasn't sure she did either. Her Heart's training taught him to always have a contingency. A plan B. His involved keeping her safe. Styx was right. If anyone would get through what lay ahead it was Daire... and he'd drag her along with him. Even if she was broken. Useless. Dying. He planned to be there at her side.

Thank you for letting me read your last London letter; the one you gave me at the same time H got his. Seems like you've told me we're over more times than I can count. You said ending us was the only hope for my survival. I don't worry about mine, baby, I worry about yours. What was it you said after our last time together? You didn't care who I had to kill or what I had to do if it meant getting out alive. That's why I live. For you. I live to serve you. To keep you alive. To keep the wolf from your door.

Love doesn't even cover it, LR. I know it's too little, too late. There's no way you can see past the horrific things I've done and the things I'll have to do. You said if anything happened to me, there wouldn't be a you left. That's my reality. I need you, baby. I need you out there. Living. Breathing. Happy. I understand that means you can't be with me. That I have to get you free of this.

If I can stop Z, if we can figure out how far his plan reaches, I'll spend my life eliminating every threat against you. Your letter said my primary mission was to survive. My life is only worthwhile if it's in service of yours. If I have to die, I will, if it means protecting you.

I try to put us aside and focus like you said. I try. I do. Knowing the intimate ties between us have been severed helps my focus, but you will always be my something. You are the paradise I'll live in after this life. That's what I'm running toward.

You didn't want to say goodbye. I don't want to disappoint you more than I already have, but that's the only way this ends, LR. I will not be the weight around your neck. People thought you were my weakness, yet it's me who keeps you tangled in the Olympus web. You need to break free. We have to set you free. I understand why H did what he did now. Yes, you are my meaning and my reason, but it's not enough. My love for you isn't big enough to raise you higher than the danger. I can battle it, hold it back as long as I can, give you the freedom to run, to hide, to live.

It's the one thing I promised myself I'd never do: let history repeat itself. But that's exactly what's happening. If by some miracle we do succeed in toppling Z's regime, I'll find you a new life, give you a new name, let you live free of it all… As free as you can be. My enemies will become yours in a way that will make me your enemy too. My actions have brought this about. This end.

And the pain you must've felt in Vegas when you saw the Scepter…

Her first thought hadn't been against her Heart, she'd feared Zeus had hurt him, not that he'd turned him.

…You had no forewarning. I suppose it made your reaction genuine, but I have never had a more challenging mission.

When you watched me in the ring… Shit, baby, the heat of you near burned in my blood. I wanted you closer. Away from the asshole at your side. Knowing I put you there, my actions led you into that trap… I'll never forgive myself. I'll never forgive myself for what you've endured. You are a light. Warm. Pure. Honest. You are the beacon for all of us in this. Your pedestal raises you above us all. You are a goddess. Once mine. Never again. Temptation is overpowering, it will be, but if I taste you again… if you ever let me in… I won't get out again. I won't be able to do what I have to, I will be selfish, and that'll spell disaster for us all.

In the lab, when you were carried in… I took you from them ready to fight. Ready to murder every man there with my bare hands. That's the biggest obstacle to my mission. Maintaining my cover around you will be impossible. Maybe I didn't manage it. Maybe I failed. Providing you got out, I'm happy. The taste of your lips is worth dying for, a hundred thousand times over.

Her lip wobbled and she had to look away. Her Heart was saying goodbye. In spite of knowing they'd meet that night, that she would see him again, she heard his silent plea. His mission weighed heavy on his shoulders. While his focus was her, she had to see beyond that and think about the greater population. His words implored her to make it easier for him. They couldn't be together in front of others, couldn't be familiar, but even if they were alone…

Could she be alone with him without touching him? All she wanted to do was trace her thumb over his cheek, to beg his dimple to meet her fingertips, to see his smile, to hold the man she loved. The man with the world on his shoulders. Her man. Her Heart.

She'd never been so proud and so devastated at the same time. This was what Styx was trying to tell her. Going undercover meant being the other person, being the alter ego. No breaks. No pauses. No stolen moments or whispered words. Any hope she'd had of seeking her Heart out while in captivity were shutting down. She couldn't do it. She had to be strong. For him. To help him. But…

This could all end bad. It could end with her losing her life. Or him. They may never have a chance to be together again. To be them. To declare their love and say goodbye.

I want to write more. Want to maintain this connection for as long as I can. This could be the last chance I ever have to speak to you, from my heart to yours, Temptress. But it has to stop. I have to put that period at the end, just like you told me. For my sanity and yours. I'm running out of time but haven't said all I want to.

Love. Desire. Even if I had all the time in the world, I'd never be able to express how much I want you, how I crave you and dream of you every night. How I wake up sweating sure your body is beneath mine. The memory of sliding into you, the way your body closes around mine, how your breath changes, I remember every detail. Thank you, baby. Thank you for giving me what I was never supposed to have. I was supposed to be the machine they created. Nothing more. My mission means returning to that permanently, but for a minute there… For I minute I was someone else. I was yours. And it was more than I could ever deserve. You are more than I deserve. Better than all of us. A piece of me will live in you long after I'm gone. You feared dying alone? Now know I guarantee you won't. Even if I'm not there, if I left the world long before you, you won't be alone, my Heart. I will be with you every second you breathe and will be waiting for you on the other side when this world is no longer big enough to contain your beauty and heart.

You are my truth. My only. My Heart. Always. In this life and the next.

Her yelp of grief probably got the attention of others. She didn't care. Pulling her feet to the edge of her seat, she held his letter close. How could he say goodbye to her like that? How could he…? They'd never have each other again. Never be free to live and love as they had when they first met. Danny or not, that life was meant to be theirs. They were meant to be together. Except they wouldn't be. Life. Circumstance. Everything conspired against them. What was she supposed to do? Just accept that? Just forget them? That was impossible. Would be impossible, especially when she'd be living in Beta probably until the moment Z bled her dry.

Opening his letter, she read the words again, her tears dripping onto the paper, blurring the words. He loved her. He did. Had she doubted it? Reading his sentiments over and over, it became impossible to believe. He loved her. Of course he did. And she…

Sniffing in her grief, she pushed it aside and thought for a second.

This could be the last chance.

With purpose, she took the notepad from her bag and began to write, sparing only a brief thought for Styx who was probably wondering where she'd gotten to. No, he would know where she was, but was smart enough to give her space.

She had to get her words out, to say something, to respond. Maybe he'd never read the letter, but maybe he would. Everything she felt was too much to keep inside.

Time didn't mean anything. She didn't care how long it took. She got out everything she needed to say and folded the letter to slip it back into the secret compartment in the locker. One day he'd get it… she hoped.

Daire's letter was important too and she couldn't risk taking it to Beta with her. Anyone could find it. So she sat on the bench and sealed the envelope with the letter inside, writing her own address on the front.

She didn't even need to go to the milkshake bar, Styx was waiting for her at the top of the entrance stairs when she was done.

"Can we stop to mail this… please?" she asked, flashing the envelope.

"Mail it to who?" he asked, reading the nameless address.

"Me," she said and shrugged at his surprise. "Just if I make it out of this…"

"Okay," he said. "Is it secure? Do a long list of people know about this address or is it classified?"

Resting her head against him, she looped her arm through his. "Just me."

"Me and you," he said. "How do you pay for our little secret?"

Because if she had a running tab, maybe it was

traceable? "I paid for like three years in advance," she said and glanced up at him. "But I guess if the apocalypse is coming, I might get a refund."

"Something to hope for, right?"

His smile was slow, and it took her another second to register it. Her lips curled, reciprocating, yet they wobbled.

New tears blurred her eyes. "Sorry," she said on a sob.

"Shit," he said, throwing an arm around her neck to pull her against him, probably to hide her upset. "He really fucked you up."

"This is not his fault," she mumbled against him. "We just didn't say goodbye like we should've... until now."

"He really fucked you up," he said again, his lips warm in her hair. "Want me to kill him? I can do it. He won't see it coming."

Through her tears, she laughed. Everything about the situation was fucked up. They were all in danger of losing something, their lives if nothing else. So much was unknown. So much wasn't what it appeared. So little could be anticipated. How would this end?

THIRTY-FIVE

WHEN THEY GOT BACK, Harry was sitting in a truck in the hotel parking lot, window down, arm raised toward them. "Where the hell have you been?"

They'd asked the cab to drop them off a couple of blocks early and walked the rest of the way. Of course they did.

"We're not late," she said without knowing whether they were or not given they didn't know where the meet was meant to take place.

Her father was out of patience. "Hurry up, get in."

Styx went around to get in the front while she slipped into the backseat. The new vehicle was much more spacious than their last one. Especially given the doctor's junk was all gone.

"Everything go okay?" she asked and got no response.

Harry was tense. Made sense. He was about to hand over his only child to the enemy. After a few streets went by, he started to relax. Returning to an empty hotel room must've unsettled him. Had he feared they'd betrayed him and taken off?

"Do I have to tell you to do what you're told, Light-

Sprite? We're only going along with this because we know they'll keep you safe. They need you."

Styx chimed in. "Remember there's a spectrum between alive and dead. The more you speak out, the closer the needle tilts toward the latter."

"You don't have to speak to me like I'm five," she said, which was an improvement on her father speaking to her like she was two. "I know what I have to do."

"Live," her father said. "That's all you have to do. We'll be working on things out here. Stashing you there is just as good as stashing you anywhere."

As long as Zeus didn't have Harry and Styx, she couldn't be used as a weapon against them. "Are we sure this isn't an ambush? That they're not just going to take us all again?"

"Zeus knows how to adapt. It didn't work the first time. There's no reason to suggest it would work a second time. If he tries it, he has to either follow through and kill us, or admit that the death threats were a bluff. Then he loses all credibility."

So he didn't want to torture them and face another stonewall. They'd proved their resolve to keep their secrets no matter how far their needle tilted toward death.

"He's using us. We're useful out here setting up Gamma for him. We're not naïve. He doesn't have any intention of everyone falling back into ranks and everything being like it used to be. He's using us to prepare his secondary site, so when he's done with the primary one, he can move right in to the new base."

"Yeah, we're just labor," Styx said. "Skilled labor, but labor all the same."

It was hideous. Disgusting. Revolting that anyone could be so exploitative. That Zeus could use so many people to achieve his own ends, aware all along he had no intention of letting them live.

He couldn't do it himself. He couldn't do it without the skills of Harry and Styx, and Ares too, especially Ares. It was some comfort to know her Heart wasn't truly on the other side. Somewhat gratifying knowing Zeus stood next to him believing his loyalty when all the time Daire would just as soon slit his throat and watch him bleed out.

"Where did you go?" Harry asked. "You were out. Where?"

"Your daughter had some crazy idea about checking out our previous SPs," Styx said without missing a beat. "The apartment. Some RV park looking for his Airstream."

"It's not there," Harry said.

"I knew it wouldn't be there," Styx said. "She didn't believe me that he wouldn't be that stupid. Why would he leave anything that might help us out? He's playing for the other side. We all have to accept that."

His lies were impressive. They were important but horrifying too. Yet, they were all capable of it. Hadn't her doubt of Daire's love proved that being with an Olympus operative meant trust was never guaranteed? She hated to think back to how she'd doubted him. The man was just too good at his job. Daire wanted her to believe the lie because if she believed it, why wouldn't Zeus? The principal had never reached inside him the way she had.

"Where is this meet?" she asked, changing the subject. "How do you know where it is? Zeus didn't say it out loud, did he send coordinates to your base unit when you had it?"

"He didn't need to," Harry said, negotiating a turn.

Minutes past and her father didn't elaborate. "That doesn't tell us where it is or how you knew," she said, aware that he was aware, but calling him out anyway.

"If you thought about it long enough, you'd figure it out too."

Why did people keep saying that to her? Why couldn't people just be honest? Open their mouths and tell the truth rather than talking in riddles?

"It's where he took her from the last time," Styx said, saving her taxed brain. "He's taking your daughter from you, which he's done before. Miami means something to you and Carrie, you met here. I don't know how many places you stayed in the year and a half you lived with them, but it's not a stretch to think you spent some time here... The location is a '*fuck you*' too because it's kinda the last place Zeus would look."

A bluff? Double bluff? Triple bluff? She was losing count.

"Is it?" she asked. "Is the meet the same place I was kidnapped as a child?"

"Yes," Harry said. "And it's not far."

If she had to hand Zeus one thing, it would be his amazing capacity to hold a grudge. Olympus was his world, she got it, Harry threatened that world and Zeus resented that he couldn't hold power without Harry commanding the men. He didn't get the same respect. Maybe he was doing it differently with his new soldiers and Ares.

She'd been taken prisoner as a child, more than two decades ago. Her memory from that time was blank. Zeus hadn't forgotten, neither had her father.

It must've been terrifying for a parent to have their child abducted. At least he didn't have to look far to know who'd done the abducting. Knowing the man was dangerous was one thing, but if he'd wanted to kill her even as a child, Zeus wouldn't have been squeamish about leaving her body exactly where her father would find it and to maximum effect.

Then, as like now, she was useful, a cog in Zeus's machine. Hers turned to ensure Styx and Harry's would too. Take her out the mechanism and the whole thing would grind to a halt. Power. Was that power? No. Not power. Manipulation. A frustrating truth, but not one she could change. Her father with all his years of super-agent experience couldn't do it. Her lover with his immense ability couldn't find a way around it. What chance did she have?

They were going to this place to give Zeus what he wanted, biding their time until they could strike. If such an opportunity ever came.

Their destination was a quiet suburb. Windows glowed with artificial light beyond their closed curtains, indicating people lived there. Close by. Oblivious people. Children slept. Adults pondered their bills, their jobs, their whatever, without any awareness of the encroaching danger.

Danger was a relative term. With confirmation that

her Heart still had his mind, she wasn't scared of the meet or the handover. Beta didn't scare her either. As people kept reminding her, they needed her, she wouldn't lose her life. Daire would tug on Zeus's strings if the need arose. She had someone in her corner. Even if Zeus didn't know it.

They drove to the end of the block and turned into a narrow alley, no streetlights there. Yards on either side were protected by fences and walls.

"Two exits," Harry said. "In front and behind. Any of the yards will get you out if necessary. No dogs or dead ends, no weapons or security systems."

Styx just nodded. They were planning escape while people in their homes considered themselves safe.

They drove out of the alley and parked near the side of a house at the end.

"Want me to find them?" Styx asked.

"No, we're early. We don't want to start on the wrong foot."

"Trust," Styx said. "Is that what we're relying on, Stratego?"

"Common sense," Harry said, taking off his seatbelt. "Let's do this."

They all got out. As the men huddled, probably exchanging intel and loading weapons, she headed for the corner eager to see if anything sparked a memory.

"Pandora!" Harry barked. "Stay put."

She smiled. "What's the worst thing that happens? They take me? That's why we're here."

"The worst thing that happens is you get taken out in a random drive by," Styx said, crooking a brow, reminding her of earlier in the day.

"We're not going that way," Harry said.

Okay, that was a good reason to stop her. Her father gestured her over and she went. The men flanked her as they returned to the alley they'd just driven down.

"We're going in the back door?" she asked.

"We don't want to draw attention to ourselves."

Three unknown people walking down a suburban street at night might do exactly that.

They stopped at a brick wall. Not just a regular brick wall, a wall of dark grey cinderblocks, towering to at least eight feet.

"Not surprised this was your pad, Stratego." Styx bent his knees to jump up and catch the edge of the wall. "Got a laser net on the other side?" he asked while hauling himself up like it was no big deal.

"You expect me to do that?" she asked her father as Styx's hand appeared in front of her.

Harry gave her the nod. "Go on."

Gripping Styx's wrist, she didn't have to exert much effort given her father boosted her up from beneath. Styx jumped down on the other side. She sat there on top of the wall with her legs dangling until Harry appeared next to her. Waiting wasn't an option. Rather than overthink it, she jumped down, grabbing Styx to steady herself as her father landed too.

"Not an easy way out," she said.

Styx bowed closer. "You won't be the one running for your life. It's easy for the rest of us."

"There's a gate to the next property," Harry said, pointing to the overgrown bush that ran along the side of the yard, towering to the same height as the back wall.

The men made eye contact and Harry's head moved, presumably communicating the location of the secret escape route.

"Why didn't we come through that way, Dad?"

"Can you see it?"

"No."

"Then why reveal it to our enemy?"

"Our enemy," she said, locking on to Styx. "Ares. He means Ares."

"Yeah," Styx drawled, drawing out the word with a dubious intonation.

Just one word could freak him out. Was he worried she would reveal the truth of Ares's loyalty?

"Do we really think that he hasn't scouted this location himself?" she asked. "That he doesn't know everything we know?"

"Depends if he did it himself," Styx said.

"Of course he did it himself," Harry said, striding away, his obvious purpose led her and Styx to follow. "He won't trust Zeus's mercs with a job this important. Shit, he barely trusted us."

"Which means he's doing everything important himself… Everything himself… Sounds like him."

No light came from the house up ahead. The long yard was a mess, whoever lived there didn't care about curb appeal. That or no one lived in the two-story structure at all.

They ascended the stairs to the porch and her father entered the building as if he'd never left.

"Are we doing this inside?" Styx asked. "Where was she taken from?"

"Backyard," Harry said, glancing around. "I want to check if there's signs of them being here since I left."

Wandering through the kitchen, that had apparently once been hers, was curious. Maybe the décor was different or the whole place had been remodeled, but it didn't provoke any memories. The shadowy abode wasn't filled with homely trinkets.

Cabinet doors hung from broken hinges or were completely gone. She went into the room beyond, a living room, stripped bare. Graffiti adorned the walls. In the corner was a pile of trash and balled-up carpet confirming this was no one's permanent address.

"Nobody lives here."

"Not now."

"Who owns it?"

"Now?" Harry asked. "I do."

She couldn't have been more shocked. "You own it?"

"He owns various properties," Styx said.

"Isn't that a liability? Having property like this in your name?"

"Who said it was in his name?"

Her father left the room and they heard him running up stairs.

"I don't get it," she said. "Why would he want to own this mess?"

Styx smiled, incredulous and amused as his head shook the tiniest fraction. "This was his home. You were his home. It didn't matter that he could never be here or live here. Owning this allows him to own the memories, a piece of the past. A past no one experienced with him except you."

No one living. She didn't say that. Thankfully, because Harry was on his way back down the stairs. At a slower, more plodding pace, she heard every thump of his boot on each step before he got back in the room.

"They're here."

She expected a knock at the door. The three of them stood on pause. The men didn't seem anxious despite the pulsing tension in the air pressing into them from every angle. She wasn't scared and yet, standing there in the dark, listening to her allies breathe, it seemed danger was nearby.

"Are you gonna invite us in?"

That shout came from the yard. The backyard.

Harry started out, Styx waited for her to follow, and then fell in behind. That was Ares's voice. Daire's voice. Hearing the disdain dripping from it caused such confusion. He didn't disdain them, he loved them, but he had the act down pat.

At the top of the stairs on the back porch, Harry stopped. Styx stalled her with a hand on her waist, sliding it around to her abdomen to pull her back against him.

The heat of his breath warmed the top of her ear. "You're in the field."

No kidding.

She slid a hand over his, linking their fingers. Having spent so much time thinking about how it would be staying at Beta, being around Daire and Zeus and so many others she didn't know, there hadn't been time to think about those she was leaving behind. These men had been her support in her darkest time. Losing Daire had hit her harder and faster than losing her mom.

Out there, on that porch, when Harry went down the stairs, opening her view of the yard, it was almost like her Heart had come back from the dead. Surrounded by half a dozen guys in black, it was difficult to comprehend that was the man she loved.

"You don't want to do this inside," Harry said from the bottom of the stairs. "This is where he took her. Not far from where you're standing."

Had her father seen it happen? He couldn't have. Whether or not he'd witnessed it, the trauma had obviously bedded itself deep.

"Surprised you brought so many amateurs," Styx called, his hand pressing tighter against her belly, reminding her to stay wary. "Are we gonna have some fun?"

"No," she said, despite his note of teasing. "No fighting. I don't want anyone fighting."

"There's no need to fight," her father agreed. "We all know why we're here. Where are my men?"

"Out front."

"That wasn't the deal."

"That's where I left them. If they split, that's on them."

Noise behind them unnerved her until it was accompanied by a familiar male shout. "We're here."

One figure came out and then another, taking positions at either of Styx's shoulders.

"You have what you want," Ares said. "Time for you to hand over my prize."

If only. If only she was going there to be with him, to be his prize, to a place where they could be together open and free. She wasn't his prize. Not in that minute. She was Zeus's. While the principal might be eager to declare himself the winner, the game wasn't over yet.

Even when she tried to step away, Styx wasn't ready to let go. It might have been an act, a sign of reluctance that would play well to the crowd. Squeezing his hand, she pried his forearm from her waist and turned, still semi in his embrace.

The ferocity in his eyes was the only communication she needed. They were doing this for the greater good. Anything could happen to any of them at any time. She didn't want to lose Styx or her father, any more than she'd wanted to lose Daire.

Forcing herself to smile, she hoped Styx understood that she wasn't afraid, that she didn't blame him for this turn of events… and that she'd forgiven him for his misdirection… forgiven him a little.

He pulled her close to kiss her hairline, then let her go. Everyone watched her descend the stairs to her father.

"I'll be okay," she whispered, knowing others would likely hear it anyway.

This was hardest on him. Her father didn't know Ares hadn't switched sides. He didn't know she'd have an ally at Beta or that she'd be looked after. He was handing over his daughter, the one he'd fought to get back and protected with his life.

"At least this time I don't have to tell your mother." Shit. If there had been an absolutely wrong thing to say in that moment, it was those words. Immediately, her eyes stung and sinuses tightened. Her father cupped her face to raise her jaw. "Keep burning bright."

"For as long as I can."

Throwing her arms around him, she held on tight. Not so long ago their relationship was so damaged she didn't think there was any way back. Despite the heartache they'd all endured, one thing had come out of it stronger.

Just like with Styx, she let go first. Her father had lost her from that site once before, it couldn't be easy to do it all over again.

Still, stepping back, she wiped her cheeks and took a deep breath, smiling at Harry once before turning her sights to their enemy.

The time had come to go to him, to cross the yard, ignoring the mercs in black. Passing through those in front, she stopped in their leader's personal space.

"Ares," she said, her eyes finding his.

"Pandora."

TO BE CONTINUED…

Thank you for reading this tale!
If you can, please take the time to review.

~

Ask your local library for more Scarlett Finn novels!

~

For all things Scarlett Finn
check out:

www.scarlettfinn.com